Meet Meda. She eats people.

Well, technically, she eats their soul. But she totally promises to only go for people who deserve it. She's special. It's not her fault she enjoys it. She can't help being a bad guy. Besides, what else can she do? Her mother was killed and it's not like there are any other "soul-eaters" around to show her how to be different. That is, until the three men in suits show up.

They can do what she can do. They're like her. Meda might finally have a chance to figure out what she is. The problem? They kind of want to kill her. Before they get the chance Meda is rescued by crusaders, members of an elite group dedicated to wiping out Meda's kind. This is her chance! Play along with the "good guys" and she'll finally figure out what, exactly, her 'kind' is.

Be careful what you wish for. Playing capture the flag with her mortal enemies, babysitting a teenage boy with a hero complex, and trying to keep one step ahead of a too-clever girl are bad enough. But the Hunger is gaining on her.

The more she learns, the worse it gets. And when Meda uncovers a shocking secret about her mother, her past, and her destiny… she may finally give into it.

CRACKED

ELIZA CREWE

Cracked

STRANGE CHEMISTRY
An Angry Robot imprint
and a member of the Osprey Group

Lace Market House
54-56 High Pavement
Nottingham NG1 1HW
UK

www.strangechemistrybooks.com
Strange Chemistry #20

First published in India by Penguin India 2013
This edition published by Strange Chemistry 2013
1

A catalogue record for this book is available
from the British Library.

ISBN 978 1 90884 466 8
Ebook ISBN 978 1 90884 468 2

Typeset in Sabon by EpubServices.

For Adam & Madeleine

One

There are some people you know you shouldn't anger because it isn't right. Like your mom – if she's the nice sort.

There are other people you know you shouldn't anger because they have the authority to punish you. Police officers, politicians, insane asylum wardens, your mom – if she's the bad sort.

But there are some people you shouldn't anger that you *don't* know about, because no one ever survived to warn you.

I'm the third kind.

I eat souls. The packaging can be tricky, but fortunately I am blessed with special skills to pry my meals from their pesky shells. My teeth rip skin; my jaws snap bones. I am fast, lightning-fast, snuff – oh-was-that-your-life? – fast. I try to stick to bad souls, in the memory of my own mom (the nice sort). There were other reasons, reasons I used to understand, but they are reasons for a good person. I am not *that*.

That might be why I feel so at home here.

Small rooms, thick walls. Hushed whispers and ear-grating wails. A symphony of misery set to the beat of beatings.

The Mulligan Residential Mental Health Facility – an insane asylum, but with better promotional materials – prison of the cracked and grey.

Cracked windows, cracked walls, cracked minds. Don't make them angry or there will be cracked skulls.

Grey-painted walls, grey-tiled floors. Once-white nightgowns, now grey. The skin of the inmates. Grey. The metal-framed bed. The bedding. Grey, grey, grey. The bars on the window…

Black.

Imagery ruined.

Correction – prison of the cracked, grey and *black*.

The sound of a slamming door vibrates down the darkened hall and I draw up to my elbows. As the loud bang fades, dead silence takes its place. It's the middle of the night, maybe even early morning, and nothing else stirs. My ears ache as I listen, waiting. When they start, the heavy tap of boots on linoleum is loud, like drumbeats.

Someone's coming. My hands tighten on the faded coverlet. I hope it's *him*.

Two nurses work the night shift, so there's a fifty-fifty chance it's only Gideon, the other one. Samson's the one I'm after, the reason I'm here. The ghost-girl, Callie, pointed him out to me. I wasn't in the mood to help her at first, but she insisted. Then she insisted again and again, until I wanted to kill her. They're like that, ghosts, once they realize I can hear them. Demanding – and impossible to kill.

I turn, finding Callie's translucent form in the shadows. She stands rigid, her semi-transparent head bent away from me, staring through the wall at something I can't see. Something that wears large, linoleum-tapping boots. She twists the strap of her pack in her hands, and, as the boots tap closer, she takes a step backwards, then another. The cell is tiny so it's only a few steps until she bumps against the wall. Well, bumps *through* the wall, actually.

One look at her pulls me upright, electric excitement shooting along my veins. The nurse coming down the hall is Samson. Her murderer.

I could have snatched the naughty nurse from his house, lurked in the parking lot by his car, called him claiming to want his Craigs-listed couch. I didn't need to have myself committed to the asylum like I did. But there's something poetic about recreating the scene the nurse played out with his own victim, only this time, with a very different ending.

Callie doesn't approve. She wanted me to take care of him weeks ago. She's spent most of our time here drifting around the room, running her silvery fingers along the dingy grey walls and giving me impatient glares. But if she doesn't like my plan, she can find another ghost-seeing, soul-eating monster – I haven't come across one in seventeen years, but she's welcome to try. As Mom always said, there's an easy way to do something, and the right way.

Then again, she also said I shouldn't play with my food.

I wouldn't say Callie and I are friends. More to the point, *she* wouldn't say we're friends – even if she could speak, instead of just bombarding me with memories. She was committed to the asylum because she couldn't deal with the horribleness of the world. I am the horribleness of the world.

It doesn't give us a whole lot in common.

But right now, I'm all she has and as her murderer tromps down the hall she looks to me for comfort.

I give it a shot. "Relax," I whisper. "You're already dead."

Her eyes fill with tears and I roll mine. Ghosts.

My hall-mates are silent, barely breathing, and I imagine I can hear their broken minds screaming, "Not me, not me." The boots pause somewhere down the hallway. I imagine the short, bullish Samson peering through a mesh-enforced window and terrifying the room's occupant. There's a soft, deliberate knocking – he wants to make sure he has the inhabitant's attention. At the sound, Callie cringes and then, forcing courage, sticks up her chin, her eyes as fierce as a scared little dead girl can manage. But then the steps start again and she shrinks into the wall. Her eyes dart back to me.

I can take a hint. I hop off the bed and prance into position, in perfect line of sight from the door, then, with a little spin, drop down so I'm curled against the wall with my head on my knees – a delicious little dish of déjà vu. When he came for her, Callie was curled up just like this, crying into her knees. Broken-hearted, until he was done. Then she was just broken.

The linoleum is icy through the thin material of my institute-issued nightgown, but the heat swelling under my skin more than makes up for it. The Hunger has been very patient, waiting quietly for weeks while I laid my trap, but now it yawns and stretches, tingling out to my fingers and gnawing on my soul.

Samson's tapping feet come closer, but again he pauses and knocks on a door. I don't mind. The pauses make it better. They make me wonder whether he's going to come to me, like the anticipation before a kiss. Will he or won't he?

But this is not a love story.

The boots begin to tap again, coming closer, and a little thrill runs down my spine. The ghost girl sinks further into the wall and slides as far away as possible, into the corner.

Shadows block the crack under my door and a river of fire washes over me, staining the world red. I have a guest.

Delightful.

I don't dare look up. Not yet. I feel his eyes creep across my skin. I know what he sees. Small, thin, pointy, frail. Curled on the floor. My dark hair is shorn into raggedy tufts on one side, left long on the other. I did that to myself. As with all the best places, they don't just let anyone in. This is an exclusive little hellhole. He sees a human teenager – which is half right. I am a teenager but, as for the other, no. Whatever I am, it is not *that*.

My eyes I don't let him see. They say the eyes are the windows to the soul and I wouldn't want to give myself away. There's a sharp knock on the glass – he wants my attention. He has it, but I don't let him see. He knocks again, more insistent. It's not very often he doesn't get what he wants, but if he wants my attention, he must come and take it. The shadows of his boots stay paused at the door and the crouching darkness in my soul shifts and flutters, unable to hold still under the agony of aching anticipation.

I hold my breath but it escapes when I hear the jangling of keys. The Hunger howls and I bite back a giggle. The lock opens with a metallic thunk and he steps into the room. He pauses. His bully-bright rational side tells him I am nothing to fear, but his animalistic side knows better.

Danger! his instincts scream.

Nonsense, his rationality remarks.

I am big! his bully side brags.

In the silence, I hear him swallow; then the door clicks closed behind him. I quiver and he sees a tremble. Finally he takes a step, then two more, until he is at my side.

He waits and I wait, both excited but for very different reasons. The moment draws thin and long and sweet, like pulled sugar, savored by us both. The Hunger pulses in the silence and, though he's just a garden-variety monster, not special like me, I know he feels it too.

Then the sugar snaps and he grips me by the hair, jerking my face up. His florid face is just as it was in Callie's memories: middle-aged, with large pores and sagging jowls.

Only now his eyes don't have the delighted gleam they had then. Instead the bushy brows are lifted in surprise.

I suspect I'm the first victim to ever smile at him.

I'm positive I'm the first to ever leap up and slam him into the wall by his throat. He tries to scream but I squeeze his neck until the noise dies with a wheezy gurgle. Confusion and shock riot in his eyes. He doesn't understand how my small, weak arms are strong enough. He doesn't understand a lot of things.

I can't wait to enlighten him.

I shove, sliding him up the wall until his feet leave the ground. His eyes are wide and panicked, and I pause to enjoy that perfect moment when the hunter realizes he's become the hunted, when he tries to reconcile what he knows to be true with what just happened.

When he makes the horrified face reserved for the bitter taste of just desserts.

I turn and see that Callie's enjoying it too. Her hands are clasped before her and her little face is lit up at the justice of the moment.

Samson's ineffectual clawing at my hand draws my attention back. He's taller than I am, and he manages to touch his foot to the ground, just his toe, but it's enough to take some pressure off his throat. I allow it.

"Whaa–?" he gasps out.

"You like to hurt people, Samson." I say it calmly but I'm on fire. The Hunger has burst into a conflagration.

"Nnnn–"

I squeeze. He pulls at my wrist and his feet swing and kick.

"Shhhhh, it's OK," I say softly, sweetly, as if I care. Then I drop down to a whisper. "I like to hurt people, too." I squeeze harder and he shoves off with that toe, trying to get away, to get air. My own foot snaps out and smashes it.

I let go and he falls screaming to the floor. He scrambles away, gasping and coughing. I shift to cut off the path to the door and he scurries backwards into the corner.

"Wha–?" he wheezes, then grabs his mangled throat. I step forward and he back-pedals madly, uselessly shoving with his heels, trying to wedge his bulk further into the corner. I can hear his heart race. It's pounding wildly and yet no blood reaches his face. It's deathly pale.

A preview.

"Wha–what are you?" he finally gasps through his damaged throat.

I just shake my head. Even if I knew, I wouldn't tell him. That's not what I'm here for. I take a few slithery steps forward.

"Please, no!" he screams and holds out a hand, as if to keep me away. I consider ripping it off. "I've never hurt you! I've never hurt anyone!"

"Don't lie to me."

He draws back. "Please…" his jaw works, his jowls trembling as he searches desperately for something to say. Then the words come bubbling out, tripping over themselves in his haste. "There must be a mistake."

I shake my head slowly and with purpose.

"Please… I don't even know you!"

I squat down so we're eye to eye and he shrinks away. I cock my head and my words slide out silkily. "No.

But you know Callie." I glance in her direction. She no longer looks excited. Instead, her eyes are wide and her hand covers her mouth. "Or rather, *knew* Callie."

Genuine confusion flashes across his face. His mouth moves as he tries to place the name.

"Callie Bellemore," I snarl.

Realization dawns on his face.

"It was an accident."

"What did I say about lying?" My hand snaps out and slashes his face, drawing four red lines across his cheek. The sharp scent of blood fills the room. I dance a little, in my squat, and my lips curve into a smile.

He becomes very still at that smile. The false innocence is replaced by calculation. "You're enjoying this."

My smile spreads wider. I know somewhere my mother hides her face in shame.

"You love killing as much as I do." He straightens as if he thinks he's talking to an equal. "Not, not just the killing, the…" He gropes for a word to describe it.

"Power," I supply.

His face lights up at my participation. "I don't know what you are, but I know we're alike." He puts his hands up and hurries, as if he's afraid he insulted me. "I'm not… special like you, but the kill…" His eyes drift off and a creepy smile turns up the edges of his mouth.

A smile not unlike my own. I swallow the shame and let it be eaten by the Hunger.

He continues dreamily. "I couldn't help it, she just…" He shivers, then his attention switches back to me. "I couldn't stop even if I wanted to." His hands open and close, turning from claw to fist and back again. "It's too strong." He looks to me for understanding.

And I do understand. I understand better than he could ever possibly imagine. Because, for me, it's more than power. I eat souls. Without them, I die.

Of course, that doesn't explain why I so love to collect them. I run a finger down Samson's cheek and he squeaks. Mom never understood the monstrous darkness that craves the kill. She wanted my need to eat souls to be like my need to eat vegetables. Necessary, but not desirable.

Samson, this foul piece of slime, understands me better than she ever did. But unlike him, at least I'm ashamed of my wickedness – when I'm not reveling in it. Like a dog wallowing in a mud pool, I love the glop and splash of ick. It's not until after, when the stink dries stiff and itchy that I regret it. Other wicked things, like Samson, don't feel the guilt. They don't have a memory-mom tsking and shaking her head.

Instead, they have me.

I suspect they never really feel guilt, but I make sure they drown in regret. Red, sticky regret.

So Samson's right, I am like him. But unfortunately for him, hypocrisy is the least of my many sins. He thinks our shared trait will make me like him, but it only makes me hate myself.

I lean in until mere inches separate us and close my eyes. I feel him tremble and inhale the intoxicating cocktail of fear and blood and I'm flooded with a hot joy. He moves and my eyes snap open, freezing him in place. "You're right. I am like you." I breathe, then shake my head very slowly, holding his eyes. "But that doesn't help you any."

His eyes widen and his mouth opens and closes wordlessly. I let him have one more moment of life, spent in panicked realization.

Then the Hunger howls through my veins, sweeping everything up in its frenzied tide. I jerk him from the corner, popping him free like a hermit crab from its shell, and he comes apart in my hands. So easily. Imagine a child at their first birthday.

He is the cake.

I hear myself laughing, screeching, cackling. The world is red hot and pulsing. On fire.

His soul erupts from his carcass, a roiling grey gas, like a thundercloud. The Hunger roars and I dive for the soul. It pours through me, sparkling and beautiful, filling me, stretching me, until it feels as though my skin can't contain it. I arch my back, my arms wide. I am a canyon surrounding a river of beauty.

The water recedes and I am left a bubbling mess of contentment, burbling with victory.

As I stand among the wreckage, frothing with delight, drunk on a sweet soul, I catch a flicker out of the corner of my eye – the horrified face of the ghost girl as she slips away through the wall.

Her eyes, once again, filled with tears.

I leave behind a mess, the walls painted in a style reminiscent of Jackson Pollock. Red, grey, black, brown.

Mostly red.

I prefer a more neo-Impressionistic style myself – Seurat, Signac! – but my medium has its limitations. Usually I try to be a little tidier – mustn't see my face on the news (especially with this haircut). But this is not a place that wants an investigation and I like the message only a rearranged corpse can deliver (Picasso!). Well, a corpse and a message written in blood – just in case I was too subtle:

I am watching.

Underneath it, I prop a little love note to the administration letting them know I know where the bodies are buried – in at least one case, literally. They won't be calling anyone.

I'm soul-drunk. The world's too bright; I feel too strong. A soul doesn't sit heavy in the gut, but bubbles through the veins like champagne, tingling the nerve endings. For at least an hour it cocoons my brain in cotton, protecting it from the talons of shame and worry. Later they'll dive back down and dig in their beaks, but for now they can only circle uselessly above. I laugh and sneer, able to forget for now that they'll have their revenge.

I stroll down the corridor and the flickering fluorescents celebrate my passing, humming in praise. I spin, bow and hum along. Bloody footprints trail; bloody fingers smear the walls. I reach the door to the stairwell and spin, heading back the way I'd come.

I'm in no hurry, because Gideon won't be. He's a good wingman and wouldn't want to interrupt Samson's fun.

Which is exactly what I want to discuss.

I reach a locked doorknob and I snap it off, then the next. Most of the inhabitants won't run far – they were sent to an insane asylum for a reason, after all. But they have the opportunity and, if they get far enough away, they might end up at a different facility, one with a different philosophy.

Some I leave in their cages. Even an animal rights activist wouldn't loose a tiger.

I'm swollen with the sweetness of Samson's dark soul, filled with it. Strong with it. It has been too long since I fed the Hunger. Like anyone on a diet, I've found that complete abstention never works – it just leads to poor decision-making later. Of course, my binges don't result in weight gain, but rather indiscriminate homicide. I'd say the stakes are higher, but then a Twinkie would no doubt disagree.

Hinges creak behind me; then I hear the pitter-pat of bare feet as someone flees, away from me – their savior.

Come back, we can be friends!

A door slams. Guess not. Ah, well, Spider-Man didn't have any friends either.

Creak-creak, pitter-pat. Another escape.

Come now, Gideon, investigate!

I prance, I dance on the gritty floor. Vengeance is sweet, sweet music. I spin, arms outstretched. The walls pass by in a blur of grey-white-grey-white-grey.

Then, suddenly, a spot of black enters my spinning vision – a figure at the door. The nurse has arrived! I stop and hiss.

Not Gideon – times three. Three strangers stand at the end of the hall.

And they are hissing back.

Two

Humans don't hiss. Well, except trashy girls fighting over equally trashy men. But grown men, respectable in black suits, do not hiss at their enemies. I blink and shake my head, trying to clear the fuzzy soul-drunk and, when I open my eyes the strangers are still there, though there's no hissing. Maybe it was a disapproving hiss, a what-are-you-doing-out-of-your-cage? hiss. Maybe I imagined it, the soul-drunk playing with my mind to turn this into a fight. It's a violent thing, the soul-drunk.

The three men stand at the end of the long hallway, in front of the stairs leading down to the ground floor. Respectable-looking men in neat suits with tidily trimmed hair – modern, urban men, incongruous in this dark and dirty dwelling for the insane. The one on the left is short with puffy, soft-dough cheeks, while the one on the right is tall and hawkish. The one in the center has the pitted face of an acne survivor, but is otherwise middle-aged unmemorable. The grey expanse of the narrow hallway separates their skin from my claws and my feet from the exit.

"What are you doing here?" asks the man in the middle. He straightens and tugs his suit smooth.

Yes – I, the girl with the ridiculous haircut and blood-splashed nightgown – am the one who doesn't belong in the insane asylum.

"Have you been reassigned?" he continues. "Why wasn't I made aware of this?"

Um. I straighten out of my own crouch.

"Did zi-Ben send you?" Hawkish asks.

Who?

"Is this some kind of joke?" demands Puffy.

That zi-Ben – he's such a kidder.

"And what on earth have you been doing?" demands the one in the middle.

Better not answer that, though they'll probably notice soon enough. No way to hide it. I eye the three of them, considering. They'll need a lesson in discretion before I go. Not a lethal lesson. Mom wouldn't like that.

But, if there's a fight… accidents happen. The Hunger hums.

The leader's still ranting. "I don't know where you've come from, but we're near the Templars here. You tripped every alarm we set – if they have any of their own…"

Right, the Templars… who? Not that it matters.

"I told zi-Ben we could handle it," he continues, shaking his head. "Even while helping in The Search… I mean we have Skype – this isn't the dark ages any more. The asylum practically runs itself, anyway. We don't need some junior associate in here screwing things up!" He waves at me.

Do I look corporate? Maybe they belong here more than I thought.

Puffy swipes a finger through a blood smear I left on the wall and licks it.

Holy crap. Maybe they do belong here.

At the taste of the blood, a shocked look comes over his face – mirroring the shock on mine no doubt. But I'm trying to hide my confusion, so maybe he doesn't notice. He's been largely quiet, but now he explodes.

"This is… this is – did you eat Samson?" Puffy ends in a bellow. "I've been working on him for months. I almost had his soul, I was this friggin' close!" Pinched fingers, red face. "All these easy vics around and you eat Samson! Unbelievable! Not to mention, who am I going to get to work the damn midnight shift?"

I've never been caught "eating" people before, but somehow I imagined a different reaction. For the barest moment the world sharpens and something tingles in my mind, a worry trying to work its way through the cotton.

But worries are for people who can't pull grown men apart with their bare hands.

Puffy storms forward and I drop back down and hiss again. He draws up short and they share meaningful glances.

"What did you say your name was?" The leader again, his eyes narrowed.

Should I lie? But what would be the point? Even if I leave them alive (*I will, Mom, really!*), they would be foolish to follow me once they know what I can do.

"Meda," I say and they exchange glances again.

"Zi-Meda or hal-Meda?" the middle one asks slowly.

Hmmm... fifty-fifty chance to get this one right. "Zi," I say. Judging by the way they all just bared their teeth, that was the wrong answer. I'm pretty sure they just figured out zi-Ben didn't send me. It looks like we are going to fight after all. *Sorry, Mom, I tried.*

Did you? Her voice drifts across my mind.

Yes! I can almost see her arms cross and hear her foot begin to tap. I can't see her expression. Time has washed it away. *Fine, no.*

I really wish she was still alive. I can't lie to a memory.

"Zi-Ben didn't send you, did he?" Suspicion confirmed. "Who did you say you are?"

Your death, strange human. I mean, your injury. No murder, just a little maiming. So I can leave. Maiming's not so bad.

They crouch themselves, mimicking my stance, spreading out across the narrow hallway. They creep forward in smooth, slithery steps. That's fine, I like my food delivered – especially when I don't need to tip the driver.

Not food, foe. I'm not going to kill them. Really.

Here piggy, piggy, piggy.

They come closer. I could attack them from here, but they can't reach me yet. Not with little human leaps, not from there. Closer they come, their footsteps so quiet I almost can't hear them over the growl in my throat. Come in, come in, closer. I will leap over. Maybe a leap ⌐⌐⌐⌐⌐⌐s. Just a few! Just to mess up those ⌐⌐⌐⌐hem know *what* was here, *what* they escaped. It's rather humanitarian of me, helping them to count their blessings. Appreciate what they have – like their heads. Too many people take them for granted.

I crouch even lower as they approach, while rising on the balls of my feet. Ready to leap, ready to dive over. Ready to show these fools that they do not control me. I am not some weak little human. I am unique, special. Powerful in a way they could never anticipate. In fact, I've never felt more powerful. Samson's fresh soul must have been extra strong.

They move in. Twelve feet, ten feet, eight. Their teeth show through snarls and the narrow hallway vibrates with the sound of our enmity. Their fingers curve like claws, just like mine. Do they mock me? I hope so. Deflated arrogance fits beautifully on a plate of defeat.

They're close.

Six feet. I leap, perfectly measured, towards the gap between their heads and the drop ceiling. In the dance of death I am a ballerina, a leaping lady. I want to see the widening eyes, the shock, the awe. I look down and instead see a fist and an explosion of red.

I hear a crunch, a chorus of cackles.

I fly backwards and slam into the wall, then collapse, face first, to the floor, gasping. I can't catch my breath. I push myself on to my back, blinking the confused clouds from my eyes.

How…? My boggled mind clings to the word with a death grip. *How?* I'm one of a kind. Mom said I was special. But evidence to the contrary stands over me, burbling with wicked giggles, erupting with maniacal cackles.

My prey doesn't cackle, *I* cackle.

Instead, I lie in a pool of my own deflated arrogance and a horrible sneaking suspicion dawns.

They are like me. *Like me*.

"What was *that*? Did you just try to *jump* over us?" The leader's jeering voice cuts into my confusion, and I focus on his face. "And you're only a halfling? 'Zi', my ass." He howls with laughter.

They're also assholes. I leap to my feet with a growl, but unfortunately my knees are a little wobbly and I stagger, setting off another round of loud guffaws.

Puffy bends over, trying to catch his breath but Hawkish catches his eye and makes like he's going to dive, giving a girlish little jump, and Puffy loses it again.

My eyes narrow.

"Oooooh, don't make her mad!" the leader gasps around his laughter.

Rage replaces thought, carried to my brain in an effervescent stream, and I dive at his fat mouth. Quick as lightning, he side-steps and slams me into the wall, without even the slightest pause in his laughter. Hawkish claps him on the back, holding his stomach as the mirth bubbles forth.

You. Will. Stop. Laughing.

I whip around and make a motion like I'm going to dive at him again, but, at the last possible second, I jump at his unsuspecting companion instead, punching Hawkish hard in the face. My thumbnail slides across his cheek, and a red line wells. I land, and grin.

Then realize I'm an idiot. A soul-drunk idiot.

What was I thinking? I finally get the opportunity for some answers and what do I do? I punch it in the face.

Dammit.

They stop laughing and, as the crouching and snarling resume, I realize that failing to get answers is now the least of my problems. They outnumber me, they're stronger than me and they're pissed.

Shit.

As they leap, I cut sharp and run, bent low, my feet flying. Snarls and stomps follow behind me. I hit the stairs and leap down to the first landing, then turn and leap to the bottom. They race right behind me. I blast through the door and it explodes out of its frame at the contact. It slows me, only a half-second, but it's enough. I'm tackled from behind. A blur of brightly patterned furniture and warm orange wall paint flashes across my vision as we crash and skid across the floor. The lobby is the only inviting room in the asylum and, not coincidentally, the only room visitors are allowed to see. I find it sadly ironic that I'm going to die in the only room worth living in.

I twist so I'm facing my captor – the man I clawed, Hawkish. He slams me into the wall, and the stud gives under my back.

It *hurts*.

He wraps his hand around my throat. Blood dribbles down his face.

"You think you can attack me, halfling?" Hawkish leans in, his beaky nose nearly touching mine.

I'm a halfling. Half-something. Half of whatever they are. He slowly strokes my cheek in the same place where I cut him, pulling the skin with each pass. I open my mouth to apologize, to ask the questions I've been dying to know the answers to my whole life.

But his question beats mine out of my mouth, his black eyes hard on my face. "Think you can *cut* me, halfling?" His thumb presses into my cheek and the nail bites into the skin. The sting becomes a burn as he pushes harder. As the blood begins to crawl down my cheek, the questions of "who" and "what" shrivel and die on my tongue. He's going to kill me.

As if to prove my point, he jerks his thumb across my face. My steel skin parts like silk. I squeal and scramble, fighting his hold. He leans forward, menace radiating from him. Was this what my victims felt like? Powerless? Sweaty? Heart pounding?

"Hal-Karim, we aren't supposed to kill our own," the leader says, stepping into the lobby.

Yes, you can't kill your own! Own *what* is suddenly an unimportant detail.

"But accidents do happen," my captor snarls.

My heart stops.

"She's only a halfling. We'll say she's a traitor. That she flipped sides," Puffy offers. Apparently he's still pissed about Samson.

"That might even be true," Hawkish says and strokes the other side of my face, his nails rasping against my skin. I squirm to get away. "Why else would she pick Samson?"

Flip from what side? I have no idea but it's my only chance. "I didn't flip sides! I just couldn't resist! He attacked me first!"

He isn't buying and I recognize the look in his eye. Bloodlust. I often see it in the mirror. It's too late. How ironic I learn I'm not alone as I die.

When Mom told me I was special and unique, I thought she literally meant I was special and unique. After all, I never met any other children who could lift cars or chew on steel bolts.

Turns out I'm only 'mom-special'. Special like a snowflake is special. Special like a school kid on honor roll.

There are others like me. And they want to kill me.

That would have been good to know, Mom!

"Please…" I won't give up. "It's the truth. I didn't flip–"

"Shhhh." The hungry eyes gobble mine. "The truth doesn't matter when you look so… delicious." He leans in, breathing deep. His tongue snakes out and slithers wetly across my cheek, licking the blood trickling down my face. He sneers, he smiles. Then he freezes. His eyes widen and his tongue darts out to lick me again.

Those wide, wicked eyes meet mine. "Are you…?"

A loud bang echoes through the room and we all turn to face the entrance. The front door has been kicked open.

Someone else has come to join the party.

Three

As parties go, the food is good but the hosts are complete assholes.

The new attendee, a man, crouches in the doorway. Well, not really a man, a human teenager. One of God's most misbegotten creatures – big like grown-ups and yet dumb like children. Selfish, moody, reckless, with a tendency to sleep too much and complain too often. I'm a teenager too, but I take exception to the human part.

He's around eighteen. Grungy jeans, faded black hoodie under a leather sleeveless jacket. Blond, shoulder-length hair. An attempt at a beard (fail).

The million-dollar question – whose side is he on? Unlikely to be mine, as I've never really been much of a team player.

"Crusader!" hisses one of my attackers.

The words have no sooner slithered from his lips than the boy lobs a brown, grapefruit-sized ball into the room. As it arches over us, he raises a gun and shoots it. The ball explodes and liquid showers down. I duck behind Hawkish, but some still finds my exposed shoulder and it burns. My captor screams and collapses on the floor writhing – he took the brunt of the flying liquid. I don't see the other two – they must have taken cover in the stairwell or one of the several hallways feeding off the main room.

"Do you want to be demon-chow? Come on!" the boy shouts to me.

Demon-chow? But that's a thought for another moment. I need no further encouragement and race towards the entryway. Towards my savior.

It's an unusual feeling.

The clip of shoes behind me alerts me that one of the "demons" is chasing me. His claws brush my back and I dive past the boy, out of the lobby and into the entryway, bringing my savior and the demon into a collision course. They crash with a meaty thud. I jump to my feet and back away from where they grapple. The boy shoves the demon back into the lobby and they go rolling. I creep back towards the door to keep an eye on the action.

The leader kneels by his fallen comrade, who still writhes on the floor. The leader half-rises, but Hawkish clutches at his neck and whispers in his ear. With a shocked look at his friend, then a final snarl at me, he chalks something on the linoleum and, with a crack like thunder, the two of them disappear.

Poof. Just like that.

A crashing noise drags my attention to where the newcomer and Puffy face off. A rust-colored couch is tipped on its back and the combatants roll around on the remains of what was once a coffee table. The boy scrambles free of Puffy and jumps to his feet. He pulls a wicked-looking knife, long and curved, from his belt. I creep back into the lobby, but keep my distance while I debate my options. I pull the door to the entryway closed. No matter what I decide, I don't want any additional audience members.

Desire for revenge pulses in my veins. I want to punish the demon. Crush! Kill! And above all – cackle! They claim revenge is a dish best served cold, but I've found it to be equally delicious hot – not unlike fried chicken. Two-on-one, the boy and I could probably take him. If nothing else, the boy can serve as a distraction as the demon tears him to shreds.

But a strong dose of self-preservation holds me back. I've already learnt the hard way that the demons are stronger than me – or at least a lot more accustomed to fighting people who can fight back.

So I stand. Indecisive.

The demon looks similarly indecisive, his eyes shooting between the two of us, then back to where his friends disappeared. The boy steps in his way, obviously blocking him off.

"You're not thinking of running, are you?" the boy taunts, blue eyes narrow as he passes the blade back and forth between his hands. "I'm not even a full Crusader, just a kid. You're not afraid of a kid, are you?"

The snarling leap seems to indicate "no". In a move too fast to be merely human, the boy jumps to the side as the demon streaks by. With a smooth motion, the boy rolls back to his feet and dives at the demon's back, slashing hard across its spine. The demon shrieks to shatter glass, his back arching as if someone had pulled his bowstring. The boy pins the demon face down as it flails and puts his hands on its bare neck. Inky black smoke billows out of the demon where the boy makes contact with its skin. The smoke then disappears into the boy's fingertips, like he's some demon-smoke-sucking sponge. Once all the smoke is absorbed, the boy releases the now-limp demon and stands. He's a little wobbly and he puts a bracing hand on the wall. Then he tips back his head and exhales a long stream of light grey fog that I instantly recognize. I recognize it because I routinely eat it.

It is the essence of a human soul.

I sit down. Hard.

The boy pushes himself off the wall and his forehead scrunches with concern. Concern's good. Concern means he's not going to turn on me now that the others are out of the way. "Are you OK?" he asks.

OK? I've gone from thinking I'm Superwoman (OK, so maybe her evil twin) to having my ass handed to me. I learnt my beloved mom was one big, fat liar and now here's a boy *exhaling* souls who might try to kill me any minute. It's been one hell of a day.

But, it occurs to me he's probably asking about all the blood and not my emotional turmoil.

I nod, then hold out my gown. "It's not mine. Another man was attacked." The boy makes to take off for the stairs – can't have that! "Don't leave me!" He pauses and I shake my head. "He's dead. He was... torn apart."

The Hunger flares at the memory, and I look down to hide my exhilaration.

"I'm sorry," he says, and I sneak a peek at him. "That must have been hard."

I try not to snort.

I examine the boy from beneath a ragged curtain of hair. He still doesn't look as if he suspects anything and an idea takes root. Despite his grungy appearance, the eyes are guileless and the face open. Giddiness sweeps through me. A second chance for some answers stands in front of me, wrapped in a simple-minded package.

I'll need to tread carefully. Just because he's against my enemies doesn't mean he's for me. In fact, had he shown up half an hour earlier, I suspect this would have been a very different conversation. If he senses I'm more than some hapless victim, this could still go sideways.

But the opportunity for some answers…

My… *specialness* was one of those we'll-talk-about-it-when-you're-older topics. Turns out, it wasn't *my* getting older that became the issue, but my mom's. Unfortunately there aren't any equivalent books to *How Babies Are Made* to cover these particular gaps in my education. I know Mom didn't plan to get murdered, but I still curse her lack of foresight. Never more so than today.

This boy might have the answers; I just have to take them from him. I consider the many tools at my disposal, eyeing his large blood-splattered frame, and settle on my weapon of choice – one so infrequently used I need to dust it off first.

My eyes fill with tears. "Wha–" I swallow hard "– what were those things?"

"Demons." Thanks, Einstein. I got that part. "Turns out spiritual warfare is a lot less theoretical than you probably think."

How many times had he practiced that line? I wouldn't make judgments on what *I* think, silly boy. I let a tear trickle over.

He hurries to reassure me. "Don't cry – I'll protect you."

Humiliating. Absolutely humiliating.

"What do they want?" I ask. The boy sits down on the floor next to me and pats my bruised back reassuringly. I try not to wince and look up at him like he's my hero – which is equally painful.

"To destroy the world," he says. Apparently wannabe monster-hunters tend towards the dramatic. I turn my attention to the body lying across from us to hide my irritation.

"Destroy the world?" I push. The boy sees where I'm looking and stands. He walks to where it lies and pulls a rustic-looking, clay globe from his belt. I recognize it as the same kind he had lobbed into the room; the kind that burned my shoulder. He pops a cork and pours liquid all over the corpse. The body starts to smoke and bubble. He turns back to me, holds the ball to his lips and takes a swig. I gasp.

"Don't worry! It's just water! Well, holy water. But it only hurts demons."

I discreetly tug my nightgown's neckline to more completely cover the burns on my shoulder.

He offers the ball to me. "Thirsty?"

I try not to look appalled.

"So, how do they try to destroy the world?" I ask again. He's starting to make me consider the other tools in my arsenal. *Speak, boy!*

He squats next to me and tucks his hair behind his ear with his free hand. We both watch the body dissolve. "By taking it over. Outnumbering the good guys till there aren't any left. Most demons were once regular people who were convinced to sell their souls. Then, when they died, they became demons and started convincing others."

Finally, some helpful information. I didn't sell my soul – but maybe that doesn't count for halflings. I feel as though the definition of that's pretty self-explanatory. And colossal fibber though Mom's turning out to be, I'm pretty sure she wasn't a demon. "And the rest? How are the other demons made?"

"Some demons just are. I don't really know the specifics, though there are a bunch of theories. Angels that sided with Lucifer during the fall, minions created by Satan the way God made Adam." He shrugs. "I don't really worry too much about theories – just enough so I know who to kill." He grins toothily.

Under different circumstances, maybe we could have been friends.

He continues. "There are halflings, too – they're born. Succubae and incubi trying to inflate the ranks 'naturally'."

Ding-ding-ding! I try to dial down the curiosity in my expression from tell-me-now-before-I-rip-your-head-off-

and-try-to-suck-the-truth-out-of-it to "Please, do go on." It must have worked because he keeps talking instead of trying to run.

"Demons also feed on souls, good people that they couldn't turn – gives 'em kind of a high. They especially try to murder Beacons – people who are particularly good or who will have a positive impact on the world. Da Vinci, Gandhi, Betty White and Mother Teresa are the classic examples, but there's a bunch of other, much less well-known ones." He gives me a meaningful glance and I freeze. He can't know I eat souls. There's no way. All he saw was the demons trying to kill *me*. Oh my God, he must mean...

Bahahahahahaha. He thinks I'm a Beacon. I look down to hide my twinkling eyes. Bad day or not, that's hilarious.

"It's OK. You don't have to be scared, I'll protect you."

Big brawny man, protect this damsel! I try to look angelic and helpless – Beacon-ish. The haircut and the blood can't be helping. Fortunately he seems particularly thick. "And wh– what are you, exactly?" My voice is sweet. Timid. Awed.

"Malachi Dupaynes, but you can call me Chi."

I said *what*, not who. Funny, though, that his nickname rhymes with "die". A sign, I wonder? We shake and our hands stick a little, because of all the blood.

"I'm a Crusader. Or at least I will be, once I graduate." His chest puffs in that way of young men.

"But you're so strong." I fawn, I flutter. "Strong enough to fight that monster... you can't be just a normal *student*." I saw how he moved – he isn't just a human.

"No, that's in the blood. My ancestors have been fighting demons for centuries. We've been given certain… gifts… to help us."

Crap. That doesn't sound good. "How did you know I needed help?"

"I can sense demons – that's part of it too." Double crap. That doesn't sound good at all. If this "demon-sensing" thing kicks in, I'm screwed. "I knew they were here so I came to rescue you." His chest inflates. "It's what Crusaders do."

As he crouches biting distance away from this half-demon, I can't help but think he has a startlingly short and unimpressive career ahead of him. Because, although he just saved my life, he makes a career out of hunting my kind. Not that I feel the teeniest bit of loyalty towards my "kind", but it is going to be a problem once he senses what I am. There's no choice really.

I'm going to have to kill him.

Four

Mom wouldn't have liked it, but I find my near-death encounter has left me a little peeved with Mom at the moment. The killer part (ha, other than me) is it's my *second* opportunity to learn who I am. I've been wandering aimlessly around North Carolina for almost two months without a single break and now I've had the opportunity to learn the truth twice in two hours.

And for the second time in two hours, I'm going to punch that opportunity in the face.

If my shoulder didn't smart so bad, I'd reach up and pull my hair out.

But I don't really have a choice. He managed three demons on his own – three demons who handily whooped my ass. Answers don't mean a whole lot to a dead girl.

Even with Mom on mute, I still feel a little guilty about killing my rescuer. But what can I say? I've been known to bite the hand that feeds me. And anyway, he wouldn't have saved me if he had known the truth. My savior would quickly try to become my murderer if he did.

I'll compromise and make it quick. Having experienced the whole fear-and-pain thing, it's the least I can do. I just need him to turn his back and it'll be over before he knows it's happening. I cast around for a distraction – and my eye lands on the most obvious in the room.

I point to the smoldering corpse, "Are you sure it's dead?" It's mostly slime and smoke, so yes, yes it is. I'm banking on the fact that he seems more like the physically gifted type than the mentally.

"Yes."

"Maybe you should make sure."

"No, I'm pretty sure." His eyes twinkle.

"I think I saw it move."

"Unlikely."

"Just go look at it!" I snap, then cough and bring my order back down to a whimper, placing a hand on his arm. I look up through my lashes, then bat them a few times for good measure. "I'm sorry, I just want to make sure it can't come back to get me." He smiles like a boy asked to stomp on a spider for a silly girl and I know I've won.

It's a shame, he has a really pretty smile.

He hops to his feet and I put out a hand so he can pull me to mine. He strolls the few feet to the body while I hang back.

I look at his broad back and think about death. The colors, the flavors, the squelching and splashing. I think about the Hunger and the power. The control. The bloodlust grows and pulses through my veins, spreading like a hot, heady poison. I let it take over, glee replacing the little twinges of regret.

I crouch and I roll on to the balls of my feet. I tense. My legs are springs, my hands are claws.

I narrow my eyes, focusing on the back of his neck, where the brain stem becomes spine. The thin column that is so vitally, vitally important and yet so very, very fragile.

I draw back, preparing to spring. Lower, lower, lower. I am a sleek black leopard, a silent predator who delivers pouncing, painless death...

WHAM! The door bangs open *again*. I jump behind the overturned loveseat instead of towards my victim.

Five intruders in one night? This really is turning into a party.

Chi spins around at the sound, one hand flying towards a holy-water globe on his belt, the other for his gun. When he sees who it is he relaxes and straightens.

"What are you doing here?" he demands.

Limping in from the entryway is another teenager. A girl this time, with a metal brace wrapped from hip to ankle over her tatty jeans. She has wild-woman hair, olive skin and a glare that makes me marvel at Chi's courage. Her leather coat matches his, but hers has sleeves. A knife's sheath peeps out from beneath her jacket.

"What am I doing here? What the hell are you doing here?" She starts forward and I creep deeper into the loveseat's shadow. "*I* came to drag you back, you're not supposed to be – is that a demon?" She picks up her pace until she's standing over the bubbling mess. "You actually fought demons?" She says it as an accusation, but Chi's chest swells.

"There were three of them. I injured another but he escaped with the third," Chi brags.

In spite of herself, the girl can't contain her curiosity. "Did you—" she puts out her hands and wiggles her fingers "—purify him?"

"I did." Chi grabs the sides of his leather jacket and rocks forward a little. "He won't be reborn."

She looks impressed for about three seconds, then her scowl returns. "Well, it was stupid, coming out here by yourself. Everyone's too busy to rescue some idiot who likes to play hero. Besides, you're supposed to be guarding the school."

"Really? Then why didn't you stay at the school if they need protection so bad? Or did you plan on playing a little 'hero' yourself?"

"I'm not sure saving your stupid ass counts as heroic. Besides—" her mouth twists into a bitter shape and she smacks her leg-brace "—they wouldn't let me help even if the school was under siege. They wouldn't even let me fetch you if they knew."

Chi's eyes slide to her leg then awkwardly away. Then he's back on the offensive. "Why *did* you come? I had it under control. I don't need help."

She crosses her arms. "It's not always about you, Mr Hero. The Crusaders are away, so upperclassmen—" she snorts and corrects herself "—*able-bodied* upperclassmen are supposed to be guarding."

Chi rolls his eyes. "That's a BS job and you know it."

"Your orders are to protect the school, whether you like it or not."

"A Crusader school hasn't been attacked in centuries, if ever. I'm needed in the field – I'm better than anyone who graduated last year, they should have let me finish early."

She's unimpressed. "Well, they didn't."

"Aw, come on Jo, the demons were practically on our turf this time," Chi argues. "There wasn't anyone else to take care of it, so I needed to."

"You didn't *need* to do anything – demons are attacking people everywhere." She scolds him like he's a naughty schoolboy. A neat trick since he's at least six inches taller than she is. "You only went after these because you could make it back to school before you were caught." She narrows her eyes at him. "Or so you thought."

Chi switches tracks and looks charmingly sheepish. He takes a step closer and scratches the back of his head, making his triceps bulge gloriously. "Well, I'm not going to say it didn't help that it was so convenient…"

Unfortunately for him, she's not easily charmed.

"It was reckless and irresponsible–"

He cuts her off with a groan and an eye-roll. "You used to be more fun, Jo – you used to have balls."

"Yeah, well, I traded them for brains. I see you're still thinking with yours."

Haha, I fight the urge to like her.

"If I hadn't, she would have died." He points to where I crouch, peeking around the loveseat. I let my crouch collapse into a cower. Jo turns, obviously surprised to see me.

"Who is that?" If a fish could be furious, it would gape like Jo.

"The girl I rescued," Chi brags.

Ah, my poor ego, to be so defined!

"What's your name?" she demands.

I consider lying, but don't – they're both going to die anyway. Besides, Mom always said honesty is the best policy. I frown. Obviously not a policy she kept.

"Meda," I whisper, back to playing the innocent victim. I shuffle out from behind the loveseat, keeping my head lowered and my eyes on the floor.

"You live here?" she demands with all the gentleness of a fifteenth-century Spanish priest.

"Yes." That's sort of true. I've been here two weeks, which is longer than I stay anywhere these days. Silent seconds pass and I peek to see what is happening. Jo is examining me, taking in the cut on my face and my bloodstained nightgown.

"What happened to you?" Her tone is edged with suspicion.

I let my voice tremble when I answer. I actually am a little trembly – the attack *was* traumatic. "I was attacked by demons." Also sort of true, though not where the blood came from. She eyes me and I don't like the expression I see there. Analyzing, calculating.

"Whose blood is that?"

"A nurse here," I say, again lowering my eyes. "He didn't make it." Both true.

"Why would the demons come here?"

"To kill me." That one's barely true. They came because of some alarm I triggered, but I don't really know whether they planned to kill me. That's just how things ended up going. Dancing closer to that edge!

"Why?" How to answer that one without lying? Blast.

I open my mouth to lie when Chi cuts in, saving the day. "It's obvious. She's a Beacon."

That isn't true at all, but I didn't say it. I guess it really depends where you stand on the whole lie-by-omission thing. Personally, I'm on the fence.

"We need to bring her back to the school with us," Chi adds.

Jo stares at me for a few more awkward seconds before turning to him. "Can I talk to you for a minute? *Alone?*" She tosses a brittle smile in my direction before limping around the corner, from the lobby into a hallway. Chi smiles more genuinely, then follows her.

"We'll be right back," he assures me as they disappear around the corner.

Now's the time to kill them, while they talk. Although, if left alone long enough, there's a good chance they'll kill each other.

Chi will be first, as the bigger threat, then the gimp. I creep towards the corner, padding on silent feet. I peek around and can't see them, but I can hear them. I move towards the voices, coming from a room a few doors down.

"You met her for, like, two seconds – how can you possibly not like her?" Incredulous, from Chi, my stalwart defender.

"I didn't say I don't *like* her, I said I don't *trust* her."

"Still!"

There's a pause then Jo says, "She's too... slick. Smooth." Jo knows I'm wrong, but she can't quite put her finger on it.

Hehe, because it's too slippery.

"What? What does that even mean?"

Ah, the dismissive tone of know-it-all boys. But I know what she means. Of course I'm slick, smooth. My soul slithers, my face is a porcelain mask. All the evidence of my flaws is spackled over and sanded smooth – like a home-seller hiding the wicked cracks that evidence a poor foundation. Lies are smooth, deceit is smooth, slime is smooth, slithery slick smoothness of something very, very wrong.

Jo growls in frustration – at her inability to find the words or Chi's inability to find a brain, I'm not sure. I creep closer and peer into the room. They're in my sights, just feet away, standing in front of the only furniture in the room, a grey metal bed. Chi's back is to me. Ideal.

"Well, why do you trust her so much? You only just met her."

"I just have a feeling about her."

A silent beat from Jo. "You're an idiot."

I'm in complete agreement, but she seems to think it's a bad thing.

"She could be a demon for all you know!" Jo continues.

Yes, yes, she could. A wicked, crouching demon about to dive from the dark.

"No, she couldn't. I would know if she was a demon." He holds out something chained to his jeans and waves it at her. I roll up on the balls of my feet. Now, before he uses that thing...

"Well, you wouldn't know if she's a halfling, now, would you?"

Wait, what? He wouldn't?

WHAM. The front door again. You've got to be kidding me – this is getting ridiculous.

I take two giant bounds down the hallway, almost bringing me into the lobby, then turn one-eighty and pretend that I'm running away from the lobby just as Chi and Jo race out of the bedroom, holy globes and guns in hand. I decide to let the two of them discover the identity of lucky guest number six, so drop behind them.

My eyes are on the entryway, but my mind is somewhere else. The gimp said Chi can't sense halflings. Opportunity wars with risk as possibilities play out in my mind. I could infiltrate the Crusaders, snatch the secrets out from under their noses and then disappear. If they catch me, I'm toast. But if they don't…

Can I really afford not to? There's an entire society trained to kill me and I have no clue. Not to mention some very pissed-off demons.

And besides, it sounds like a lot of fun. Oh, and I won't have to kill Chi. That's a plus. Of course, it also means I won't get to kill the girl. Minus.

But Mom'll be happy.

Hmmm.

"Hello?" a girlish-boy voice warbles from the lobby, calling my attention back to the present. I watch Jo and Chi from where I crouch behind them and their eyes meet. "Hello? Anyone there?" The guns and globes go down.

"Uri?" Chi calls out.

"Chi?" It ends on a squeak.

"It's fine," Chi assures me.

Jo is already striding forward, out into the lobby. Well, as best as she can "stride" on that damaged leg. "Uriel Green, what are you doing here?" she demands as she disappears around the corner.

"Errr – gugh, ah…" Uri stammers. Jo must be treating him to the death stare. "I, uh, thought Chi was here."

"That didn't answer my question." It's a scolding growl, like the one Mom used on me when she found me… well, suffice to say she was angry. Chi and I come around the corner and there stands a beet-red boy, as shamefaced as a puppy who piddled on the floor. He has floppy, brown cocker-spaniel hair and paws too big for his body. I'd put him at twelve or thirteen, just barely sticking his toes in the puberty pool. No match for Jo's glorious fury. She'll eat him alive – not literally of course.

Unfortunately.

"Hey, buddy," Chi calls out.

"Chi!" The relief that floods from the boy would drown a lesser man. Chi takes it in his stride and claps hands with him.

"Whatcha doing here?" Chi asks. It's the same question Jo asked but without the undertone of impending violence. That makes all the difference and now Uri is bubbling to speak.

"I wanted to see you fight, and, you know, be your backup." Then he hurriedly adds, "Not that you'd need it!" There is a low growl from Jo and Uri inches away from her and points at me. "Who's that?"

"A Beacon I rescued," Chi says too casually. Uri provides all the awe and hero worship Jo did not deliver.

"Wow! Really?" The boy blinks at me like I'm a fascinating zoo animal, then looks to Chi like he's a rock star.

"That smear over there is all that's left of the demon I toasted." Chi points and Uri's too overcome to speak. He just gasps excitedly and dances around the slime pool like he has to pee.

Jo snorts in disgust. "Can we go? Those demons might come back with friends. Besides I would like to make it back before someone notices we're gone. I don't really want to spend the rest of my life in detention."

I'm pretty sure I hear Chi mutter "Spoilsport" under his breath. By the death beams shooting from Jo's eyes, I'm guessing she heard him too.

"Come on, Meda," Chi says. "You can ride with me."

Jo opens her mouth, but I beat her to it. "Where are we going?"

"Home, to the Templar headquarters and Crusader school," Chi answers.

"Wait, Templar like the *Knights* Templar?" I'm a well-educated monster. Home-schooled, of course. I don't play well with others.

"Exactly." He smiles, happy I've heard of them, I guess. "We're still around, only the Templars are a secret society these days, we–"

"*Secret*, Chi. *Secret* society," Jo cuts in, flinging her hands into the air.

Chi rolls his eyes. "She's a *Beacon*. We can tell her."

"You don't even know that! You're just assuming."

"She was being hunted by demons. Demons hunt *Beacons*. Plus I found her in an insane asylum. You know Beacons often end up in insane asylums because their genius is confused with insanity."

"You know who ends up in insane asylums even more often?" Jo asks, sharply sweet. "Crazy people!"

Chi continues as if she hasn't spoken, but I see his lips tighten. "We can't just leave her here. Besides, look at her. What do you think she's going to do – wipe out the entire school?"

Cue innocence! My sweet lashes flutter against my helpless cheeks, my useless hands wring the edge of my guiltless, blood-soaked nightgown. My lovely lips quiver over my pearly white teeth.

Jo isn't buying. "Demons do all sorts of crazy stuff. It could be a trap."

Damn, that gimp bitch is a hard sell. Chi hesitates; is he seeing reason instead of my harmlessness? I reach out a gentle claw – err, hand – and place it on his forearm, tugging his attention from her smarts to my lovely-little-girl helplessness. My lower lip trembles and I hear Jo snort in disgust. Now for the *pièce de résistance*!

"You…" Faux-brave sacrifice always chokes me up! "You can leave me behind. I–" deploy waterworks, hard swallow "–understand."

He crumbles, my tiny tears beat him down like powerful waves. "No," he says. "You're coming with us."

Victory! Take that, you clever cripple!

He turns towards her. "We'll test to make sure she's a Beacon as soon as we can."

What? Gulp.

Grrrr.

A draw.

Five

The mention of the Beacon test dumps a few more pebbles on the "risk" side of the scale, but not enough to outweigh the opportunity. Whatever the Beacon test is, it's obviously something they don't have with them, or that girl would no doubt whip it out and zap me on the spot. Or whatever. In any case, I can disappear or, better, make it disappear before it becomes an issue.

They say curiosity killed the cat, but I am unconcerned. I am smarter, though slightly less evil, than any cat.

Jo rummages in the office and comes up with a first-aid kit for my face. She wipes my cut with all the gentleness of a marauding invader and slaps it with a Band-Aid, sharing the happy news that I won't need stitches. My shoulder smarts, but I don't mention it – and not just because her bedside manner sucks.

We exit the lobby, tromping down the crumbling cement stairs. The other nurse I'd been so eager to play with, Gideon, is bound, blindfolded and stashed in the shadows. I can smell his fear – it's a good thing I'm already full.

"Where are you guys parked?" Chi whispers. I'm not sure who he's afraid will hear us. The insane asylum is located in the foothills of North Carolina, about thirty minutes outside of Marion, aka Nowhere, NC. Prospective asylums always seem to make the neighbors scream in protest.

"I parked next to you," Jo answers.

"Me too," pipes Uri.

"Well, that makes it easy," Chi says and we take off down the twisting black drive, an odd parade. A grungy young man, a girl in a blood-soaked nightgown, a prancing puppy and a cyborg.

The asylum is right off the highway, albeit back a half-mile at the end of a long drive. The unkempt property is lined with a chain-link fence entangled with thorny vines and saplings from the encroaching forest. The gate blocking the drive is chained closed, but as we get closer I see recently cut metal shine silver-bright among the rusty links. My rescuers must have cut it to get in, then draped the chain to make it appear as if it still held the gate closed. We stop to unwrap the chain, Uri rushing forward, eager to help.

"Geez, you must be freezing!" Chi says to me as we wait. I'm not, even though it's only mid-March. The cold never bothers me when I'm filled with the hot soup of bad souls. Nevertheless I make a show of shivering. Chi strips off his leather vest and I hold it as he peels off his hoodie, pulling his shirt up with it. I get an eyeful of carved six-pack abs and bite back a whistle. Demon-hunting must be good for the physique. The looks of an angel and yet all it makes me want to do is sin.

I catch Jo's expression. I'm pretty sure she's thinking the same thing.

Interesting.

Chi tosses me his hoodie and I put it on, trying not to let on that my arm hurts. It's still warm from him and a little icky with demon blood, but so am I – on the inside. He slips his vest back on over a plain white tee, and we take off again to find our getaway cars.

Our getaway cars are, in fact, getaway motorcycles, the big American kind with high handlebars and lots of chrome. Three are parked right in a row, tucked into the shrubs lining the highway. The leather jackets make sense now, and the patches on them obviously marked them as bikers, had I been paying attention. A black cross in the middle lined with red. Night's Knights arches across the top, and underneath Mountain Park MC.

Upon closer inspection there are actually only two motorcycles and one giant tricycle pretending to be a motorcycle.

"Motorcycles?" I whisper.

"Crusaders were knights, cavalry – the closest thing we have these days," Chi explains, waving at the bikes.

"Plus they're small enough for a Crusader to teleport, can go places cars can't, they're cheaper and the mileage is great," Jo adds wryly. "The Crusaders have a stable of cars too."

Motorcycles. I could crush them in my little hands, pop them as if they were balloons. Quite possibly I could eat them, though passing them might be uncomfortable. I could probably outrun them. But Human Meda yelps and whimpers.

"Aren't motorcycles… *dangerous*?"

Bahahahahaha.

"Not if you know how to drive one." Chi winks.

Jo turns to Uri, "Speaking of which, you don't even have your license yet."

"Well, no, not exactly…" He shoots SOS eyes at Chi.

"Aw, come on, Jo. You and I were sneaking out on our bikes when we were much younger–"

Her death glare is back, killing his words. "And, if an adult had caught us, we would have been chewed out."

"So you're an adult now?"

"One of us ought to be."

"Says the girl who snuck out to fight demons."

"I did not–" Jo starts, then clamps her jaw and takes a breath. "Put on your helmet, let's go." She climbs on the tricycle. I guess they gave her an extra wheel since she's short a leg.

"You sure you want me to wear my helmet?" Chi taunts. "You might choke the next time you bite my head off."

Jo doesn't dignify that with an answer and instead guns her trike and roars off. Chi actually doesn't wear his helmet but passes it to me. I put it on and climb on behind him. I'm pretty durable, but concrete and I have faced off before. While I didn't die, I wouldn't say I won, either. Chi waits as Uri gets situated on his bike and we follow.

The whistling wind steals my attempts to talk, so I give up and think instead. Any lasting effects of the soul-drunk are long gone – there's no brain-cotton cocooning me from my thoughts now.

Like any fatherless child, I've wondered about the man responsible for the glory that is me. Needless to say, it's disappointing to learn he's the kind who'd probably eat his young.

I've always known I'm a monster. My skin is as tough as sheet metal, my bones are almost impossible to break. I can run faster and jump higher than any Olympian. My strength is unreal. And let's not forget, I eat people (though I was exaggerating about the whole motorcycle thing).

But somehow it's different, knowing I'm not just any monster, but the walking embodiment of evil. Though again, I still shouldn't be shocked. Not with the things I've done. My conscience is such a pathetic, silent thing I had to share off Mom's like a parasite, sucking the goodness out of her because I have none of my own.

Mom knew. I don't know how much she knew exactly, but she always knew I was different. Bad. She watched me for signs of wickedness, for violent tendencies. The Hunger. She was never surprised when the naughty traits appeared but she was always dismayed. I guess she didn't know how much of my DNA soup was going to come from dear old Dad's pot.

It makes sense now, why she wanted to wait until I was older to tell me. She didn't want to tell her grade-schooler she was a child of evil. Maybe she thought if I knew I was half-demon, I'd give in to the demonic side. Use it as a justification to do all the naughty things I dream about.

Not a bad idea...

Chi's spinal column is inches from my mouth. It screams, "Bite me!" I don't, though. He's driving.

I wouldn't anyway, now that there's a good chance he isn't going to kill me – or try, rather. Mom only wanted me to kill people who deserved it, and my morality's flexible enough to toss in self-defense (and everyone knows the best defense is a good offence… my morality is almost a contortionist). There were reasons why I should only kill people who deserve it, but they don't matter to me anymore. Only for her sake do I try to launder my dark and dirty soul, keep it as clean as my nature will allow. I try, I really do, but it's getting harder, without the bright light of my mother's goodness to shine on the stains. It's why I came to North Carolina, where my mom grew up, to try to feel closer to her, to try to find some truths, maybe even some family. Because even if she did lie, Mom's sin against me is minuscule compared to mine against her… but I don't want to think about that. I scuttle away.

What other secrets did you keep, Mom? Is my father really dead? What would it mean if he's not? Mom kept me from him for a reason, but was it to keep me safe or to keep the world safe from me? I just don't know.

I asked about him, of course, especially when I was younger. She always refused to answer, but the questions alone were enough to fill her face with shadows. I imagined some sort of tragic love story caused that look, but now I see it was more likely a horror.

I don't like to think what it meant, then, raising me.

The miles fly, street lights zinging past. Occasionally I see the sparkling silver mist of a ghost. They always lift their heads like startled deer as we pass. Somehow they know I can see them. I look away; I don't want to deal with any of their baggage now.

We head further west on I-40, into the mountains. I pay close attention to our route. As a demon, it seems prudent to know where the demon hunters hang out.

The air grows colder as we climb. Chi wears gloves but his arms are still bare. If he was a regular human his arms would have frozen off by now. As it is, he takes turns tucking one arm then the other against his chest.

We take I-74 into Waynesville, then even further into the mountains on Highway 23. We wind through the giant metropolis of Sylva (population 2,435, the sign proudly proclaims), then on to one twisty mountain road after another. The sky starts to lighten behind us and Jo's tail-lights slow. She pulls to the shoulder and we join her. Uri as well.

Jo pulls off her helmet, her curly hair sticking up wildly now that it's been set free. "We need to get our stories straight," she says. It appears I wasn't the only one thinking during the drive.

Chi dismounts and holds the motorcycle steady so I can climb off. "I figured we could pass her off as my cousin, Cassia," he says. "Say she came to visit. She goes to the school in California and hasn't visited in years. No one would recognize her."

"And then do what with her?"

Chi shrugs. Apparently that's as far as his plan goes.

Jo doesn't appreciate his nonchalance. "You can't just keep her."

"Why not?" Chi asks too innocently.

Jo doesn't fall for his needling, and says, her voice sweet, "Well, for one, the school has a policy about pets."

I stick out my tongue and Chi laughs.

"They'll figure out she doesn't belong eventually and then we'll be busted." Jo winces.

Chi thinks for a minute, then his face lights up. "Asa's due back in a week or so. He's unassigned; he'll take care of her for us." Chi turns to me. "He's my older brother and he doesn't have a Beacon yet. He's also the wild one in the family, so he won't rat."

Asa's the wild one? God help the good guys.

Jo lets out a gust and her shoulders relax. Apparently she really was worried about getting caught. "That'll work."

Hmmm. That only gives me a week. I was hoping for more. With Samson's soul bubbling fresh in my blood, I won't need to feed for four, possibly six weeks if I push it. But a week's better than nothing. And really, pretending to be some kind of saint is going to stretch even my truth-warping abilities. Everyone has limits – saintliness is definitely one of mine.

Jo cocks her head and examines me. "But she can't be Cassia. Cassia's a total goody-goody."

"So?" Chi asks.

I know the problem and pull off my helmet. Fashion guru he may not be, but Chi recognizes my hairstyle as not exactly de rigueur for goody-goodies these days.

"She can be my cousin Emma," Jo suggests.

"Emma? But Emma refused the Inheritance, why would she come visit here…" Realization dawns. "…

which is why she *can* be here even though she's not a Crusader." Chi smiles and Jo smiles back, almost involuntarily. Chi's smile stretches wider and Jo must have realized what she did because she pulls back with a cough and looks away.

Interesting.

"Right, well." She turns to me. "Think you could pretend to be a bad girl? She's kind of a bitch."

The laughter almost chokes me in its attempt to burst free. Through sheer force of will I manage to answer solemnly. "I can try." I even manage to keep a straight face as I add, "Maybe you could give me some pointers?"

Chi and Uri are less talented than I am and do choke on their laughter. To my surprise Jo isn't angry. She won't give me the satisfaction of acknowledging a point well-earned but she can't stop her eyes from laughing.

"We'll have to get you something else to wear."

"You don't like it?" I hold out the grey and gory mess.

"The bloody nightgown is so last year."

"Where are we going to get clothes?" Chi asks.

"My parents' place. I have some old stuff still there."

Something about that answer must have come as a surprise because Chi starts. There's a pause, but all he says is, "We gotta get the bikes back in the garage before someone sees they're gone first."

"We'd better push them from here. I bet Professor Palmer is already up," Jo says.

Chi makes the mistake of asking her, "Can you push?" and receives the Return of the Death Stare.

And we'd all been playing so nicely.

Jo shoves off with a huff. The others push their bikes along and I trail, weak human that I am. It's not far before we turn off the main paved road on to a gravel one cut into the woods. The road is more of a path really, two deep ruts where wheels have cut into the dirt, half-assedly scattered with gravel. The road arches up, making the bikes harder to push, and the boys and I pass Jo in the left rut. None of us are stupid enough to ask if she needs help. Well, they aren't stupid enough. I just don't want to.

I'm a little excited now that we're getting close. A secret society of demon-killing superhumans hidden in the North Carolina Mountains? Wild. What will their hideout look like? Will they have a castle, being Knights Templar? Or maybe a state-of-the-art underground complex like in spy movies? We come around a bend and I can see it. Spread out before us is...

A trailer park.

No, I am not kidding. Total letdown.

A small valley spreads out before us, overflowing with trailers, as if they had been poured in and splattered on the nearby hills. A smattering of bigger, metal-sided buildings, carports and aluminum sheds dot the property and one enormous building squats on the far side, but I can't make out any details. The sun is just rising and no sunlight reaches down into the valley yet, giving it the appearance of a dusky bowl of trailer soup.

"You live in a trailer park?" I ask Uri, who happens to be closest. The road slopes downward now, meandering back and forth down into the valley.

"I don't," Uri answers. "I still board at the school. But my parents do, when they're here, and all my brothers and sisters. They're older." He gives a funny little skip, skids on the gravel and almost loses control of his bike. He catches it with a grunt, before adding, "A lot older."

"Uri here was an 'uh-oh baby'," Chi inserts. "Don't worry." He tosses a look over his shoulder, sending his blond hair swinging. "The best of us are."

"'Uh-oh baby'?" I ask.

"Yeah, you know, when the parents find out they're pregnant and they say, 'Uh-oh.' Uri's parents were like forty when he was born."

"I'll have you know, I am not an 'uh-oh baby'," Uri says loftily, but ruins it with a grin. "I asked my dad and he said I was more like an 'oh shit'."

Chi laughs and I can't help it, I do too.

"Anyway, about the trailer park," Chi explains, "Crusaders take oaths of poverty and our chapter, at least, takes that seriously."

"Chapter?" There're multiple demon-killing training facilities?

"Yeah, this is the Mountain Park base, but there're other branches spread out across the country – and the world."

I see the sign now. "Mountain Park" painted on a wooden sign. Some enterprising character has inserted a spray-painted "Trailer" between the two words.

"And they aren't all trailer-park biker gangs?"

Chi smiles. "No. The Crusader who founded Mountain Park was a bit of a nonconformist. He and his buddies were into bikes, and it made a convenient cover when they started their own chapter. Not too many people poke around a biker-run trailer park."

"Hey, guys," this from Jo, bringing up the rear, "we're trying *not* to get caught." We all get quiet as we enter trailer-town; the only sound is the gravel road crunching under our feet and tires. Light shines from a few trailers, but, for the most part, it's dark.

Eventually we come to three large metal-sided buildings in a row. A large porcelain sign with evident age proclaims: "Dinkin's Motorcycle Repair". Chi rolls up the garage door. Jo opens her mouth like she wants to shush him but then shuts it. She must realize there's no quiet way to reel up a garage door.

Inside are motorcycles. Lots and lots of motorcycles. An enthusiast's wet-dream number of motorcycles, and all the equipment necessary to fix them. Most of them have some version of the same motif – a cross, usually red on a white background. Chi, Jo and Uri quickly wheel their bikes into position, casting furtive looks around them. Chi rolls the door down and we move on to task number two: my makeover. What does a bad girl wear when pretending to be a good girl pretending to be bad?

Jo leads the way, sticking to the outskirts now that we don't have the bikes to push. Her limp is more pronounced – pushing that bike must have been harder for her than she let on. The sky gets brighter, highlighting the unkempt look of the trailer park. The closer I look the more I realize the trailers are more than just neglected, they're abandoned. Weeds sprout in front of doors, too many windows stay dark. You'd expect more cars, maybe some scattered toys. Something. Whoever lives in most of these trailers has been gone for a while.

We eventually cut back towards the main road and come to a stop in front of a beige-and-red trailer that was probably new in the 1970s. Weeds cluster at its base and the wooden porch looks rotten.

Home Sweet Home.

Chi, brave lad, hops on to the frail porch in two bounds. He holds up his hand and a tense Jo flips him a card from her pocket. He snatches it from the air and sets to jimmying the lock with an ease that speaks of long practice.

And these are supposed to be the good guys? The human race is doomed.

"Just like old times, eh, Jo?" That earns him a tense smile, but Jo is obviously not happy to be home.

"Hey, Chi, will you teach me how to do that?" Uri asks, gingerly climbing up the broken stairs to peer over Chi's shoulder.

"Of course, buddy."

"Why are you picking the lock? I thought you said this was your house?" I ask.

"It was my parents', and I guess it's mine now." She shrugs like she doesn't care, but the movement is too tight. "But I don't live here. I can't until I graduate."

"You don't even have a key?" I ask her.

"Most of the parents are off guarding Beacons. That's why all the kids live up at the school. They don't want us having a bunch of unsupervised hang-outs, so we don't get keys till we graduate." That seems to be working well – instead the kids have unsupervised hang-outs *and* know how to pick locks. The door opens with a soft click and Chi slips inside. Uri and I follow.

Stale, musty air smacks me in the face. This place obviously hasn't been used in a while. *It* was *my parents'*, she said. I look back at Jo and she stands at the door unmoving. Chi is watching her too.

"Jo? You OK?" Chi asks, softer than I would have thought him capable of.

Jo looks up. "Yeah, of course I am," she snaps, but still hesitates before stepping in.

The trailer is like most homes, just smaller and crappier. It has a couch and a TV – no flat screen here. A tiny kitchen. The usual shrine to family life hangs on the wall leading down the hallway. A smiling man and woman dominate most of the pictures. Judging by her wild curls and his hazel eyes, I assume they must be responsible for spawning Jo. A younger Jo grins from school photos or plays softball. A happier Jo, complete with two happy, healthy little legs.

Chi disappears into a side door and I follow. Jo's childhood bedroom. Well, bed-*closet*. Real bedrooms are bigger. I inspect the place – I wouldn't have pictured her as the lilac type.

A bed takes up almost the entire space, neatly made with a faded purple comforter. A boom box (and here I'd thought dinosaurs were extinct) sits on a low table along with a collection of tatty paperbacks, hairbands,

CDs and other evidence of childhood. On one wall is a cork board covered in posters, dated birthday cards and photographs. Some are again of family or school shots, but most are dominated by two people through the years. One is Jo and the other...

Chi.

Hmmm. From what I've seen, I wouldn't have pegged them for BFFs.

The boy in question is digging in the closet. "Jo! Are you coming? I don't know what to give her!" Jo limps in. The tiny room can't fit us all. I sit on the bed.

"Go get the scissors from the kitchen, and my..." Jo swallows. "...my dad's clippers out from under the bathroom sink. We're gonna have to do something about her hair." She eyes me. "No girl's *that* rebellious." Nice to see her sunny personality is back. "What happened to your hair anyway?" Then the more obvious question occurs to her. "Why were you in the asylum, for that matter?"

I'm tempted to say, "Because I'm crazy," just to see her reaction, but manage to bite it back. Instead I borrow a story I'd heard from a girl I met on the streets. "I didn't have anywhere to go." I shrug. "I thought the shelter would be... safer... than my last foster home, so I..." I finger my jagged locks and trail off, letting her fill in the blanks.

Her face says, "Bullshit," but her mouth stays closed.

Chi squeezes by her into the hallway and Jo takes his place digging in the closet. She comes up with jeans, which she lobs blindly in my direction, followed by a black T-shirt dominated by a neon-green high-top sneaker radiating more neon-green lightning bolts. Random. She digs deeper and produces a ratty military-style jacket. Army green with grommets and a belted waist. It's frayed around the edges but is actually pretty cool. Mom liked to keep me in pastels, as if their sweetness would eventually soak in.

"Change," Jo orders and gimps out, closing the door behind her. I do. Jo's taller than me and bustier, so I have to roll the jeans up and the shirt's a little loose, but it all fits well enough.

Chi and Jo are waiting for me in the bathroom. Well, Jo's in the bathroom but it's so tiny, Chi only has a foot in. To be fair, it's a big foot.

Jo's holding the scissors she sent Chi for. As a general policy I don't let girls who don't like me near my head with blades and I especially don't let them cut my hair. I squeeze into the bathroom and take the scissors from her. She shrugs, sets some clippers on the avocado sink and leaves me to it.

I'd really done a number on my lovely black locks. Jagged and short to a couple of inches on one side and long on the other. Fortunately, I'm an artist. I set to work.

My new haircut is still long on one side and short on the other, but it looks like it was done on purpose. There is always a fine line between fashionable and crazy. I think I am on the right side, if barely. The long side ends in a blunt edge at my jaw. The short side is feathered and layered. Very bad-girl chic.

I take advantage of the toiletries, lining my eyes heavily with eyeliner, above and below, and ink my lashes with mascara. Unfortunately there's no black nail polish, so I slap on a quick coat of dark purple.

I'm too thin, almost gaunt from my stay at the asylum, and pale. Crack-addict thin and pale. The cut on my cheek's no longer bleeding and adds a nice element of disreputableness, so I peel off the Band-Aid to show it off. With the black haircut, black-inked eyes and outfit I look like the kind of high-schooler that makes parents appreciate their own children. Perfect.

I join the rest of them in the living-closet where there's (slightly) more room.

"Wow!" Uri gapes. The peanut gallery approves. "How did you do that?"

"I'm good at cutting" – briefest pause – "hair." I think Jo catches my cleverness as the sharpness returns to her eyes. She says nothing, though, as she passes me a pair of men's socks and a beat-up pair of black Converses.

Chi's flopped on the couch trying to keep a pen standing on the tip of his tongue. He pauses long enough to check out my outfit, which earns a "Badass!" Uri plops down next to him and looks around, probably for a pen.

Jo slumps in the bile-beige recliner, eyes on her lap. "We need to hang out here till breakfast, then we'll join everyone else in the cafeteria."

I sit on the floor and put on my footwear. Uri finds a pen and he and Chi compete in the pen-tongue balancing game. Jo rips the Velcro on her leg brace, pats it back down, then rips it up again. Silent minutes, save for the repeated ripping, pass.

"How long till breakfast?" I ask.

"Ine-eerty," offers Uri, losing his pen mid-worthless answer. He rubs the slobber off his face. "9.30." It has to be close to 8. Kill me.

"So, what do I need to know to be Emma?" I ask. That seems to crack Jo out of her shell. She blinks up out of her misery, but doesn't answer. "Jo?"

"Right." She sits up straighter. "Fortunately no one likes Emma so you shouldn't have to say much."

"How can they not like her if they can't even recognize her?"

Jo shrugs. "She refused the Inheritance." I have no idea what that means so Jo clarifies. "She doesn't want to be a Crusader."

Smart girl. From what I can tell, the life of a Crusader sucks. "That seems harsh," I say.

That's enough to make Chi remove the pen. "How can you decide *not* to fight evil?" Chi really does have a good heart, but then maybe his bravery is influenced by the fact that he doesn't know how many times he almost died tonight.

And let's be honest, there's still a possibility.

Meda!

Kidding, Mom. Kidding.

"We're already outnumbered. The more who refuse to help, the more dangerous it is for the rest of us." This from Jo, the pragmatist. "In any case, you're the shame of your parents, your community – no one likes you.

Your dad, Elijah, and my dad are brothers. Your mom, Becka, became a Templar when they married, so you have lots of normal non-Templar cousins."

"And a weird name," adds the kid named Uriel. Seriously.

I'm lost. "What?"

They explain that Templars descended from the original Knights Templar, a religious order formed in the twelfth century. Their original goal was to protect pilgrims who wanted to visit the holy lands. Pilgrims were often good people willing to risk their lives to worship God. Some of them even had the potential to improve the world – Beacons. Demons figured this out and started picking them off, not that they needed a lot of help in those dark and dangerous days.

To even the odds, the original core group of Templars were granted special abilities by heaven along with special responsibilities – defeat demons, protect Beacons. The problem was, they were good at their job. Too good, though they managed to keep the reason a secret. Religious and world leaders took interest and started using the Templars for their own purposes. They forced them to recruit new members to expand their ranks, but these new members weren't given the secrets or powers that the originals and their descendants had. Eventually they were infiltrated by evil people controlled by demons and the whole thing went awry. The original Templars tried to restore its original purpose and, as a result, were violently disbanded in the fourteenth century. Many were executed, but some escaped underground. The surviving descendants regrouped. So only descendants of the originals have special powers.

"Oh, and anyone who marries a Templar," Uri adds.

"But how?" I ask.

They all blink at me.

Finally Uri answers, "Because God says so."

Fair enough.

"Templars are born with minimal extra powers – a little stronger, a little faster – until we undergo a ceremony on our thirteenth birthday," Jo continues.

"Some descendants of the original Templars are still out there, but they just don't know what they are," Chi explains, leaning forward with his elbows on his knees. "We try to keep an eye out and bring them back into the fold when we spot them. Usually families where all the kids have uncanny athletic ability. Unfortunately, sometimes we can't get to them soon enough."

"Do the demons get them?"

"Sometimes, but sometimes it's fame."

"Fame?" Now that's an enemy I wouldn't mind catching me.

"Yeah, like Serena and Venus Williams," Chi says. "We're pretty sure they're Templars."

"Or Peyton and Eli Manning," adds Uri and Chi nods.

"Their profiles are way too high to bring them in now." Chi shakes his head in regret. Somehow I doubt the superstar millionaires are as disappointed not to have traded their lives for a short, violent one accompanied by a vow of poverty.

"Are Templars ever Beacons?" I ask.

Chi thinks about it then shakes his head. "Not that I've ever heard of."

"In any case," good ol' Jo, keeping us on track, "on our thirteenth birthday, or when they are otherwise brought in, we undergo a ceremony when we come into the Inheritance and get all our super abilities. Or in Emma's case, don't."

"So I won't be expected to have any super abilities?"

"Nope. Maybe just a little extra athleticism." Chi winks. "We'll make sure no one asks you to play a sport."

This seems like the perfect opportunity to wrest more prudent information on my natural enemies. "So what kind of special abilities do Templars get during the ceremony?"

Chi and Uri both open their mouths to answer but Jo cuts them off, her sharp eyes on my face. "It doesn't matter, you don't have any."

Blast. It's becoming quite clear I'll have to lose my darling cuz in order to get more information. I only have a week and it'd take longer than that to get her to trust me. I wonder if she traded her leg for extra brains.

Fortunately, the boys spill information like I spill blood. Unfortunately, I don't think I will have to merge our two hobbies; I just need to separate her from the rest of us.

They spend the rest of the time explaining the rather dull specifics of Emma's background. She's seventeen (though no one can remember her birthday), she has a brother and a cat (gross to both), yadda yadda, snore, who cares.

Finally the clock rolls around to 9.15 and it's time to leave the dump and head to the school. Chi and Uri lead, while Gimpy brings up the rear. I think she wanted to take the lead – so far she hasn't struck me as a real good follower – but her leg slows her significantly. So significantly that she drops behind, unnoticed by the boys. She'd choke before she'd ask us to slow down for her and pretty soon she's out of sight.

Hehe.

We snake between trailers at a half-run, keeping bent below window height. The sun's fully up now, but it's still cold at this altitude and our breath comes out in little puffs. We cut left towards the opposite end of the valley from where we entered and straight ahead between the trailers I can now see the big building, which must be the school. I have to slow down to take it all in.

It's a crumbling brick box four storeys high with sprawling two- and three-storey appendages that shoot off at odd angles. When the extensions were added no one consulted the style of the original building (if "big box" can be considered a style), and the brick doesn't match. One wing looks as if it was poured from straight cement – or airlifted from the USSR, back when there *was* a USSR. Some wings look closed altogether, dressed with caution tape and boards over the lower windows. The rusting corpse of a swing set leans pathetically out front.

It's a monster, created by the architect Frankenstein.

Project Enlightenment Charitable School, a large and largely rotten wooden sign proclaims.

You've got to be kidding me.

I'm staring, offended at the school's ugliness, so I don't notice the wire-mesh enclosure at my feet until I stumble into it. It rattles and clanks at contact – waking the sleeping monster within, a scrawny little ankle-biter with a stumpy snout and wiry grey hair. It goes bonkers, barking like mad and attacking the wire-mesh fence like it wants to rip me to shreds. The feeling is mutual, but this isn't the time for that.

I look to where Chi and Uri stand twenty feet ahead of me, frozen in indecision, not wanting to run without me. The trailer's front door bangs open. I'm still behind the trailer with the demented beast, but Uri and Chi are directly in front. They tense to run, but it's too late.

"Don't move, I'm armed," a voice says from the front of the trailer.

Crap, we're caught.

Six

Yip, yip, yip, yip, yip.

"Malachi? Uriel? Is that you?" At least that's what I think the man said. I can barely hear over the stupid barking of the drowned-rat dog.

From where I stand behind the trailer, I can see Chi and Uri, but not the trailer's owner, who's at his front door. Chi's stance goes from bent and furtive to hands-behind-the-back angelic. A pleasant smile moves across his face and Uri tries to copy it, with less success. What little I can hear of the voice sounds old, so maybe his eyesight is bad enough that Uri looks convincing. It looks like they're exchanging pleasantries, but even my superb hearing is no match for that damn dog.

With a quick look at Chi and Uri to ensure their attention is elsewhere, I snake out my arm and snap up the little dog. Before I can do anything, Chi shoots a glance in my direction and I'm forced to smile innocently and pat the obnoxious beast on the head. The beast repays my kindness by twisting and snarling and trying to rip my hand from my wrist. Once Chi's attention turns back to the man, I grab the animal by its scruff and swing him around until his wet black nose is inches from mine. We lock eyes and I watch his widen as I snarl ferociously into its face. The dog pisses itself, but is blessedly silent. I toss him back into his pen. Sometimes bad things need to be reminded they're not the only ones who can bite. Chi turns at the dog's sudden silence. My smile is made of spun sugar.

Just to end a few debates, I can conclusively say dogs do have souls. Not deliciously large and filling souls like humans, but they are there. Nutritionally I'd say there're a dozen dog souls to one human. I suppose I could make the trade and survive, but I won't. A good dog is worth more than a bad human any day. I can also end another debate: all dogs do not go to Heaven, plenty of them are just as awful as they seem.

Uneven footsteps come from behind me and I turn to see Jo, catching up.

"They get caught?" she whispers. I nod. "Well, at least it's just Fredrick. He won't remember five minutes after it happened. Let's just hope no one else notices." She looks down at the dog, which is whining and scrabbling in the dirt. She scoots a step or two further away from it.

"Ugh, I hate pets," she mutters.

Interesting. Most girls love animals. Pets specifically. I look at her curiously.

"Why would anyone pay that much money for a *chore*?" she whispers. Wow, she just might be less human than I am. I, at least, appreciate a good dog. Actually, I even enjoy a bad one – just not in the same way.

We wait while Chi and Uri finish lying to Fredrick and cheerfully wave him goodbye. We hear a door close and the boys beckon us to follow. There are no more unwanted encounters as we make our way to the most dilapidated wing of the school, then around to its back, coming to a stop at a heavily rusted door. Someone slid a piece of cardboard in the doorjamb to keep the lock from catching and it opens easily at Chi's tug. He peers in then slips through the opening, motioning for us to follow.

And so I take a deep breath and step into the Meda-killing training facility.

Finally. This is more like it.

The interior is the polar opposite of the cracked and decrepit exterior. The lower windows are boarded because they wouldn't want anyone to see what's inside. After all, most high schools don't include a combat training center. At least not on purpose – some inner-city playgrounds functionally qualify.

The two-storey gymnasium looks like a typical school gym with a shiny but scuffed wood floor, white block walls and folding bleachers, except it's filled with not-so-typical training implements – punching bags, shooting targets, a fighting cage, a boxing ring – along with the standard mats, hurdles and climbing ropes.

But most intriguing are the walls lined with practice weapons. Wooden blades of all sorts hang from racks that most suburbanites use for garage tools, while a whole collection of real ones fill a metal cage – locked, I'm guessing. Brown clay holy-water globes fill a wire-mesh bin, stored like most gyms would keep kickballs.

We creep across the empty gym into a hallway. I can hear kids tromping and shouting in the distance, but we don't go that way. Instead we take a sharp left and head down another hallway. We slip into a stairwell and head up to the second floor landing. Instead of going into the hallway, Chi leads us out of a window on to the roof of an abutting wing.

"Cool!" chirps Uri. Apparently the upperclassmen hadn't filled him in on their escape route.

Chi offers me a muscular forearm and hauls me up after him while Uri boosts me from below. (*So. Freaking. Embarrassing.*) Chi offers similarly to help Jo and gets a cold stare in return. Really, doesn't he see that coming by now? Even Uri's smart enough not to offer help. But then, I can't imagine anyone brave enough to touch Jo's ass uninvited, good intentions or not. Jo levers herself out, unassisted, then Uri scrambles out and we're off across the slanted roof. We approach the main box of the building and Chi waves us to wait while he peeks in through a window. When the coast is clear, we climb into a men's bathroom.

"Cool, cool!" Uri again.

"Go make sure it's clear," Chi says with a nod towards the door and a paternal smile. Uri practically glows with the privilege bestowed on him. He peeps out, then waves us into the hallway. Jo slips out right behind him.

Chi pauses at the door and quirks a blond eyebrow at me. "You ready to play the bad girl?"

I give him a vicious grin, all teeth, and he draws back. I wrinkle my forehead and ask, "Was that good?"

There's a beat as he blinks, "Um, yeah, good."

Hehe.

He holds the door open for me and we join the others dodging from their rooms and down to breakfast.

And just that easily, this little half-demon learnt how to break into the Templars' home base.

No, Mom, of course not. I would never!

She shakes her head; she knows me too well. I sulk.

The main box must be open to the public because it looks like any low-income, particularly crappy school. Not that I was ever allowed to attend one – Mom probably wanted to minimize potential negative influences. The walls are beige-painted cement blocks; the floor is black-and-white patterned linoleum. The halls have cork boards with seemingly benign reminders and advertisements. *Practice, Fridays 2–4*, one says simply. In a school for professional killers, I can only imagine practice for what. There is even a horrible collection of cheesy motivational posters. One brightly colored announcement contains a collection of smiling, gap-toothed children with the words "Be Yourself" in big block letters. Worst advice I've ever been given by a poster. I look at the deliriously smiling children featured. It's probably a bad idea for them, too.

This hall contains boys' dormitories, their names chalked on boards next to the doors, many of them horrifically biblical. Ezekiel, Abraham, Methuselah (really?). Even a Judas. Who thought *that* was a good idea? Mom was big on the Bible, now knowing she gave birth to a half-demon, I'm starting to see why.

We troop down to the first floor and the sounds of humanity get louder – talking, giggling, a few screams. Their origin is a pair of battered wooden doors at the end of the hallway. I smell breakfast and assume it's the cafeteria, though there's no sign. As we get closer, nervousness twists in my belly like a snake. I suppose it's natural to be nervous on your first day of school, even if the other students won't try to kill you.

We push through the doors.

It's a typical cafeteria, if TV can be trusted. Long tables with attached benches stretch across a room dotted with cement pillars. The room teems with swarms of human larvae – there have to be over a hundred. Children are everywhere, outnumbering adults twenty-to-one. Anywhere from toddler to eighteen. They shout, tumble and fight, mostly in good fun. Like a room full of energetic puppies. One kid socks another who then dives on him, grinning madly. Wolf puppies.

The few adults here to handle them are unimpressive – two ancient geezers with more facial hair than muscles and a guy with one arm. They need whips and chairs, not walkers. Certainly all their limbs, at least. I can't help but think I left one asylum for another, but this time the inmates were running it. Their free-range babies have gone feral. I guess the Crusaders figured their kids were the good guys, so how much supervision did they really need? Idiots. A good teenager is like a good demon – a contradiction in terms.

This is madness.

I wondered how they were going to explain my appearance to the adults. The chaos makes me stop worrying. Well, almost.

As we walk in, the other students turn to greet us. Or rather, greet Chi.

"Hi, Chi!"

"Chi!"

"Good morning, Chi!"

Apparently I'm the guest of the prom king of Demon Hunter High.

No one says hi to Jo. There's a double take when they notice her at Chi's side, right before their eyes slide away from her as if she's coated in Teflon. I'd blame it on her less-than-charming personality, but their eyes snag slightly on the leg brace.

Even I get my share of attention.

"Who's that?" one red-headed, freckled mess of a kid asks, pointing.

"Jo's cousin, Emma," Uri blurts out, rushing into the lie. There's a gasp and some tittering, and just like that I'm the class pariah. They sneer and turn away. I bare my teeth in a convincingly evil smile.

What can I say? I'm a natural.

A line of empty-handed students disappears through a door on one end of the far wall and exit a door on the other, this time carrying plates piled with food. We join the end of it, collecting trays and silverware, napkins, crackers and condiments. Chi falls back, chatting with some friends. Uri, close on his heels, basks in the glow of his acquaintance. Gimpy stomps along behind me. I'd like to think it's to protect me from her hateful classmates, but suspect it's to keep an eye on me. I'm definitely going to have to lose her if I'm to learn anything.

The line ahead of me shuffles as students try not to stand near me, as if my imagined disgrace is contagious. Eventually someone slides a near-toddler in front of me and the line settles down. He's obviously too young to care that I am evil. He turns as if to see what all the fuss is about.

I wasn't allowed to play with children. Not since that little incident with Amelia. Hey – she bit me first.

I study the little creature in front of me. What is it about these dwarfish little humans? They lack smarts, lack skills and they never seem to have much money. Yet they are powerful little monsters – adults dance to the tunes played by their chubby little fingers. Is it the disproportionately big head? Or the eyes too big for that head? Did I have this effect on my own mother? Was that why she believed in my goodness, despite all evidence to the contrary?

Suddenly the lower lip pokes out and the eyes grow even bigger. I feel a tug in the region where my heart should be… I want to give it things…

Ahhhhhh! Look away! Look away! Evil, ensnaring, hypnotic monster.

Just kidding, but it is kind of cute. I feed it a cracker.

We shuffle through the line, and I scoop food on to my plate. It's all horrifyingly healthy fare, omelets heavy on the veggies, mixed fruit and Canadian "bacon". Ha, it is as much bacon as I am human. We are both liars, but I feel it committed the greater offence. I spear a piece with a little extra violence as punishment. No wonder all the kids are lean and mean, eating this kind of food. They have to be kept in fighting condition, I guess.

I do eat. I mean, other than souls. When I am full with a fresh soul, I tend to eat less, but I eat a lot more when I'm running on empty. Usually I wouldn't eat much the day after but, as they'd been pretty much starving me during my time as a happy inmate of the house of horrors, I'm hungry.

I'm first through the line and pause at its end, not knowing where to sit in the full cafeteria. I scan the long tables for empty seats and see eyes alternately dodge mine or glare. The message couldn't be clearer if they'd shouted, "Seat's taken."

Jo limps up next to me, her plastic tray mounded with food. She, too, scans the room and halts when her eyes land on a table full of girls, bright with pinks and pastels and shiny with product-treated hair. She looks at me and a wicked little smile curves up her mouth. "Come on," she says and leads the way. I feel eyes track our progress and the gym gets quieter as we reach our destination.

The girls pretend not to see us. No one wants to be seen buddying up to the class pariah. Or me, either.

"Hey, guys," Jo says brightly. Too brightly. There's a pause as the girls pray we'll disappear. Not surprisingly, Jo's not the prayer-granting type and she waits. A little blonde thing turns red.

A snooty brunette with offensively perfect eyebrows is the first to look up. "Jo," her mouth says; *Loser*, her tone says. Our table choice suddenly becomes clear.

"Hannah, you remember my cousin, Emma?"

Their faces say they know all about Emma.

"Oh," says the brunette. "You mean the other Buchard girl who'll never fight demons?" Up goes a perfect eyebrow and she turns to me. "No, I don't believe we've met." Her face says, *Back off, I'm not afraid of you.*

Being short, thin and female, it's an expression I'm used to receiving. Being mean and borderline-indestructible, it's also one I have no problem erasing. Without any prodding from Jo, I shove my leg between Hannah and the blonde thing, wedging myself between them on the bench, as they gasp and squeal.

Had I pooed in my pants, the table couldn't have emptied faster, or by people with more disgusted looks on their faces. Hannah stands, tray in hand, and for a half-breath I think she's about to smash Jo with it. I'm pretty sure everyone close enough to be eavesdropping joins in my mental chant: *Catfight, catfight!*

Jo smiles a fat smile, leaning in. "Please, don't get up on our account."

Hannah's hands tighten. Long pause. Then they loosen and she turns on her heel, the rest of the posies following her.

They're beaten, but not beat. A blonde says, loud enough to carry, "What was Chi doing with *her*?" I assume they're talking about me, but then she adds, even louder, "I thought he dumped her years ago."

Jo turns a little pink.

"Some people can't take a hint," Hannah says, even louder. "It's so pathetic."

Ahhhh, I always knew I'd like high school.

We plop down at the now-empty table. Chi and Uri catch up with us, dropping on to the bench.

Chi waggles his elbows. "Roomy."

Not for the first time, I wonder just how much he's aware of.

I fork a scoop of eggs, but a sharp elbow from Jo makes me realize no one's eating. There's a loud clap and I twist around, searching for the sound. My eyes land on the table for grown-ups at the far side of the cafeteria where a compact, bearded man stands talking with a tall, frizzy-haired lady. They're average grandparent age, but unlike any grandparent I've ever seen. Instead of squishy and bent, they're lean and hard and decked out in denim and leather. His face looks as if it were carved by someone new to the craft. It's uneven and heavily creased, with random lines where it looks like the tools slipped. I can only see half of the woman's face, but it looks like it fared somewhat better. Wrinkled, but the creases are fine, as if in paper. Then the two stop talking and face the crowd. A scar drags across her face from forehead to cheek, twisting an eyelid that doesn't open.

"Headmaster and the sergeant at arms, or 'The Sarge'," Uri volunteers. "Though don't let her hear you call her that. She's in charge of the field Crusaders based out of here." Dreams of dealing with doughty administrators if my Emma cover gets blown go up in smoke. I hope Chi and Jo know what they're doing.

The headmaster bows his head and the room, except me, follows his lead. He prays, something about duty,

honor, yadda, yadda, way too long, then some Latin at
the end I don't understand. The crowd chants "Amen"
and the room bursts back into noisy chatter and forks
scraping plates.

We've barely started eating when a group of boys
approach His Royal Highness, Chi the Magnificent.
They're a ragtag bunch – but really, who isn't here? There
are four of them, a little younger than us. Sweatpants
and stained T-shirts seem to be the uniform.

"Chi," the tallest one says meaningfully, looking from
Jo to me and back again. I'm not sure which one of us
appalls them more. "Don't you want to sit with us?"

I glare at him and he shifts a step back. Side by side, Jo
and I must be terrifying.

"Oh, that's OK, guys. Not today." Chi smiles like
there's nothing out of the ordinary.

"Are you sure?" he pushes. "We saved you a seat."

"It's cool."

"But–" cuts in a younger, dark-haired kid in a green
hoodie, looking at me in disgust. I squirt water at him
through my teeth and I feel Jo turn to give me a look.
Maybe I've overdone my performance, but her eyes
dance. It's fun to finally be myself, even if it is a lie. Mom
was always making me play nice.

The boys sidle closer to their hero and change the
topic.

"Chi," the tallest one, who's lanky but muscular,
whispers excitedly. He tries to shove his shaggy brown
hair behind his ear, but it's not quite long enough and
it flops back in his face. He must be trying to grow it

out. Oh God, like Chi's. "Where did you go last night? I swung by, but…"

Chi grins then looks around conspiratorially. "Can you guys keep a secret?" he asks and Jo rolls her eyes. They all nod, creeping closer to our table. Chi pitches his voice low, "I had to take care of a little demon problem."

I didn't know boys could swoon, but I swear to God one did. Jo meets my eyes and I try not to laugh as she rolls them again.

"What happened?" an awestruck youngster asks. Chi gives them a dramatic and barely true summary of the evening. Chi leaves Jo and me out of the story – presumably to preserve my cover. He includes Uri and somehow makes him sound like a helpful sidekick instead of a needless latecomer. Uri glows.

It occurs to me that Chi is probably the kid on the basketball team that never passes the ball – but who is never asked to since everyone acknowledges he is the best. I hope his inevitable crash with reality doesn't hurt too badly.

A bell rings in the distance and Chi waves the guys off with a "Well, I gotta finish eating." They're dismissed, but in a friendly manner. I decide to take advantage of the free moment between supplicants to pump the boys for more information.

"So – what can you tell me about demons?" That earns me a suspicious look from Jo. Apparently our embarrass-the-bimbos truce is over. "What? Shouldn't I know something about the people trying to kill me?"

Jo shrugs, accepting my argument but not buying it. Chi answers despite his full mouth. He's having eggs. "They're super strong, really fast – as you saw. They can rip a person, even a Templar, to shreds with their bare hands. But they need to, because fortunately they can't use weapons at all."

"What do you mean, can't use weapons?"

"They can't. They won't touch a knife or a gun or anything. It's always bare hands only."

Now that I think about it, I've never used a weapon on any of my kills, either. It just never really occurred to me. Using a weapon is just… unnecessary. Like someone with 20/20 vision wanting to wear glasses. Actually it's a little worse than that. The thought of shooting someone is just vaguely unsettling. Unnatural. I'm not saying I've never touched a knife before – it's not like I eat with my hands – but the thought of sticking it in someone. Just… yuck.

"Why?" I ask.

"Don't know." Chi shrugs then smiles. "Probably because nukes in the hands of Satan's minions would make their job too easy."

True.

"We're limited too – we can only kill them with holy blades or holy water. It's their skin; it's impossible to saw through with anything else."

He's wrong. Apparently demon fingernails also work quite nicely. I fight the urge to touch my cheek.

Chi's still talking. "Those were the weapons the original Templars were given to fight the demons and we've never gotten an upgrade. But even if you do kill them, they'll just be reborn unless you purify them. That's their greatest advantage."

"The smoke?" I ask, and Chi looks pleased.

"That's right. As a Templar, we can suck the tainted soul out of the body and purify it – stripping the soul of its false life. They still go to Hell, but they can't come back as a demon."

"Whoa, what? False *life*?"

"Yeah," Chi says, like it should be obvious. "Demons are dead."

"*What?*"

Jo groans. She's made it clear she doesn't want to tell me anything, but listening to Chi try to teach is tortuous. "Most demons are people who sold their soul while they were alive. Then, when they die, they're conscripted to Hell's army. So they're dead. Hell brings them back to life by giving them what we call 'false life' – corporeal existence. Bodies."

That would explain my eating habits. I mean, I don't actually eat *souls*, not really. After all, ghosts are souls and I can't eat them. Believe me – I've tried.

I eat what leaves with the soul at the kill. The life. The demons get it from Hell; I get it from assholes.

I look up and they're all watching me. I wonder what I let slip across my face, but no one looks suspicious except Jo and, really, that's normal for her. "Anything else?" I ask.

Chi answers. "Well, they have magic." This perks me up. "You saw those two teleport out of there."

But can half-demons do magic? I'm dying to ask but it's too dangerous with Jo listening. That girl has trust issues. I have to limit myself to a generic "Magic?" and I still feel the weight of her eyes. It's a reasonable question for both my personas, so I ignore her.

"We spend years studying the types of stuff they can do. Fortunately, it seems to work a lot like ours – they need artifacts and spell books, although theirs aren't grimoires, obviously." Chi changes the subject before Jo changes it for him, "Anyway, teleportation and possession are the most common. Also…"

Please say fly, please say fly.

"…they feed off each other. The more there are, the stronger they are, but it maxes out at some point."

Damn. But at least that explains the extra burst of power at the asylum – it was more than just a delicious shot of life.

"That's why you can't usually catch one alone. They travel in packs. It's also why it's so dangerous in the demon headquarters. Not only are there more of them, they're also stronger."

Sounds like a place to avoid, at least until I know more. "Where are the demon headquarters?"

"You can't guess?" Jo gives me a look that says it should be obvious.

"How would I know? I'm new to all this demon stuff." This part of it, at least.

"Demons are attracted by sin, corruption and power. They always build their headquarters where there's the highest concentration," Chi explains.

When he puts it like that, it *is* obvious.

"Washington, DC."

Chi nods. "At least that's the East Coast headquarters – LA's another big one, Chicago too, but they're spread out all over the world. That's why we're in the North Carolina Mountains – close enough to keep an eye on the DC branch, but far enough away to hide."

"The demons at the asylum – they said something about 'zi' and 'hal'. What were they talking about?" I ask.

"Oh, those are just titles," Chi says, then scoops another forkful of eggs into his mouth. He swallows, then finishes, "'Zi' is a demon in management, while 'hal' is essentially a lackey."

So the demons didn't believe I looked like management material. That stings.

I open my mouth to ask another question, but apparently Jo thinks I've learnt enough for the day and cuts me off. "I'll need to let Mrs Lee know of my dear cousin's arrival."

But that raises other questions. "What's the plan for today?" I ask. Even Jo can't quibble with my interest in that one.

Chi answers. "It's Sunday, no class, no chores – just the games this afternoon. Sunday," he says happily, "the day of rest."

Not for this little monster. As they say, there's no rest for the wicked.

Chi yawns hugely. "I say we catch some sleep and meet back up at lunch."

His yawn is contagious. Maybe a *little* rest for the wicked, but then it's back to scheming.

I need to get rid of Jo if I'm going to get all the info I need before I have to evacuate and, to do that, I'll need a little more intel on my nemesis. When Uri's the first to finish his food and takes up his tray, I follow him. Jo and Chi are too busy bickering to notice.

I nudge him conspiratorially with my elbow. "Hey Uri, those two always fight so much?"

"What, Chi and Jo?"

No, the other two people here I know. I nod.

"No," he says. "Actually, they used to be best friends."

I raise my eyebrows in "surprise" but I already expected as much from the photos at Jo's. "Really?"

"Yeah – I mean, they still fought all the time, but it was different. More, like, competitive, you know? Chi was stronger, but Jo was faster and smarter – though not as nerdy as she is now. They were the best at *everything*." His voice is filled with awe.

"So what happened?" But I can kind of already guess – the posies already let slip he ditched her and I think I can guess why. I just need to check my timeline.

Uri shifts uncomfortably, but at my encouragement he answers anyway, leaning forward to whisper. "About two years ago, she got hurt." He won't meet my eyes and his floppy hair hangs in his face. "She almost died. She couldn't even walk for a year... she wasn't the same. She–" He closes his mouth abruptly because Jo herself clomps up to join us. But it's fine, I know the rest of the story. Super-athletic Chi stuck with a best friend who can't even walk? He ditched her and she's pissed, understandably. I'm a serial killer and *I* think that's pretty heartless, though he probably doesn't see it that way. Probably doesn't even recognize his abandonment for what it was, just drifted away when they no longer had so much in common. He's still nice to her – he's not a monster, after all. But then, it's easy to be magnanimous when you're the one doing the ditching.

And even though she hates him for it, she still has feelings for her former best friend – although, I suspect they're no longer the friendly sort. That must piss her off no end. It's kind of sad really.

Ah well, not my problem. In fact, I fully intend to use it against her. He's obviously her weak spot. I just need to figure out how.

Uri practically tosses his tray on the pile of dirty ones and scurries away, not looking at either of us. There wasn't a chance Jo heard us, so I'm not sure what he's embarrassed about. I scrape my plate – I have blasé down to an art – and Jo does the same.

Then she turns and looks at me. "Come on, *Cuz*, let's go get you checked in."

I follow her gimpy stride through the school towards what I assume is the front of the building. The place is such a maze I can't be sure. We come around a corner into the lobby and there's a small, messy office with a glass wall separating it from the entryway. No one could come in and out of the front door without being seen.

Or at least, that would be the case if the woman guarding it wasn't born at least a century ago. You can barely make out her tiny, hunched form between the towering stacks of paper piled on the beat-up wooden desk. She's decked out in a faded pink floral print and glasses that probably weigh more than she does. Her remaining hair stands up wildly as if it, too, wants to flee like the rest of it has. Gnarled arthritic fingers turn the pages of a paperback novel.

"Jo?" I ask, before we reach the door.

"What?" she snaps. She's a charmer.

"Are there any Templars between the ages of eighteen and…" I nod towards the upright corpse, "a thousand years old?"

She gives me a hard look. "Yes. Tons. A whole army, literally. They're out slaughtering our enemies, but could be back within hours if they needed to be."

I'm pretty sure Jo couldn't talk about the weather without somehow including a threat. *Forecast today: cloudy with a chance I'll kick your ass.*

Jo keeps talking. "They only leave behind the kids, the elderly, the pregnant–" Her eyebrows lower. "–the cripples and the incompetents." She starts forward again with her uneven lurch. As she puts her hands on the door, she pauses and looks from Mrs Lee's floral-decked granny-sweetness back to me.

"Wait here."

I'm not sure I trust her to go through with it on her own. "What? Why?"

"Because you don't know anything about Emma." She looks me up and down. "And, if she meets you, she might just throw you off campus in good taste."

I stick out my tongue as she pushes into the office. Mrs Lee looks up as Jo enters. I can't hear what they're saying, but see Mrs Lee's eyes blink behind their bottle caps. Then her lips purse, the wrinkles around them folding up into the world's most complex origami. She turns towards me and I force a friendly wave.

She doesn't return it, instead she blinks some more and turns back to Jo. Jo says something that makes the old woman come around the desk and pat her awkwardly on the back. They wrap up while I try to look harmless. Finally Jo comes out of the office, clutching a piece of paper.

I wait until we turn a corner down another empty hallway and are out of sight of the office. "What'd you tell her?"

"That you were getting bullied at school for refusing the Inheritance." Her eyes flick to my scabby cut. "So your parents sent you away mid-semester."

"Good one." I mean it. Never having gone to school, it didn't occur to me that the middle of the semester is an odd time to take a vacation. "Do you think she bought it?"

"Probably." She shrugged. "Why would I lie?"

The question feels like a trick. I answer slowly. "Because you illegally snuck out to fight demons and rescued a Beacon you now have to hide until you get a chance to unload?" Or, rather, you mistakenly rescued a half-demon who is now under cover as a Beacon so she can learn the truth of her identity?

Turns out there are a few reasons to lie.

"No, *Chi* snuck out to fight demons. I, the cripple, couldn't do such a thing even if I wanted to. Chi might lie about sneaking out. Amoral Emma certainly would lie about running away. But the poor crippled Jo? No, she's not capable of doing anything worth lying about."

It's good news that Mrs Lee would believe that, but Jo says it like it's not. "Is that enough to make her not follow up?"

There's a long pause filled only by the sound of our sneakers on linoleum. Jo looks straight ahead. "I also told her that Aunt Becka threatened to make you come home at the slightest hint that your presence here was a problem. And that I didn't want that to happen because…" her voice gets even stiffer and she picks up her pace so I can't see her face. "I need a friend."

Embarrassing. Even the undead administration is aware how unpopular Jo is. Explains the back-patting.

She continues. "A friend who doesn't spend all her time talking about demon-hunting, since I'll never be able to."

"Guilt card, nice."

Jo makes a face, not happy with the compliment. We walk the rest of the way in silence.

Jo has a double room but numerous piles of medical equipment are her only roommates. Books are stacked haphazardly on every flat surface and clothes are scattered on the floor. The only other personal item is a single photograph of her parents on the nightstand. It's informal and they look like they're at a table having dinner. Her mom leans on the table, her chin resting on her hand. The tip of her nose looks a little pink, like she spent too much time in the sun, and her wild Jo-hair looks especially windblown. Jo's dad leans back, a satisfied smile peeping out underneath an impressive black moustache, with his arm draped around the back of her mom's chair. They look relaxed and completely carefree.

A pair of sweatpants hitting me in the head interrupts my staring. I snag them before they hit the ground and change while Jo clears the spare bed. I hope for gossiping, giggling and perhaps a pillow fight, this being my first sleepover, but am disappointed. We crash till lunch.

I shove my plate away, satisfied that the corpse is adequately picked clean. Salmon, that is, not that other kind I so enjoy, unfortunately.

I sit with my usual honor guard of Chi, Jo and Uri. As with this morning, the other students were mystified by Chi's choice of lunch companions. They're willing to stop by and talk, but only a giantess named Zebedee actually sits with us. She has a shaved head, perfect mocha skin and a self-confidence that must come from looking capable of eating entire oxen and bench-pressing semis. She isn't even afraid of Jo, who, when Zebedee arrived, made it clear she wasn't welcome. Zebedee just flashed her a bright white smile accompanied by a head-cock that said she wasn't above kicking a cripple's ass. Jo scooched.

Despite her aggressive entrance and terrifying proportions, Zebedee is actually very easy-going and chats with Chi and Uri, and even occasionally Jo, about the "games" this afternoon. Since my job is to be sulky and unlikeable, I sit there saying nothing and return her friendly "Hi" with a stink-eye.

I lean back, refreshed from my nap and more food, and scout the teeming, creeping hordes of human larvae. All of them have what I want – information. Chi and Uri are still the easiest targets, but why limit myself?

Which one's brain can I pull it from? From their brain to their mouth to my ears. I feel a tug on my sleeve. A volunteer! How opportune. I turn, but am disappointed. She is too young to be of use. A small girl, still young enough to suffer the indignity of pigtails, holds out a dead goldfish in her cupped hand.

Thanks, but I just ate.

"My fish died," she lisps around missing teeth. She looks at me expectantly.

Ah – catastrophe has struck and she's in search of an adult to handle it. My luck to be closest to the door. Fortunately, I know just how to handle this one.

"Flush it down the toilet."

Or maybe not. The girl's lower lip starts an ominous trembling and the big eyes take on the glossy sheen of a slug. Tears – danger, Will Robinson, danger! I look frantically for backup before the emotional volcano erupts, but my companions are looking at *me* horrified.

What? It's a *fish*.

Jo grunts in disgust and stands to scoop up the little girl, dead fish and all. "Aww, it's OK, Sarah. She was just teasing." She shoots me a look over the little girl's head that says clearly, *Weren't you, you evil witch?*

"Uh, yeah. Sorry." But seriously, it's a fish. The room is littered with the corpses of its cousins. Fish-ageddon in the cafeteria. Jo pats and rubs the little girl's back and I hear sniffling. Slimy sadness leaks out of the child.

"I know you miss him," Jo says.

Miss what? Their long conversations into the night? The phone calls, the rollerblading? Summers at the shore? Ah well, stupid or not, apparently my response was Not Human – even for Emma. I've always struggled with the concept of mourning the death of food.

I feel the faint niggling of a memory. Not of food, but of pets.

Scally was an ugly, vicious cat who took to hanging around our dingy dump of an apartment building when I was younger. One-eyed, half-eared, with some kind of scaly skin disease. A cat-leper. One leg was missing, like a pirate, so it became Scalawag. Mom encouraged the naming; I was content with "That Stupid Cat". I fed it. It became a hissing, clawing shadow. Even when I became a shooing, kicking human, it followed. It wasn't the cuddling kind and neither was I. One day it was kissed by a clever car.

I found it cold in the road.

I cried. I can't tell you why, now. I used to do things like that before Mom… died.

She held me, her scent of lavender mixed with strawberry shampoo in my nose, and even though I was sad and she was sad for me, I also knew she was happy. Not because Scally was dead, but because I cared. Mom suggested a funeral to honor Scally. I declined – I knew better than anyone that there was nothing left of that mean old cat. Its body was just an empty shell.

"We should have a funeral," I blurt. Everyone turns to me and their disgust morphs to much more acceptable expressions. Relief, awe at my brilliance.

OK, so maybe those are my feelings and not theirs, but at least the disgust is gone. As for Jo... she told me just this morning that she hates pets. What a hypocrite. I can't help but point it out to her as we stand half an hour later next to a gold shoebox, the spray-paint still drying, for the silly-solemn event.

"Hypocrite," I murmur for her ears only. She looks at me blankly. "You hate pets."

She quirks a brow. "Well, I didn't comfort the fish, now, did I?"

Touché. Sometimes she makes it hard to hate her.

The funeral eats up time I would have rather spent plundering information, and afterwards we have to head straight to the gymnasium for the games. I'm not sure what the game will entail but it doesn't really matter. I will be playing my own.

Knowing Chi, I'm not expecting Scrabble, but their game, once described to me, sounds like attempted homicide.

"We call it Paranoia," Jo says with a toothy grin, "because everyone *is* out to get you."

Awesome.

The game's rules are simple – they set us loose in the playing field in teams ranging from three to five. In the groups of five there's one "Beacon", who has to pretend to be weak and slow like a human or it's a foul. The difference between this game and real life is that even the other Beacon-protecting teams are trying to kill you. A team gets one point for each person they "kill" and your whole team "dies" if your Beacon does.

No one wants to be the lame Beacon so the teacher, a woman in her mid-thirties – so hugely pregnant I think she might be carrying a litter – waddles through the gym assigning Beacon roles while everyone tries not to meet her eye. No one's surprised when Jo's selected, and interspersed with her long and creative swearing is the complaint that apparently she is *always* designated a Beacon. The teacher seems unsure what to do with me, so she ignores me. I guess she assumes I won't play. I will, though. I don't have time to sit around waiting for everyone else to finish. Besides, in the confusion of the game, surely I can figure out some way to lose Jo.

Chi leans back on the bleachers but is propped up on his right elbow so he can see what Jo, one bleacher lower, is sketching as they plan their strategy. His hair's pulled back, but it's not all quite long enough, so some hangs rakishly in his face. Uri sits next to Jo, watching them both, while I sit a row above, watching them all. Zebedee was recruited to our team during lunch, but she hasn't shown up yet, so only the four of us are sprawled on the bleachers when we are approached by an optimistic fifth. She's the kind of girl all other girls are required to hate on sight. Jo certainly does, but then Jo hates everyone.

The pretty brunette tosses her pretty hair and props her pretty butt right next to Chi on the left, just behind

him. She's decked out in coordinating workout clothes.
Pink, of course. It's loud in the gym and he's so focused
on the plan, he doesn't notice until she speaks.

"Hey, Chi, I missed you in the gym this morning."

He starts, then rotates so he's leaning back on both
elbows. His faded grey T-shirt clings. "Oh, hey, Rachael."
He smiles. "Yeah, late start this morning."

"Oh, really?" she purrs. I swear she purrs. Have I
mentioned I hate cats? "Late night?"

Chi's eyes slide briefly to Jo and he catches her
watching. Chi turns back to Rachael and ratchets his
smile up from "charming" to "heartbreaker" and leans
in a little.

"Nah." Chi's eyes shoot again to where Jo sits trying
not to fume. This time Rachael notices his glance and
looks a little confused before she shrugs it off, dismissing
Jo as a threat. Which doesn't seem fair, really. Jo's pretty
in her own way – if you like the angry-violent type.

"Well, anyway, I was wondering if you wanted
someone?" the girl asks, leaning in and flashing some
cleavage. I didn't even know they made low-cut sports
bras. Chi looks surprised by the discovery as well –
rendered speechless actually. "You know, for your team?"

"No," snaps Jo. Rachael seems surprised to find her
there.

"Uh, no, that's right." Chi collects himself. "We've
got Zebedee." He grins at the little tramp. "Next time,
maybe?"

She smiles back. "I look forward to it. See you for our
workout tomorrow?"

"Wouldn't miss it," Chi says. As Rachael sashays away, her back is treated to a patented Jo death glare. It occurs to me that it would be easier to get Jo pissed enough to leave on her own than to lose her. Rachael already did half the work for me.

I stand and walk around the table. "So, Chi, what's the plan?" I ask. Jo's death glare switches to me but I think it's more from habit than anything else. It's about to be deserved. I take the designated tramp spot at Chi's elbow and look at him, big-eyed. "How are you going to protect Jo... and me?"

"You?"

"You weren't just going to leave me behind, were you? All alone?"

"Uh, no, of course not," he stumbles, but it's clear he hadn't thought about it.

"You're not just going to let them kill me, are you? I mean, I can't look out for myself." I think I hear a snort from Jo. Not the emotion I'm trying to get from her. I put a hand on Chi's bicep. "You're so strong. You can protect us both, can't you?" My lashes batter my cheeks like demented butterflies, but he seems to like it. My eyes flicker to Jo. She most definitely does not.

Bingo. She doesn't leave, but then I never thought she'd be an easy nut to crack. The best plans take time.

Chi grins as he stands up and pulls on his hoodie. "Of course. Stick by me. I'll make sure no one gets you."

"Me too!" agrees Uri from my other side.

Jo says nothing, but refuses to go back to plotting after the tramp and I play our games. Instead she stomps and fumes, radiating displeasure. Fortunately we're like a superbug, immune through prolonged exposure. Zebedee shows up and bumps fists with the boys, nods at me and returns Jo's snarl with a shrug. We join the rest of the students at the metal weapon racks to pick out our instruments of destruction.

The practice blades are all safe, dull wood with fabric, stained a bright blue, fixed along the "cutting" edges. They're all shapes and sizes, from daggers to claymores, but have in common that they all look old and hard-used. Big dents and chips are beat into them and the brightly colored designs on the hilts are flaking off. Chi selects a dagger and a sword, testing their weight in his hands and giving them a few practice swings. He snatches up what looks like a bright-blue dusty sock and rubs it along the fabric, painting it even bluer.

"Chalk, to mark all my kills," he says with relish. He holds up the chalk sock and says, "Holy globe," and slips it into his pocket, along with three others.

I have no interest in weapons, but the artist in me is curious about the designs. I mean, why bother with something that's going to be so abused? I run my finger along one, a curved sword suspended by a loop on its hilt, and realize the designs are actually stylized text. Bible references, actually. Ha, they're trying to remind the students what they're fighting for. I can't help it, I chuckle. Chi raises his eyebrows as if to ask why.

I point at the Bible verses. "So far I've seen you lie, steal and kill. That's three of the Ten Commandments and we've only just had lunch." Not that I'm complaining, as most of those sins were committed for my benefit, but still.

Chi grins, unrepentant. "So?"

"So? How can you be the good guys?"

"Well, first of all, we have a special dispensation against the last one, at least when it comes to demons. As for the lying and stealing, well, it's not ideal." He has the grace to look slightly shamefaced. "But we have good intentions. We lied and stole a little, but no one got hurt and you got saved – that's more important." Amen. Preach it. "So it comes down to intent. Good intentions equals not evil."

Jo looks up from where she's selecting knives, apparently over her anger and willing to join the conversation. I almost sigh. At this rate I'll have to kill her to get some time alone with the boys.

"I have a better example." Her hand closes on the hilt of a large knife and she jerks it from the wall, then spinning, she presses it to my chest.

Nope, still mad.

I give her a hard glare that says *I'm not scared* – then realize Human Meda would be scared and whimper.

"Jo–" Chi starts, but she ignores him.

"Look at it this way – do you want someone to stick a knife in your chest?" she asks, almost sweetly.

Mine? No. Now, *yours...* but I shake my head no. There's a heavy pause and she pushes down slightly. It's just dull wood and I don't hurt easily, but she isn't trying to hurt me. It's a warning. Silent threats bounce between us and I know she hears mine even if they are disguised under a whimper.

"Jo…" Chi again, and this time Jo steps back with an unfriendly smile.

"You would if I were a doctor performing heart surgery," she says lightly.

I don't know if I have a heart, but I get her point – both of them really.

Intent.

And she doesn't like me.

Good.

Seven

We play in a few acres of wooded mountain terrain, the outer limits marked with dingy neon-orange twine. There's lots of jumping out and scaring people, "stabbing" and screaming. They fight with a bloodthirstiness I wouldn't expect outside of a maximum-security prison or suburban PTA meeting. My only regret is I have to spend the whole time jumping frightened into Chi's arms and grabbing his hand instead of joining in the murdering mayhem around me. Chi likes all the attention, but I can't help notice his eyes sliding over to Jo when I do something particularly outrageous – like stroke his abs.

Yes I did, and they are amazing.

As for Jo, I'm pretty sure if it wasn't against the rules for a Beacon to kill her own guard, she would have skewered me. But as mad as she gets, she doesn't leave.

As time runs out, I decide to try something else. If she won't leave, I will.

My opportunity arises when we're caught in a three-way fight. Chi stashes me in some bushes while they take on a pair of lean, tween boys defending a chubby grade-school Beacon. The sound of the conflict brings along a third team made up of three tough-looking girls in camo. Our team – with Chi and Zebedee – is seen as the bigger threat so the other two teams cleverly join up against us. Jo is tossed unceremoniously up a tree, while Chi, Uri and Zebedee defend at its base.

While they're busy, I slip unnoticed through the trees.

Come along, Chi. Come find me…

I jog, wanting to put space between me and the others. If I'm too close, Chi will just bring them all. I need to get far enough away that it's not worth waiting on Jo.

Branches reach out like claws, trying to snatch my clothes and mark my skin. I reach back to them, as if to shake their hands, then I break their arms, leaving a mini-path of destruction for Chi to follow. I haven't been outside in weeks; the nurses at the asylum weren't big believers in recess. I breathe in the sweet scents of rot and sunshine. A small outcropping of rocks lies ahead, forming a little cliff with a cluster of boulders at its base. It looks like a convenient spot to wait for Chi. I run a little faster and leap on one of the smaller boulders in the pile.

And am instantly pelted by a half-dozen chalk-filled socks.

Crap. Forgot about all my pretend enemies.

The chalk dust burns my eyes and makes me cough, and I stumble, losing my footing and land hard on my back in the brush, the breath knocked out of me.

Twice. In. Two. Days.

I must be losing my edge.

I blink the dust out of my eyes in time to see a face pop over the edge of the boulder. Inky black curls, blue eyes and eyebrows up near his hairline. I guess I'm not who he was expecting.

"It's that girl!"

"Who?" another voice calls.

"The traitor!"

Maybe these enemies aren't so pretend.

"She's out here?" The body belonging to that voice comes around the corner, answering his own question. He stops when he sees me. Shadows play across his face, and not only the ones from the trees overhead. Dark thoughts. Revulsion, hate, anger.

He's taller than me, but thin, and has the look of someone who's been sick for a while. Greasy blond hair, gaunt cheeks, dark circles under his narrowed eyes. He white-knuckles the toy knife in his hand.

Definitely not a pretend enemy.

There's a rustling of dead leaves as the black-haired boy scrambles around the boulders. "Hey, Isaiah." He casts a look over his shoulder. "Come on, man, she's dead." He takes a couple steps away, but Isaiah doesn't move. "Before her team gets here."

This wakes the blond up a little and he casts around. "Where are your bodyguards?" he asks me.

"On their way." I climb to my feet.

"Really? You just wandered off?" His tone is filled with disbelief. I nod. "That's pretty stupid."

In hindsight, I have to agree with him.

He shakes his head, the greasy curls swinging. "I don't believe it."

Ha, the one time I've told the truth in days.

"I bet they decided you weren't worth guarding." He pauses, then adds with a sneer, "*Traitor*."

"Isaiah." The other boy shifts back and forth, the leaves rustling under his feet. "Come on." His voice cracks a little.

But instead of leaving, Isaiah takes a step closer to me. "I know why you're here."

Unlikely.

"I know how you got that cut on your face."

I highly doubt that, too.

"It's because everyone back home hates you. Well, we hate you too and you're not welcome here. You filthy, selfish coward."

And he spits on me.

Spits. On. Me.

I start to shake and force myself to take a deep breath. He's not even talking to me, not really. It's Emma he hates. But that doesn't stop me from being pissed. Emma, the scum of the earth because what? She doesn't want to spend her life hunting monsters?

As a monster, I can only support her position.

But it's more than that. It's the way he's trying to scare me because he thinks he can. Because he thinks no one will stop him. That Emma can't fight back. A familiar surge of giddiness threatens to stretch my mouth into a smirk. Thanks to Samson, I won't need to eat again for weeks, but what can I say?

Mistaken bully is my favorite.

My mind slips into that red-and-black place where I can see it happening. I punch Isaiah. No, I backhand him – it's more humiliating. Then I imagine spinning to kick the other one. Maybe in the head, so he sinks under while my bully and I have a little heart-to-heart. Or fist-to-face, whatever's appropriate. Then…

Isaiah's still talking. "You thought you'd come here? And then what? Then what, Emma?"

Then what, Emma? The question cuts through the red haze. Then what indeed? Emma can't kick the shit out of two Templar boys. How on earth would I explain that?

The red bites back. Not unless I don't leave any witnesses.

Isaiah shoves me.

"Isaiah!" the other one protests.

"Shut up, James."

"Come on, man."

Isaiah whips around, turning on his friend like a mad dog. "I said shut up." There's a hysterical edge to his voice. "Or do you think she belongs here? Do you think she can just do what she did and get away with it?" His eyes are wild when he turns back to me and, as his hands fist, I realize the problem is bigger than I first anticipated. He isn't going to stop at scaring me.

I flick a look at James. He won't meet my eyes. No help there.

Come on, Chi. Where the hell are you? Only the birds answer, and they don't know shit.

It's not that I can't take the beating. I'm no expert or anything, but I took a few at the asylum. I'm worried what the beating will reveal. At the asylum, they beat me bad-cop style – careful not to leave marks.

Isaiah doesn't look capable of that control.

What's going to happen when Emma's skin won't break? When the bruises don't appear? I can't run. They'll just catch me, unless I run too fast, but then they'll still know. My cover will be blown. They'll tell.

Unless they can't.

The wicked thought licks out my arms and down my spine, making me shiver. My eyes slide sideways, taking in the empty forest, the dense brush cover, the rotten boy puffed up with a bully's pride. His cowardly friend who stands by and allows it. What's the world without them? Monsters don't appear grown; every vicious man grew from a vicious boy. Why should youth protect them?

Meda, no! My memory mom weeps. Her tears drip on my anger, cooling it slightly so I can think. Even if I do kill them, I'll still have to run. I'll have longer to escape if they can't tattle, but that's all.

It means I will never know the truth.

Regardless what I do now, I've failed. It's over. That loss floors me hard enough that, when Isaiah shoves me again, it knocks me to the ground.

They've ruined everything. Rage bubbles and my fingers sink into the loamy forest floor, shoving through the frozen dirt and gravel as if it were as dense as soap bubbles. I meet his eyes.

He sees my rising anger, the way my hands fist. "What? Never say the coward wants to fight?"

Oh, yes. Yes, she does.

He jerks back his leg, but something makes him pause. His eyes flick away, away from me, away from the woods and, for a brief second, I think he's changed his mind. Then he shakes himself and the foot flies forward.

It's all I need. As if that leg were a lever, it pulls me flying to my feet.

Chalk clouds explode against Isaiah's shirt, blinding us both.

"Enough!" screeches a high-pitched voice somewhere from the rocks above.

I back out of the dust cloud, coughing, and blinking. Taking back control of the situation. Of my emotions. As it clears I see Isaiah doing the same. My/their rescuer comes climbing over the edge of the jutting cliff above us, scaling it like a monkey. It's a small girl splattered with freckles and topped with a mess of red hair. It had to be her brother I saw in the cafeteria. No two kids could be so similarly unfortunate-looking without being kin. At least, I hope there's not more than one set of genes responsible for this particular look.

"What the hell, Mags?" Isaiah says around coughs.

"What do you mean, what the hell? You guys are dead, now get out of here."

"But–" Isaiah starts.

"Get out of here before I think too hard about what I think I almost just saw." Her hands rest on her non-existent hips, just above a belt dangling with blue-chalked socks. "You two should be ashamed of yourselves."

"I–" Isaiah starts, then shakes himself, as if he's waking from a dream. "I wasn't going to…" But he doesn't finish the lie.

Mags glares.

Isaiah flushes and looks vaguely ill, while James is still not looking anyone in the eye. Both of them are heavily coated in blue chalk and shame.

"Get out of here." Mags just sounds kind of tired this time. James tugs on the sleeve of Isaiah's hoodie, pulling him away. Neither one looks at me before they jog off through the woods, leaving me alone with my pint-sized savior.

She turns to face me and her eyes are a startling, brilliant blue. Maybe all her genes don't suck. "I don't think they'll bother you again." She pauses. "Isaiah's… He's not really bad."

She must have read the blatant disagreement on my face. She makes a face. "He lost his sister a few months ago."

I recognize the crazy look in his eye now. I remember a hundred of them staring at me from a shattered bathroom mirror. Grief. My breath catches. I almost killed him for it.

But then, I've done worse.

The girl's still talking, and I come back. "It's hard for him, seeing someone who opted out, when someone he loved sacrificed everything." There's an edge to her voice. She might have saved me, but we aren't friends.

I wonder why she bothered. "You agree with them." It's not a question. "That I'm a selfish coward."

She shrugs. "It *is* selfish to turn your back on the Templars, especially given how badly the demons outnumber us." She scuffs the ground with a ratty pink sneaker, then cocks her head and studies me. I guess she decides that Emma the quitter is in no position to throw stones, because she adds, "But it's a little brave, too." A little breath escapes her. Wistful.

Oh. I wonder what it's like to be born a soldier with your future all planned out. Probably a short future, and most definitely a violent one. For Chi, it's perfect. He's a born hero. The idea of him working a regular nine-to-five office job is laughable. And Jo's so violent and angry, if she had any other career, it could only be at the DMV. Uri is Chi's mini-me, and Zebedee is wildly athletic. But Mags? Small, freckled, scrawny and apparently tender-hearted enough to rescue someone she doesn't even like? It doesn't seem like such a great fit.

"They won't actually make you fight demons, will they?"

"Hey." She wrinkles her nose. "I'm more dangerous than I look."

Which brings her up to what? Angry-kitten status? But she just saved my bacon, so I'm willing to be generous. "I mean, if you don't want to."

"Never really thought about it," she admits. "Better to fight the demons than wait around to see who doesn't come back."

Which she's spent her whole life doing. The grass is always greener, I guess.

"Anyway," she says briskly. "I'm just saying I understand why you chose what you did, even if I don't agree with it." Then, under her breath, "You'd have to be kind of crazy to want this life." She wanders around scooping up her chalk socks and tucking them back into her belt.

"Are you crazy, Mags?"

Her smile is too bright when she answers. "Most of the time."

The sound of a wild rhino charging through the underbrush pulls our attention. Chi bursts from the bushes, his eyes a little insane. His breath comes out with a whoosh when he finds me in one piece.

"Me–" he spots my companion, tries to say "Emma" instead and winds up with "Memma." Then jumps to "Mags!"

Chi. Captain Obvious. He grabs for a chalk ball in his pocket. She's on another team, after all.

Mags doesn't move. "Hey," she says, blasé. "You should keep a better eye on your friend here. Isaiah wasn't too happy to see her. I took care of it, but he's not really the only one, you know."

"Oh." Chi relaxes, his hand leaving his chalk ball. "Thanks, Mags."

"No problem. Catch you two later." She takes a few steps into the bushes, then calls, "Oh, and Chi?" He turns and a cloud of blue explodes in his face. He stumbles backwards, holding his nose where it was hit by the chalk sock. "You're dead."

She grins and disappears as Chi coughs and gags on chalk, his big body bent double, completely laid low by her perfectly aimed missile.

Maybe I didn't give Mags enough credit.

"You OK?" he asks when he can catch a breath. His sweat turned the pale blue chalk royal, and it stains his hairline and streaks in lines from his watering eyes.

Am I OK? I guess I'm better than OK, because, while I'm not sure I can claim my last plan was a complete success, I have managed to get Chi alone. Once again I find my eyes sliding sideways, looking for witnesses as another nefarious plot unfolds. All's quiet but the birds.

He lost his hoodie at some point and his faded grey T-shirt is stuck to him with sweat. I wrap a hand around his big bicep and give him my "Help me" eyes.

"I'm so glad you found me!"

"Um, well." He slants me a look. "It would have been easier if you hadn't run away."

I study him for sarcasm. It's unclear, but unlikely.

"I was so scared–" I widen my eyes. "–with all the fighting."

He studies me for sarcasm. Misses it entirely.

"Well, you're safe now. And–" He looks at my chalk-covered shirt, then his own; we're two dead smurfs. "–it looks like we're out of the game." He sighs. "No more fighting for us."

I try to look sorry.

Chi checks his watch (plastic, digital). "There's still ten minutes left in the game. Let's let the others know we're out, then we can head back in."

I let him lead the way and follow, but slowly. I plan to take advantage of the full ten. I let my clothing, hair and feet get caught on every branch, briar and twig, bringing our pace down to a crawl. Then I bust out my verbal pry bar and get to work. "So, you told me about demons. But you said something about halflings?"

He grunts an affirmative as he tries to unlatch some briars from my jeans.

"So, are they hunting me too?"

He doesn't look up. "I guess." He jerks on the briars and they come loose. He straightens and we start again. I stumble clumsily among the branches.

"So, can you tell me about them? So I know what to watch out for?"

"Don't worry; my brother will be watching out for you."

I blow some hair out of my face. "But I want to know."

My tone says I'm serious, so he shrugs and answers. "Well, we actually don't know much about them. They have some human traits, some demon traits, but you never know quite how much. I've heard one was shot before. Like with a regular gun."

Hmmm, I don't like that.

"But they only shot him because the holy water had no effect." He shakes his head like it's too crazy to believe. "They had to try something. Others though, they're just like demons, except not dead." He hops over a log and holds out a hand to help me over. I take it and step over, then release it. He starts forward again. "Not dead, *yet*, I should say. They almost always become demons when they die. Sell their soul just like the rest of them."

"Do any of them not become demons?" The question comes out softer than I intended.

He pauses and turns around. I pretend to fight with a branch and lose. He comes back and snaps it off, setting me free. "What do you mean?"

"Are there any that aren't evil?"

"I dunno." He shrugs, turning forward again. "I only ever hear about the ones we have to fight. But I wouldn't think so. Normal people have a hard enough time staying good. How could someone who's already half-evil pull it off?"

Very good question. I certainly don't have the answer.

I open my mouth to ask something else, but then hear Jo's voice through the trees. They're coming to meet us. Of course. Did I really picture Jo patiently waiting somewhere?

Dammit. I barely learnt anything and it appears my Emma cover is riskier than I first thought. I need to step it up and stop underestimating Jo. I need to go nuclear.

We meet up with the others and trek back to the gym while a blue-chalked Uri enthusiastically recounts how he fell victim, literally, to a botched surprise attack from above. Jo says nothing, but her limp is more pronounced – her version of stomping, I think. Zebedee already headed back, choosing not to wait when she was "killed". We're the last ones to reach the empty gym. Jo slams her weapons back into their spots. Losing the game, her role as the helpless victim, my disappearance and my reappearance draped all over Chi's arm, all have her simmering. I just need to push her till she boils over. There are still a few hours before dinner, a few hours I want to take advantage of – with Chi.

No, not like that, though that would be fun too.

Like any clever spider, I weave my web and set my trap. I steal the idea from an MTV drama – the best place to brainstorm diabolical schemes. I wait until Jo is about to follow us out of the gym (when angry, she moves about as silently as a cyborg elephant), then I spring it. I grab Chi by the ears and lay one on him.

Villain that I am, it's fitting that my first kiss is one I stole.

His lips are soft and salty (or maybe that's chalk?), but slack – I hope it's because of shock and not a testament to his kissing skills. Talk about a disappointment. Suddenly his brain catches up with his lips and he jumps as if electrified and just has time to put his hands on my waist – to kiss me more or push me away, who knows – when Jo walks into the hallway.

It's almost as if someone planned it.

Chi shoves me away and we both turn to face Jo, frozen in the doorway. There are horrified looks all around, two of them real. Then a white-faced Jo (finally, finally!) stomps off. To my surprise, Chi is equally white-faced. His mouth hangs open and he just shakes his head at a loss. He turns to me, baffled.

"Just happy to be alive," I say perkily and release him. He sputters and I try not to laugh. "Show me around?" I suggest.

"Gahh," he says, eloquent as always, looking at the door Jo went out of. I pull away and give his hand a tug in the opposite direction.

"Soooo," I start, letting my voice go all husky, "if you guys are outnumbered, shouldn't you go out and,

I don't know, make some more?" I wiggle my eyebrows suggestively.

That startles Chi out of his confused daze and he laughs. "No, unfortunately, it doesn't work like that. We're not allowed to defeat evil through intentional and systematic sinning."

"But you can lie and steal?"

He's thoughtful for a minute. "I think it's about how and who it hurts, and what's the trade-off. It's one thing to tell a tiny fib to save a Beacon, and another thing entirely to bring a bunch of innocent babies into the world with no family just so you can have more soldiers. Oh sure, there have been babies out of wedlock before. We're human after all. But–"

I wink at him and he blushes. "I know, I know, it's all about intent," I say.

"You're catching on. Must be the Beacon in you."

I sincerely doubt it. It works as a nice segue, though. "So how are you going to test me to find out if I'm a Beacon?"

He looks at me, and his face has a decidedly Jo-look. Either the kiss made him suspicious, or the fallout with Jo irritated him enough to make him doubt me.

I let my voice tremble as I ask, "Will it hurt?"

He smiles and shakes his head. "No, it's nothing we do to you really. It's an artifact that functions as a map of Beacons." His chest puffs a little. "Our chapter has the most powerful Beacon Map in the world. Most only cover regions, but we can track them all over the world." This doesn't really have anything to do with me, but he seems proud of it, so I let him continue. "Anyway, you'll show up on the map as light."

Unlikely.

"Where's the map now?" Somewhere easily accessible? Perhaps next to a conveniently located incinerator?

"We've loaned it out to another chapter." Even better, it's not here. "Because North America became a demon-Templar battlefield so late in the game, we don't have a lot of artifacts that originate here. Our Beacon Map, since it's the only one that shows the entire world, is the only one that works in North America. We loan it out occasionally to other chapters when they lose their Beacons or are trying to pinpoint the location of a new one. We can't test you till they bring it back, but they never keep it long."

Oh. "How long, typically?"

He shrugs, but he has that Jo-look again. I change the subject. "So, how was your chapter chosen to keep the Beacon Map?" I realize a hair too late that that question could be interpreted as insulting, but Chi doesn't look miffed. Instead he smirks.

"The Northern Chapter lost it." He sends me a sideways look. "They're the original North American chapter – from back when New York was the demon headquarters – and they used to be our parent chapter." He snorts. "They think they still are. Anyway, at the turn of the century, they lost the Beacon Map and the demons got hold of it." His smug smile dies. "The result was that almost an entire generation of Beacons was lost. Without them... well, there were two world wars, the Holocaust, the Nanking Massacre, the Cold War, Stalin, the Spanish Influenza..." he trails off, shaking his head. "It was the bloodiest period in the history of the world. They call it the Hemoclysm – the blood flood." He exhales. "Anyway, our founder rescued the Beacon Map from the demons. It was a huge deal, he basically saved the world." Chi's back to bragging. "So when he asked to be in charge of the Beacon Map and run an independent chapter, they allowed it." He smiles and swings out his arms. "So here we are."

"Interesting," I say. And it is, even if it's not particularly helpful. "So, what's it like to be a Templar?"

"Great." He grins.

"What do you like best?"

"Killing bad guys."

A great answer. I meet his roguish smile, his eyes twinkling between the hair that has fallen in his face and feel an unexpected squirm in the place where I once thought there might be a heart. I look away.

"What else?"

"Well, the powers are pretty cool."

I give him an interested look but he hesitates.

"You probably shouldn't tell me about those," I say. "Jo told you not to." *But no one is the boss of you...*

His jaw tightens and he spills. "Once a Templar accepts the Inheritance he or she gains super-strength and speed, rapid healing and the ability to purify demons. Some get lucky and have extra gifts, but they manifest erratically." He grins and wiggles his fingers in front of him like he's doing a magic trick. "Zeke can blast demon-killing light out of his fingertips. It was pretty exciting when he figured that out."

I bet. I'll keep an eye out for Zeke. I make an interested noise for him to continue.

"Most of our magic comes from grimoires – our anti-demon spell books. But we're not allowed to play with those till we graduate," he says and I give him an incredulous look. He hasn't given me any reason to believe he's a rule-follower. He catches my look and grins mischievously. "Oh, I've tried to sneak a peek before, but they're all written in ancient languages and I'm not advanced enough to read them. Now, artifacts, on the other hand, are rarer, but can be used by anyone with the Inheritance." He pulls out something from his pocket to show me. It looks like a small incense burner on a chain. "This heats up when I'm near a demon." I subtly inch away, just in case, even though Jo had said it doesn't work on half-demons. Chi slides it back into his pocket.

Up until now I'd thought we'd been strolling aimlessly, but then he leads me down a flight of stairs, then two more until we are deep underground. By the time we approach a high-tech security door, I'm antsy with curiosity.

"Where are we?" I ask.

That delightfully naughty grin crosses his face again. "Top secret." He doesn't bother to cover the security sensor as he puts in the "code". Probably because it's his own blood pricked from his finger. "Templar blood," he explains. Unlike a PIN, I guess he figures I can't steal that.

Fool.

The door opens with a click and a hiss. Chi pulls it the rest of the way and I see that it's nearly a foot thick and made of solid steel, like you'd expect on a bank vault. Inside is not what I expected – although I am not sure what I *did* expect. My experience with secret demon-fighting societies is limited.

It's a museum, long and narrow, filled with locked bookcases and glass display cases. The floors are polished wood and the walls are painted in muted greys and rusty oranges. By far the nicest place I've seen in this ratty school. Chi points out the library of grimoires, a dozen or so ancient-looking books of varying shapes and sizes. A larger collection of books concerning Templar history fill several other bookcases.

The glass cases display artifacts labeled with small plaques stating things like "Splinter of the Cross" and "Scrap of the Shroud", along with a shorthand list of uses, like "Creating Holy Blades", "Blessing Water", "Expel Demons (poss.)".

Chi nods to one of the many empty cases. "Beacon Map."

I read the plaque. "St Christopher's Skull?"

"Yeah, it's pretty cool. It works kind of like an iPad permanently set to Google Earth."

"Except it's a skull."

"Well, yeah."

I have a sudden idea. "Steve Jobs, Larry Page and Sergey Brin are Beacons?" The founders of Apple and Google. Chi just smiles.

We stroll, looking at the other relics. There have to be over two dozen cases, though many of them are empty but for the plaques. I can only guess that the relics are in use somewhere. Chi stops at one that contains a few incense burners and about two dozen spots where more should be. The lock is already undone and Chi slides the artifact from his pocket and into the case before locking it again. "Incense Burners, San Giovanni", the sign says, then in smaller print "Senses Demons".

"Borrowed it last night," he explains.

Another case has nothing but a tiny test tube. "Demon-Blight", it states. I don't know what that is, but I skirt it.

A room just filled with all sorts of tools for finding and killing demons. Seems to me like the kind of place that could use a good fire – clear out the riff-raff. I spot sprinkler heads on the ceiling.

Maybe an explosion, then.

Closed doors, plain and unmarked, leave this room in all directions. But there is one set different from all the others – huge, wooden and intricately carved.

"Where do those go?" I ask and Chi loses his lightness. I didn't know his face could do solemn. He doesn't answer but pushes them open.

They lead to a long dark hallway, lit only by unnaturally silver candlelight. The hallway stretches forever, the candles placed seemingly at random. It's like looking down a tunnel decorated with a slice of the night sky, unending inky blackness dotted with silvery twinkles.

Once my eyes adjust, I see that each candle rests on a shelf at the base of a display. Mounted above each candle is a large picture of a person with a silver plaque containing a name and dates. I put the pieces together.

I stand in a shrine to the Templar dead.

Surrounding each large photograph is a collection of smaller photographs, of weddings and babies, picnics and dances. Snapshots capturing their most perfect moments. There are also letters, some elegant, some in a childish scrawl. There are medals and teddy bears and child-drawn art. Any beloved piece of the life the departed left behind. Some have dying flowers, while others have very recently placed fresh ones. A patchwork of memories stretching forever.

When I die, there will be nothing to mark my passing. Do they still sell unclaimed bodies to science? It's ironic, but not entirely surprising, that I could do more good for the world dead than alive.

Chi is silent as we walk the hallway, our tapping footsteps echoing in the silence. The parade of dead we pass seems to never end. We reach one display and Chi stops, crossing himself and bowing his head in prayer. The shelf is strewn with flowers in various stages of wilty-ness and a happy couple smiles from the photo. I recognize them as Jo's parents.

I didn't know them and only like their daughter involuntarily, so I don't feel the urge to show respect. I certainly don't pray. God and I are giving each other the silent treatment. Instead I idly examine the shrines nearby. There's a young man on a motorcycle who looks to be in his twenties and an old woman who made it to sixty – judging from the other pictures, that's probably considered an accomplishment for a Templar. Chi's still praying, so I scuff my borrowed sneakers and wander a little further away. As if to prove my hypothesis, the next one down is another young person, a woman this time, in her late teens. I step closer and, to my deep and unending surprise, I realize I recognize her.

My mother.

Eight

When I was eleven, I fell off the second-storey landing outside our apartment and landed on concrete. Mom was struggling to unlock the door with her arms full of groceries and arguing with me all at the same time. Our argument was pretty typical tween–parent stuff – I didn't appreciate the restrictions she put on me: no school, no friends, no R-rated movies, no indiscriminate homicide.

You know, the usual.

She was tooth-grindingly calm and rational, which made my argument (basically a long-winded version of "But, I wanna!") somehow seem childish in comparison. Backed into a corner, I went nuclear. I slammed down my groceries, shattering the glass bottles with a satisfying crash, then kicked a hole in the wall, spun and shoved the second-storey banister.

Not my finest hour, but I was punished.

The banister pulled free and I dropped into a free-fall, followed by the red-black smack of my head on the cement. I lay there gasping and confused.

Mom threw aside her groceries (the crash somewhat less satisfying this time), then raced down the stairs, terrified that I was seriously injured or dead.

Then just as horrified that I was not.

That's how I feel now. Like the ground was snatched out from under me. Like concrete cracked against my skull. Like the air was stolen from my lungs. But this time, I'm the one horrified by *her* true nature.

"Meda?" Chi's concerned voice creeps through my fog.

I borrow his line. "Gah…"

"Meda, what is it?"

I point, the truth finally seeping into my brain and trickling out of my mouth. "My mom."

Chi looks at the picture, then back at me. I don't look away from my mom's smiling eyes, but I don't need to to know he's equally surprised. Well, maybe not equally – no one could be *that* surprised.

He doesn't say anything right away. He might not be especially clever, but he's pretty good at reading social cues. He realizes my world has just been rocked. My mom is a Templar. No, a *Crusader*.

And my father's a demon? The world careens out of control. I hold perfectly still waiting for it to settle. Right now it doesn't make any sense.

I check out her mementos even though that squirmy bit twists and twangs in my chest as my eyes rove over them. A whole life that I didn't share, that I never knew even existed. The only person I thought I knew is an utter stranger. A laughing, happy, smiling stranger. I've never seen any childhood photos of my mom. Not being particularly sentimental, I hadn't even noticed until now. Reddish-brown curls, brown eyes, a wide mouth, slightly crooked bottom teeth. So strange to see these familiar features in a young, fresh face. In her youth, I can pick out pieces of me. Not a lot, but some. High, rounded cheekbones, the almond-shaped eyes, but hers are golden brown, sunshiny warm. Mine are as black as my soul.

Piles of pictures of her with friends, a ribbon for first place in a science fair. That doesn't surprise me, she was always dragging me towards science and I would flee towards art. Even my name, Andromeda, is a testament to her geekiness. A ring with an oval blue star sapphire sits on her shelf. I reach a trembling hand, but stop short of touching it.

She said she grew up in the country and I guess that's true, it doesn't get more country than out here. She said my grandparents were dead. Car crash. Ha – knowing they were badass demon hunters, I now find that unlikely.

"Meda, when were you born?" Chi asks and even this question is too complicated in my current state. It takes me a minute. A minute of looking into those laughing brown eyes shaped like my own. My brain translates them from laughing to glaring in accusation. I look away.

"1994," I finally manage, then wonder why he asked. I look back at the plaque, avoiding those eyes. Mary Porter 1974–1993, it states. Not Mary Melange, as I knew her. She died the year before I was born, or so they think. I have pretty conclusive evidence they're wrong. In reality, she was murdered only two years ago. It doesn't even feel like it was that long ago. I can paint the gruesome scene in perfect, vivid detail on the back of my eyelids, as clearly as if it happened yesterday. I can recreate the feel of her lifeless hand cradled in mine.

But I don't. I can't bear to remember what some heartless monster did to her.

One face pops up in the pictures over and over again, a boy with sandy, stick-up hair. Their arms around each other, filthy, missing teeth, about seven, grinning into the camera. In a group picture, her eyes on the camera, his on her. As a couple in hideously Eighties prom outfits (puffed sleeves – eek). Again, in swimsuits as teens. Again, again, again.

One where she's got her head thrown back, laughing, almost unrecognizable in her happiness. The world's tiniest diamond is on her hand and he's kneeling, hand over his heart. A ridiculous restaging of a recent proposal. I touch a trembling finger to it.

"Who's this?" Whose voice is that? It is so croaky, it can't be mine.

Chi squints at the photo. "Luke Bergeron," he answers carefully, as if afraid I will break. And I might. The wrong note and I will shatter.

"Is he still alive?"

"Yes, he's out though, on assignment." He pauses, then excitement creeps into his voice. "Meda, do you know what this means?"

I look at him blankly. That my mom lied? That I have no idea who she is?

"You're a Templar."

That too. But to be honest, it hadn't occurred to me. I'm half-demon, half-Templar. So Mom wasn't lying when she said I'm one of a kind. The cross-bred offspring of born enemies, a mixed mutt of Good and Evil. But how did it even happen? I look back into her sunshine eyes, the eyes of the only person who had the answers.

Maybe not. I point back to Luke.

"Where is he?"

But Chi doesn't get a chance to answer. A shrill siren slaughters the silence of the shrine. The room clicks red – the candlelight is supplemented by red, ankle-height emergency lights. Before we have time to react, a sonorous boom echoes from above and the building shudders under our feet. Instinctively, Chi and I both duck and look up. My wide eyes meet his, asking the obvious question. His eyes are just as wide as he answers.

"Meda – the school's under attack."

Nine

We stand frozen, our eyes wide, like the trapped deer we are. Then Chi shakes his head and I can almost see the shock scatter off him like water droplets off a dog. He pulls himself up and trades shock for courage, and maybe the teeniest bit of excitement. The boom vibrates again and we both instinctively duck. I look up at the ceiling, checking for cracks. How much abuse can the derelict building take before it collapses? Would the weight kill me? Or worse, would I survive, crushed, trapped and starving?

"Stay here," Chi shouts over the siren. Without waiting for a response, he spins so fast his sneakers squeak and takes off running.

Like hell. I pause, snatching my mother's ring and the picture of the ridiculous wedding proposal, jamming both in my pocket, then take off after him. I'm not the wait-for-death type. I'm more the find-him-first-and-kick-his-ass type. Another boom vibrates the building and bits of cement sprinkle down like rain. I instantly cower, wrapping my hands around my head.

OK, so maybe I'm more the slip-away-from-death-unnoticed type. Still, I'm not cowering in the dark waiting to be crushed.

I blast out of the Templar shrine and the doors smack the walls with a loud crack. There's no sign of Chi and the door out of the museum is just closing. The door with the locked keypad. Shit. I make a running dive for it and it clicks closed just as my fingers curl around the handle.

Please don't lock from the inside, please don't lock from the inside.

I jerk the handle. It's locked.

Damn Chi! I kick the damn thing and slam my open palm into it, leaving marks. The damn thing is twelve inches of solid steel, even I won't be able to tear through it. At least not right away. I look around for a weapon, something, anything, and my eyes come to rest on the PIN pad. It's a good thing Chi already escaped, or I'd slaughter the idiot and drown the damn keypad in Templar blood.

Templar blood.

Oh.

I bite down on my finger until I feel the pop and burn of torn skin, then press the welling spot of blood to the pad. The door opens with a click and hiss.

Sweet.

I take off up the stairs just as another boom shakes the building and I rock into the wall of the stairwell, the handrail digging into my hip. Then I'm off again, taking as many stairs at a time as I dare. I feel a swell of power that can only mean one thing: demons.

There's still no sign of Chi, but as I cut around the fourth bend, I run into a line of children heading down. I come to an abrupt halt. I hadn't heard their feet over the screaming siren and they're surprisingly quiet and calm, talking only in murmurs. Living here, no doubt they've trained for deadly situations their whole lives. They jump when they see me – despite their forced calm, they're frightened. They hold hands and some older kids carry the littlest ones. They must be heading down into the basement to hide. They have no choice; they haven't my abilities. The tomb I fled is their best option.

I meet the eyes of the oldest-looking one, a thirteen-ish girl with black-and-blue streaked hair. A toddler with blond curls buries its face in her shoulder. She strokes its pyjama-ed back and tells it everything's going to be fine. Her eyes ask mine if that's true.

I shrug. How would I know? I slide to the right so I can continue past them up the stairs.

The trickle of children becomes a flood as I turn the final corner. Another explosion rocks the building and an involuntary squeal of fright is snatched, unwilling, from their throats. I don't hold it against them – one of the squeals is mine. I push through them, a salmon swimming upstream, until I fight my way out of the stairwell and into the lobby. It's swarming with children being herded into lines by a grotesquely pregnant woman in her mid-thirties with short blonde hair. My eyes flit to every corner, but I don't see any signs of destruction yet. I find Chi, at least two feet taller than everyone around him, wading through the children on the other side of the room.

"Chi," the blonde woman calls. He twists back to look at her and I duck into the shadows, watching. His face is angry at the attack, but also... aglow. Lit with vicious anticipation.

"Upperclassmen to the gym for orders," the blonde shouts. She turns to grab a tiny boy headed the wrong way, so Chi's reply-nod is wasted. He shoves through the crowd, heading towards the gym.

Should I follow him? If he catches me, he might try to drag me back to the basement. On the other hand, I don't really want to run out of the school blind and surely they'll be getting some information on the situation in the gym. And, though survival is of the utmost importance, I don't want to leave the Templars. Not now, not after what I just learnt. Not unless it's absolutely necessary.

I weasel after him.

He breaks into a run once he reaches the hallway and I pick up my own pace. I should slow down, a mere human couldn't keep up with Chi, but even though I've been to the gym twice now, the school is such a maze I'm not sure I'd be able to find it. I curse my stupidity in not paying closer attention to the route, and this time I do. I keep my eyes peeled for other students, but don't see any. Coming all the way from the basement must make us the last ones to the gym.

The sirens stop abruptly and the sudden silence shocks me as much as the sudden noise had, and I stumble slightly. I'm glad to have my fifth sense back and even more grateful at the timing – I can now hear other feet coming to join my hallway from an offshoot to my left. I slow, hoping it's not Jo or possibly Zebedee. I duck into an empty classroom, but it's just two random fifteen-ish boys with the same excited fervor on their faces as I saw on Chi's. I follow them, but slower. Now that I can hear, I don't have to stay quite so close on their heels.

The gym is already packed with students when I arrive. The kids shift and bounce on the balls of their feet, but keep their talking to an excited murmur. I slip in the back, keeping my eyes peeled for Jo. I'm not worried about anyone else trying to force me into the basement – they've made it clear that Emma's safety is low on their list of priorities. I see Chi moving towards the front of the gym, working his way between students. As they turn towards him, Chi gives them reassuring nods, claps them on the shoulders and grips hands. I watch them relax – Chi's confidence is catching. Unfortunately, my brains render me immune.

On the far side of the room, a mutton-chopped man stands on the bleachers. Everyone faces him as he gives orders to a group of students distributing swords, daggers and knives from the metal cage. He's younger than any of the other non-pregnant adults at the school, which is explained when I see the empty sleeve of his Templar jacket. Speaking of cripples, I roll up on to my tiptoes and again look for Jo. I'd feel safer if I knew where she was. I have no idea what my plan is yet, but I'm sure whatever it is, she'd do something to thwart it. Still nothing. I do spot Zebedee, her dark head rises above the crowd towards the front of the room.

I need more information. I hope Muttonchops will get around to explaining, but I'm not the patient sort. Windows line the wall to my immediate right and the far wall to my left. They're boarded over, but the boards are on the inside – they can't risk an outsider getting curious and pulling them back. There, one window rises from behind the fighting cage on the other side of the long room – the chain link would provide some, if not perfect, cover. With a quick look at Chi, I slither through the crowd, then around behind the cage. The wood covering the window is thin chipboard nailed into the frame and I slip my fingers under its edge. When the next boom sounds, I jerk it free then bend it back, snapping the corner off and creating a six-inch peephole. I glance around, but no one notices. I allow myself a satisfied smirk and peek out of the window. The smirk dies.

Sometimes, ignorance *is* bliss.

The school grounds have been transformed into Wall Street – black-suited, soulless men and women as far as the eye can see.

Demons. Hundreds of them.

They stand in half crouches, looking ready to pounce, hissing and snarling. It looks ridiculous really, with their forty-something bodies and conservative suits. But I don't laugh. They pack the yard in front of the school and fill the spaces between the trailers. Their human faces flicker, overlaid briefly by those of grey-faced monsters – black pits for eyes, withered, twisted skin, sunken cheeks, lipless mouths filled with sharp teeth.

There's no way I can sneak out past them. Not a chance. I should have stayed in the basement.

The only thing standing between the demons and us is a thin line of decrepit Crusaders hauled out of retirement. I recognize Mrs Lee in a Hawaiian-print muumuu (of all things), and three old people from the cafeteria, though not the headmaster or The Sarge. I can see a dozen or so others lined up with them, with several feet between each of them – spread thin so they can reach all the way around the school. Some of them I can barely see from this angle and realize they're leaning on the school, using it for support.

These are our defenders? Oh, and an army of half-trained high-schoolers. An army, I'm horrified to realize, that I just drafted myself into. I should have headed into hiding with the babies.

We cannot win. We are doomed.

"You cannot win," a hissing voice booms. "You are doomed."

Holy shit.

I scan the enemy army, looking for the voice. When they speak again I realize it isn't one voice. It's all of them speaking as one.

"But we are willing to negotiate," it/they hiss.

Please negotiate! I don't intend to become one of those wrong-time-wrong-place kind of deaths.

"Never!" croak the geezers. The old folks all reply at the same time but it lacks the eerie, impressive togetherness of the other side. That and there was a great deal of wheezing involved. Jesus, I spot a walker.

Rule of thumb: Never let people in diapers make life-or-death decisions.

The demons, starting at the very back of the crowd, raise their hands, then lower them just as the demons in front of them start to raise their hands – uncannily like "the wave" at a sporting event. The motion keeps rolling forward and, as it does, a black cloud starts forming above their hands, rolling towards the school. The air around it wavers, shimmering like the air above hot cement. As it moves towards us, the cloud gets bigger and gains definition, until it looks like it's billowing and flickering.

I blink, not believing what I'm seeing. It's a wall of fire, except painted in greys and black, taller than the school. And it's coming right at us.

My eyes fly to the elderly Templars and their stoic stance calms me. Surely they have a plan to stop it.

Then again, what they have could just be dementia and they don't realize it's a problem.

The fire reaches the row of demons closest to us and they fling it at the school. I duck, covering my head with my arms, but there's only the great roaring boom and the vibration. After a moment of shocked disbelief, I peek back out of the window. Outside, the ancient Templars have held off the black fire with a white cloud of their own. It rings the school, clinging to it, like a protective coating of cotton. It fades as the black wave dissipates.

I hope it's not gone for good, because the demons in the back are raising their hands again, building the black cloud. It comes rolling forward, gaining shape and speed.

As it gets closer, I fight the urge to duck, wanting to see what happens. At the very last second, the Templars throw up their hands and the white cotton appears, intercepting the fire with the great booming roar that seems to come from everywhere at once. Dust falls from the rafters.

"Students!" The burly cripple calls my attention back inside. He's still standing on the bleachers where everyone can see him, but now his attention is focused on the whole audience. I creep back over to join everyone else and listen to the instructions. A dark-haired boy notices me and looks surprised, then gives me a faint, approving smile.

He thinks Emma's turned a new leaf and has come to join the fight. Idiot.

The crippled Crusader is still talking. "The magical protections aren't going to hold up forever and, once that happens, you're our next line of defense. Squads, defend your zone until you hear the order to fall back." He taps his earpiece and I see baskets of them being passed through the crowd. I snatch one as a basket goes by and fit it in my ear. I can't hear anything on it yet, but I'm hoping it'll come in handy.

The students are murmuring, making protesting sounds and I realize it's at the assumption that they'll be retreating. The Crusader shakes his head and holds up his hands for them to be quiet. Then he says, matter-of-factly, "The school is lost."

The crowd gasps and rumbles. A few students shout denials and a girl in front of me covers her mouth. How could that possibly come as a surprise to them? They must not have looked outside.

The Crusader continues. "All we can do is give the younger students a head start on their evacuation."

Evacuation? The younger students are sneaking out?

He continues, "Slow the enemy, stay alive." Finally an order I'd obey – the second part I mean. "Once the children are out, you'll evacuate through the south tunnel to lead them away from the children." This was all said matter-of-factly, but now the commander draws himself up. He's taller than I first thought and he gazes somewhere over the heads of his audience. The expression on his face is as if he were looking at something beautiful. His chin sets and he looks proud; he's no longer just an old cripple, he is a noble knight who happens to be old and missing an arm.

He begins a pep talk, powerful and beautiful, full of honor and duty. His eyes – piercing blue eyes – drop and rove among the students, meeting their own as if he is calling them personally to undertake this holy mission. He plays the hearts of those in the room with the mastery of a violinist in the Philharmonic. Even my mysterious chest appendage gives a few sleepy vibrations as he plucks our strings. The words of the song are heroic, but I alone seem to recognize the title: suicide.

"This will be the first time most of you have ever fought. You're young, but you're brave and you have been training all your life for this. This is what Templars do." His eyes, blazing with purpose, burn a path through the room. "Are we afraid of demons?"

"No!" shouts the room. *Crap – was that my voice?*

"Are we afraid of death?"

"No!" I keep myself under control this time.

Throughout his speech the building shudders again and again. The faces of the students around me are serious, determined, heroic. Suicidal. I am not that person. It is time for this rat to abandon the sinking ship. The younger students are heading down, so presumably the escape tunnel is connected to the museum. I just need to get back to the door from where I came in, and I can find my way back.

I'm already on the outskirts of those gathered, thanks to my beeline for the window, so it's easy to scuttle around to the back. I catch a view of Chi, near where I left him, searching for someone in the crowd. Our eyes meet and his widen with shock. I dodge between students.

The doors out to the hallway, where I came in from, are in the far corner of the back wall. Chi's twisting his head around, scanning the crowd. He must have lost me. Good. I'm not worried about what he'd say if he caught me, I just don't care to find out. I haven't the time. I move even faster, staying low. Orders are wrapping up, the students are about to be sent to their deaths – I mean posts. The last thing I want is to get caught in the masses as they swarm towards the fight. It's a struggle to keep my pace slow enough to go unnoticed; I want to bolt, but I don't want to see the students' reactions if the cowardly Emma is seen deserting the army. It could get ugly and, again, I don't have the time. Ten feet, eight feet, six. I don't know if Chi saw me, but he heads in this direction. It doesn't matter; I'm at the door to the hallway. I ease it open and slide through. I'm out. In five minutes I'll be in the tunnels and away from the impending carnage. I take two steps, preparing to run at top speed.

"Going somewhere?"

I freeze.

It's Jo and she has a knife at my throat.

Ten

"Jo!" Not a brilliant response, but I'm taken by surprise. I take a step back, trying to put some space between my neck and the nasty eight-inch knife. If I can get far enough away, I can snatch that knife out of her hand and...

And what? I don't have time to tie her up and stash her somewhere. I can knock her unconscious, but the students will only wake her when they come stampeding from the gym in a minute. Then she'll tell. They'll know the truth about me and they'll hunt me down. *She'll* hunt me down. There's really only one option.

I have to kill her. They might figure out it was me eventually, but by then I'll be long gone.

My eyes meet her narrowed ones in the skinny space between us. I try to rally some hate to match what I see in her eyes. It'd make it easier. But I can't hate her, so I just hate myself more instead.

I ease another step backwards, trying to make the space I need. She's too clever and follows me, the razor-sharp blade steady at my jugular.

"I repeat: Going somewhere?" she hisses. I need to talk her into lowering her guard.

I don't bother to whimper and simper like I would with Chi. If I did, she'd probably run me through in disgust. Instead I'm honest – in my emotions at least. "Yes! I don't know if you've noticed but demons are attacking the school! I'm no Crusader, I need to evacuate!"

"Oh, I noticed. I thought you might have something to do with it," she accuses, pressing the knife to my skin.

So that's where this sudden aggression is coming from. Well, maybe not so "sudden"; I have been trying to make her hate me. Exaggerated aggression.

"I don't have anything to do with it! I know nothing about it!" This is all true.

"It seems awfully coincidental," she snarls, her face inches from mine. "A Templar community has *never* been attacked head on, then you show up and the very next day they're at our doorstep in droves."

When she puts it like that, it does seem awfully coincidental. Surprise registers on my face and she must sense the honesty in my confusion. She's observant like that. The blade pulls back a couple of millimeters.

My confusion is honest. I'm not. I need one more breath of space, then I'll move to take advantage of her slip. Her knife will be in her heart and I'll be on my way faster than she could tell Chi, "I told you so."

I see arguments bounce around in her head as she decides what to do. She rocks back on her heels. I try to keep my muscles relaxed; I don't want to give my intentions away.

Her eyes meet mine, consternation in them. Probably at no longer having an excuse to kill me. She backs away a hair more... Now!

I hesitate.

WHAM! The gym door slams open and students flood into the hallway. At their head – Chi.

Damn!

"Meda? *Jo*?" Although I'm the almost-murderer, Jo's the one with the knife at my throat so she gets the appalled look from Chi. She lowers the blade as Chi stops in front of us, a rock in the river of teenagers trying to get into position before the geezers give out. The hallway's narrow and we get shoved a little to the side so the students can pass. "What's going on? What are you doing here?"

Where to start? Another shudder rocks the building, with more force than the previous ones, and I decide to start with the part that gets me out of here the fastest. As delightful as it would be to rat Jo out, it's not very productive.

I open my mouth, but Chi keeps talking. "Why haven't you evacuated?"

Perfect. Exactly what I want to talk about. But then I realize he's not talking to me; he's talking to Jo.

She glares at him. She's so ungrateful, Chi, let's focus on my evacuation instead. I'll appreciate any efforts you make to get me out of here.

"I'm not leaving," Jo says, her face set in stone.

Obviously a lost cause. Me, Chi, let's talk about me.

"You're supposed to leave with the others!"

"Other what? The children and babies? I'm a little old for that." She's snide. Another boom hits the building and a piece of plaster falls from the corner. The old folks must be giving out.

"No, the other…" Chi trails off, realizing this is going to go poorly. Too late.

"Other what, Chi? The other cripples?" She's irate now, shouting in his face. "Plenty of them stayed behind, or didn't you notice Commander Heron has only one arm?"

"*They* are Crusaders, *they* have magic to protect them." Now he's angry, shouting back. "*They're* experienced in combat–"

If I don't step in, Jo's going to get some combat experience on Chi. And let's not forget, I still need to be evacuated, preferably with an escort since all the Emma-haters are on the loose – and armed. "Focus!" I shout, and they both blink at me. They'd forgotten I was here. "What are we going to do now?"

"You two are leaving. Now."

I like the sound of that. Go on.

"I'm not going anywhere," Jo says, crossing her arms. Then the building shakes again and she has to put a hand on the wall to catch herself.

"Yes, you are." Chi stands steady, feet planted wide.

"No–" Jo starts.

Good God, children. Can we focus on what's important? Me.

"Fine." Chi shoves a hand through his hair, but he must have forgotten it's in a ponytail and he messes it all up, pulling half of it out. He growls in frustration, then gets an idea and looks up. "Don't do it for yourself, but Meda needs to get down to the tunnels – and she needs an escort."

Ha. He really hasn't been paying attention. My well-being is not high on Jo's list of priorities.

"She's a Beacon," he says.

Jo rolls her eyes. "You don't–"

He cuts her off. "Fine, I don't know that for certain." This is a change to the script. "But she *is* a Templar."

"What?" Jo's shocked out of attack mode. Chi explains rapidly, looking over his shoulder. The teen river has slowed to a trickle. Two more booms rock the building, back to back.

"We were in the shrine. Her mom was Mary Porter."

"Who?" Jo asks.

"A Crusader. They thought she died eighteen years ago, before we were born. There's a memorial to her in the shrine."

Jo turns towards me, mouth agape.

"She didn't know," Chi rushes before Jo can ask.

Jo studies me, searching for the truth. I peel back my mask and let her glimpse the shock of my mom's secret. We both flinch from the experience.

"Will you get her out of here? Please?"

Jo hates it, absolutely hates it. She wants to kill demons, I can read it in every line of her body. Hell, she wants to kill *me*. She doesn't want to be sent somewhere safe with the children and cripples, a protected damsel in distress.

"Fine," she says, her shoulders slumping. Her fight is gone.

Chi relaxes slightly. "I'll take you as far as the west hall, I'm guarding the ground entrance there."

The three of us take off running, Jo in the rear as usual. I'm giddy, I'm going to escape – with a highly expendable escort to get me there. I'll evacuate, disappear. True, I didn't learn everything the Templars could teach me about my kind, actually my *kinds*, since I'm part Templar too. But I have a lead, and once I'm out I will hunt him down.

Luke Bergeron.

How I'll track him down is a worry for later – after I escape the battlefield of Good versus Evil.

The building is shuddering in earnest now and cracks are appearing in the walls. I curse the school's nonsensical construction, which means there's no direct route back to the main box and stairs to the tunnels.

"Isn't there a faster way?" I ask as we round another corner.

"No," Chi says easily, not panting despite our pace. "Everything important is in the main building – the grimoires, the artifacts, the escape routes – so there are no direct routes to get there. Makes it easier to defend."

Makes sense. Maybe I didn't give the idiots enough credit. Of course, there's one minor problem. "Um, the front door?" It leads directly into the main building.

Chi almost smiles. "It has a steel gate about a foot thick that's been dropped by now. The demons could get through it eventually, but they'll try the other entrances first. And we'll be ready for them." His grin is ugly in a sexy kind of way.

The headset crackles to life in my ear. "Squads, prepare to cover the retreating Crusaders. Crusaders, prepare for my order to fall back in ten… nine…" He continues to count down and Chi shoots a look at Jo and picks up his pace. I pretend to labor to keep up – now's not the time to blow my cover.

The voice in my earpiece finishes, "…one! Retreat!"

I hear the bang of slamming doors in the distance. Then a boom rocks the building so hard, I lose my balance, and topple over sideways. Jo, behind me, tries to catch me and goes down with me instead. We fall in a tangle of legs and profanity. Crashes echo in the distance as parts of the building collapse, and there's shouting. Chi staggers back towards us, his feet set wide, his messy, half-up hair grey with dust. Once the vibrations stop, he hauls us back to our feet, a veiny forearm for each of us.

What if the demons keep using magic? Why wouldn't they just hammer the building – and us – to dust? I open my mouth to ask, but am answered by a howling cry outside. It's a roar, but high-pitched, like a thousand squeals. It grates on my nerves like nails on a chalkboard and my hands itch to cover my ears.

Chi looks away, listening to the cry, then he and Jo exchange a look. Then he turns to me. "Battle cry," he explains. "We have to hurry."

No, really? I thought maybe we'd hang around.

He grabs my hand and starts running again, half pulling me. Jo brings up the rear, as usual. There's a pounding, like drums, then screams as battles break out all over the school. Twice we hear fighting ahead of us and Chi changes our route, taking us up not one flight of stairs, but two, until we're on the third floor. It's longer this way, but all the fighting's on the ground floor, at the entrances.

We run down the empty hall, then back down to the second floor. As we come out of the stairwell, we see a middle-aged man at the opposite end of the hallway – right where we need to go. His crisp black suit tells me he's not on our side. Somehow at least one demon has breached the defenses. He turns when we enter and, with a feral grin, runs straight towards us, his dress shoes clicking on the linoleum. Chi grins just as nastily and runs straight towards him.

I wait sensibly with Jo.

They run at each other and I wonder if Chi plans on tackling the demon. But no, at the very last second, right before the two are about to make contact, Chi shoots his feet out in front of him and baseball-slides right past him. The demon's arm whiffs over Chi's head. As he slides past, Chi brings his sword across the back of the demon's knees. The demon screams and falls, and Chi twists up to his knees and swings his sword with two hands, neatly chopping off the demon's head. Blood splatters in an arch across the wall and the momentum makes the head spin a few times before it settles.

Chi looks at me, I guess to make sure I'm OK. His eyes widen.

My lips are curved into a fierce grin – oops. Not a Nice Girl reaction to decapitation. Is it too late to faint? It isn't too late to find out. I roll my eyes and start to collapse, fighting the urge to break my fall – self-preservation has always been one of my faults.

Jo grabs my arm before I get very far. "Oh, knock it off, we don't have time for that," she snaps and I open my eyes. Chi's attention is on a new demon rushing into the hall. I shrug and stand up. Chi dispatches the newcomer with a slick feint-and-dive and we continue on our way.

We make it to the west stair, which Chi and I came up earlier. We race down it, blessedly hearing no fighting. We hit the ground floor and blast through the doors, one more hallway to the main box, then the basement stair and my freedom.

Chi comes to a complete stop. I slam into his back and Jo hits me, making a bruised-Meda sandwich. Filled with foreboding, I peek around Chi and the reason we didn't hear any fighting becomes clear.

The demons have already won this fight.

They've taken the hallway. Three men who could be accountants and a woman with the soft figure of an overeater stand over a mixed pile of student Templars and dissolving demons. Blood splatters the demons – red splashes on white skin and sensible, professional shirts. On their suits as well, no doubt, but it doesn't show against the black. Our entry did not go unnoticed and they all turn, in sync, to stare at us, their heads twisting smoothly on their necks like snakes'.

Chi just stands there. Frozen. His curved sword hangs loose in his hand and his eyes are fixed on the bodies. He knew theoretically that students could die, but I don't think he really understood what that meant. Friends' bodies still on the linoleum, blank stares and gore on teenage T-shirts. After all, as far as he knew, his last demon fight had gone perfectly.

I'm not so naive and dive for a nearby classroom. Jo isn't either and shoves Chi out of the way just as one of the males leaps at them.

The wall gives Chi a wake-up slap and he whirls with catlike grace. Jo's not nearly as graceful, but her dive was more controlled so she manages to stand only a second after he does. I cower safely in my classroom waiting for them to clear our way.

Chi has another curved sword hooked into his waistband and he pulls it free so he has one in each hand. Jo also has a sword in addition to the knife I got to know earlier. They stand, back to back, and face-off with the demons. The demons spread out, surrounding them. The demons and Chi take a couple of feints at the other, trying to get a feel for the other's ability. Finally the pudgy woman dives in, faster than I would have thought her capable of, and the fight begins in earnest.

Death is my art form – when I fight, I'm a ballerina. Graceful. Chi lacks my grace, but makes up for it in energy and enthusiasm. His fighting style is like breakdancing – strong and frenetic with some really sweet moves. Jo's is… the Macarena. Ugly, but it gets the job done. They're outnumbered two to one, but are holding their own.

But then a fifth demon comes sneaking down the hall, a burly black man in a pinstripe suit. Crap. I don't want them to die. Not now, anyway. The demon is intent on the battle and doesn't notice where I crouch in the darkness. I wait until he's between my door and the empty door directly across from mine. In a move like lightning, I dive and shove him into the classroom across the way where I twist his head off with a wet pop. His black soul pours from his body, inky compared to the silvery grey of a normal human's. I'm full, but I step back quickly anyway. I don't know if I can eat demon souls and now's not the time to risk experimenting.

This happens three more times, back and forth, back and forth, as more demons seep in. Dive, squish, pop. When there aren't new targets sneaking down the hallway, I vicariously fight through Chi and Jo, which may involve the tiniest bit of shadow-boxing. Occasionally I hear updates crackle through my earbud. We're not winning, but we are holding our own.

Finally, with a blindingly fast spin move, Chi takes out one demon, then adds his attack to one of Jo's. She takes advantage of the momentary distraction and smashes a holy-water globe into her other demon's face. Chi skewers a third and I do a fist pump.

But that was a mistake. I was so caught up in the fighting that I failed to notice the new demons creeping down the hall.

They do not fail to notice me.

My fist is still in the air when I catch their arrival out of the corner of my eye. I turn my head. Eight of them, four men, four women, all eyes on me. One of them smiles, white teeth bright against too-red lips.

I jump back into the classroom and slam the door, but it's pointless. It explodes off its hinges as the demons stomp through. Not one, not two, but three have come after me – two men and Red Lips. That leaves five plus the one still alive to attack Jo and Chi. Not that I'm worried about them – I clearly have my own problems.

I back to the wall and shoot a quick glance out of the window, but there are only hordes more demons outside. There's no escape; I'm going to have to fight.

So be it.

Just because I'm going to die is no reason not to enjoy inflicting as much damage as possible. What can I say? I'm a glass-half-full kind of girl.

I crouch down and let the hot joy of an impending slaughter fill me. The inner monster, whom I kept on a tight leash while the others got to play, dances in delight. I grin and it's all teeth. They crouch, ridiculous in suits. She's even in heels.

I remember my hard-learnt lesson the last time I fought demons and decide to start with the feint this time. I spring right for the girl, then, at the last second, twist and come down on the man in the middle. He screams as I rake his face. My hand closes on his scalp as he jerks, twisting away from me. I come away with a fistful of hair. Without pausing, I spin and dive at the woman, slamming her into the wall. I wrap my hand around her throat as the third one rips me off her. Her throat comes with me.

One down, two to go, but unfortunately it's all downhill after that. I twist like a wild thing in the arms of the man who grabbed me and manage to take a piece of his hand with my teeth. He releases me abruptly and I stumble backwards, off balance. The other man dives at me from behind, catching me around the waist and slamming me into the wall hard enough for it, and possibly my skull, to crack. I see the flickering candles of the Templar shrine – stars.

I blink back into reality and they each have an arm. I tense, preparing to be ripped in half. The taller of the two, the one with a new bald spot courtesy of me, growls in my face. I focus on the blood running down the side of his bulbous nose.

"You're lucky we're not supposed to kill the girls."

They're not? I perk up. I've never been quite so happy to be a girl before.

He grins nastily and it's almost funny, that expression on such an unremarkable, middle-aged face. "At least, we aren't supposed to *yet*."

Ah well, where there's life there's hope. I'll take what I can get.

They haul me, one on each arm, to the hallway where the battle continues. I hope for rescue, but am disappointed. Jo is captive like me but thrashing wildly. I don't bother wasting the energy. They're stronger than me, so I wait for an opportunity.

Chi's facing three alone. His hair is stuck to his face with sweat and his once-white T-shirt is a red-and-pink tie-dye. From the way he's starting to flag, I think a lot of the blood is his. He's not a girl, so there's no reason to leave him alive. Once they kill him, there will be no hope of rescue. We're dead, we're all dead.

And the demons know they've won. They're cackling and squealing, taunting Chi with dancing steps and giggles. A male lunges for Chi's side. Chi lowers his left blade to block him, while swinging his other one around blindly to block any right-side attack. Another demon, a red-haired woman, weaves in and then dances out of the way as Chi thrusts. While he's distracted, the first demon dives back towards Chi's side and this time manages to claw him across the ribs. Chi grunts and Jo screams, struggling even more madly. Chi swings his blade around to protect himself, but, in his exhaustion, is thrown off balance. He over-corrects, pulling himself backwards, but has to wheel his arms for balance.

He's done and he knows it. His eyes jump to Jo's.

A demon lunges for Chi's exposed throat. Jo screams.

I do, too.

Then the demons all freeze.

All of them. Just. Freeze.

The leaping one falls mid-lunge; my captors might as well be cardboard cut-outs. The look on Chi's face is priceless and I imagine mine matches his. I twist – Jo's certainly does. Victorious shouts echo throughout the building. The demons everywhere are frozen, we won! Somehow, someone managed to freeze the demons.

Jo jerks from her demon's hold and with two big steps, throws herself into Chi's arms. I think that shocks him more than the demons suddenly freezing. He looks as stiff as they do, his eyebrows up near his hairline and his mouth in a mystified "O". He just starts to wrap his arms around Jo when she realizes what she's doing and jerks out of his arms, turning away and, if I'm not mistaken, rubbing her eyes.

Then, her gaze lands on the demons. With a ferocious snarl, she snatches her sword from the floor and cuts off one of her captors' heads.

That's more like the Jo I know. She then kills the other captor and both of mine.

Chi's had too many shocks in the last couple of minutes and it takes him a moment to process what's going on. When he does, he protests. "Jo, what are you doing? They can't fight back."

She just looks at him, her chest heaving and a crazy wildness in her eyes. Her hand flexes on the hilt of her sword. It occurs to me that Jo really, *really* hates demons. Not in an enemy-combatant kind of way, but in a no-holds-barred-rip-them-to-pieces-and-dance-on-the-corpse kind of way.

I need to remember that.

But for now, I think it's a good idea to kill our enemies. I jump on her side. "But she's not really killing them, is she? I mean, they'll just be reborn, right, as long as she doesn't purify them?"

Chi thinks about that, then with a shrug and a swing he takes another demon's head off. I force myself to hang back while they finish the slaughter, even though my blood pounds hot and heavy with violence. I look away as black souls pour from the demons' bodies, then dissipate into the air.

Over the earpiece people are asking who froze the demons and how, but I care only about whether they can continue freezing them, not about who or how.

But I should have.

Because then we hear clapping. Not from us, from outside the walls. We exchange confused looks, then run into the nearest classroom, dodging desks to get to the large windows. Outside, the demons all clap, politely, as if at the intermission of an opera. There are still hundreds of them. Maybe a thousand. Chi, Jo and I look to each other for an explanation, but none of us have one to offer. Then the voice comes out of all the demons' mouths.

"Had enough yet?" The voice is dry; the question is patronizing.

Understanding punches me in the gut and I stumble back a few steps, bumping into a desk. We didn't win because we didn't freeze the demons. They froze themselves, or the voice froze them. Because they can, because there are hundreds more to replace the few we just killed. And if the voice is willing to kill his own people just to get our attention, what more would he do to us? It's meant to intimidate us. It works, on me at least.

"Now are you ready to negotiate?" the voice asks.

I look at Chi and Jo and read in their faces the same realization. I feel a little panicky, but they're stoic.

"They'll negotiate, won't they, Chi?" I ask, but I already know the answer.

"No," Jo says.

"Never." Chi.

"But we'll all die!" I argue with them as if they make the decision.

Chi looks at me and manages to quirk up a corner of his mouth. "Weren't you ever taught not to make a deal with the devil? You never win."

I can only sputter.

"At least all the children escaped. That's all that matters," Jo says with a stiff nod.

But I don't care about the children. "You're willing to die? Just like that?"

Jo turns towards me. Her voice is calm but now I see her eyes blaze in a holy hazel fire. She doesn't want to die, but she will, for what she believes in.

I need new friends.

"We still have a few tricks up our sleeve," Chi says, patting me on the shoulder. "There's still a chance we'll escape."

"How?" That battle we already almost lost was just the demons toying with us. He's insane.

Chi smiles and his eyes go to the ceiling. "Well, for one, we still have the holy-water sprinklers."

"*What?*" I recall the burn on my shoulder with searing intensity. Please let him be kidding. I hear a creaking in the pipes overhead. For the first time in my life, I feel faint.

The voice pulls our attention back out of the window.

"Well?" demands the voice from a thousand mouths. "Do we negotiate?"

"Never," whispers Chi again. The two of them exchange deliciously violent looks, jaws set.

"Bet I kill more than you do," Jo teases.

"You're on."

They're insane.

But then a voice comes over the PA system, startling us all.

"Yes, we'll negotiate," the voice says. Chi and Jo gasp, and my earbud kicks to life with people shouting their disagreement. They can't all talk at the same time and the earpiece clicks around to different voices.

"What–"

"No–"

"But–"

Then the voices in my earbud all go mute. All except the voice that recently came from the PA system, our mysterious leader behind the curtain. Now he's talking right into our ears. "The exodus failed, the tunnel is blocked. All the children are on their way back."

Chi's face whitens and Jo sinks to her knees, her inner candle blown out. Silence echoes as the news is digested.

The voice clicks out of our earpieces and back on to the PA system. "We'll hear your terms."

"Excellent," the demons all hiss. "It's really quite simple. Just one life in exchange for all the rest. That's it, just one. Surely that's a fair deal. One we are going to take regardless – you just get to decide whether or not it's done over your dead bodies."

They were ordered not to kill girls, the coincidence of their attack the day after I arrived. My stomach sinks before they even say it.

"Give us the girl. Give us... *Meda*."

Eleven

My first instinct is to run. Jo's first instinct is to stop me. She tackles me as I bolt for the door. We go down, her on my back, and I feel her knife on my neck. I freeze, cursing.

"Meda, Jo – stop!" Chi says, grabbing me by the arm and pulling me out from under Jo. She allows it, but pulls her sword free and keeps it to my chest. "Meda, calm down. They won't turn you over!"

My eyes dart, searching for an escape route. I'll have to fight them. But I don't know if I can win. They're tough and Jo, at least, will be expecting it.

"Meda." Chi shakes my arm until I look at him. "I promise, they're stalling – they'll never turn you over. There has to be a reason the demons want you so badly. I told you, you can never make a deal with the devil, you'll never win."

What he says starts to sink in. It makes sense in Templar-world. My eyes flick to Jo.

"He's right." She looks disappointed so I know she means it. "I don't know what their plan is, but they aren't going to turn you over."

Chi releases me slowly and I don't run. I'm not sure where I thought I was going to go anyway, I'm surrounded by two armies with one common enemy – me.

Meanwhile our earpieces crackle with Templars trying to figure out who the mysterious Meda is. Chi ends the debate with a press of a button and a few words. "Sir, Malachi Dupaynes here. We have her."

"Bring her to headquarters." Nothing else. I imagine an implied, "So we can keep her safe even if it kills us all," so I don't completely freak out.

"Yes, sir." Chi takes the lead – he absolutely loves turning his unprotected back to me. Jo doesn't, she falls behind and I'm extremely conscious of the point of her sword on my spine. We start down the hallway and the light flickers, damaged in the magical attacks. As we pass the bodies of the Templar students, I notice that Chi and Jo keep their eyes averted. I don't. I examine them, relieved not to find a splash of bright red hair or dark mocha skin. Chi looks in the room where I had my little scuffle. Two headless bodies sprawl inside the door and a throat-less one leans drunkenly against the wall, her blood-soaked shirt as scarlet as her lips. Chi stops abruptly, but I'm too alert to bump into the back of him. Thank God, Jo is too.

"Did you do that?" I hear the confusion in his voice but he doesn't turn around.

"No…" The other guy did?

I don't know whether he buys it, but he moves on and we follow. My eyes crawl along the wall and dodge into doorways, searching for both threats and potential escapes. Bodies litter the hallway, both demon and Templar, and the living come to watch us as we pass. The rest of the Crusaders don't have Chi's restraint and the demons are being hacked to pieces and their false life drained, so they can never be reborn. The earbud crackles with more updates and a defense strategy in case the demons attack again. People start moving along the hallways with us. We've lost so many defenders, those who remain are being consolidated to protect the main building. As more people join us we start picking up pace. I'm the focus of curious stares – apparently everyone heard Chi's comment about having the girl. A blood-splattered boy catches my eye, his expression is… bewildered. Trying to figure out whether I'm worth it, maybe.

That one's easy. I'm not.

I look away.

The headquarters are in the central section of the building, on the ground floor. Chi drags his thumb across his sword as we approach the security sensor. He goes a little overboard with the cut and leaves a smear on the little glass screen.

We enter a small room with no windows and the walls covered in flat screens showing footage of the school grounds. Each one is filled with a black-suited ocean. Below the monitors, desks with computers are shoved against the wall. Six adults are in the room – two women and four men. All of them waved their middle age goodbye so long ago they probably forgot about it. Four are watching the computer screens and talking into earbuds, calling the immediate moves in the death game.

The headmaster and The Sarge stand over a map on a table in the center of the room. Her frizzy hair is pulled sloppily back into a half-assed bun, giving an unimpeded view of the mottled scar that twists her face. The headmaster has half-moon spectacles perched on his nose. Coupled with his beard and biker get-up, he looks like Santa gone bad. Their lips move rapidly, too fast for me to make out what they are saying. Chi clears his throat and they turn on us – *to* us. I mean, turn *to* us. I hang back, close to the door.

"Malachi, explain," the man barks and I recognize his voice as the one from over the PA system, the man behind the curtain.

Please, Mr Wizard, if I could only have a heart!

Chi opens his mouth and vomits the truth. (*And please, Mr Wizard, perhaps a brain for my friend?*) He leaves nothing out, not breaking the rules, lying or disguising me to sneak me in. Personally I feel it could have used some editing. Although the headmaster turns an angry red and The Sarge's lips thin, they do not interrupt. Chi wraps it up with the disclosure regarding my mom and the headmaster is visibly shocked. A couple of the old people at the computer screens turn at the revelation. The others are probably too deaf to hear.

Chi ends with a sheepish, "I'm sorry, sir."

"You should be. I'm disappointed in you, Malachi. And you, Jo." He turns hard eyes on her. We'd all forgotten she was there, lingering in the back. She probably figured she'd be sent out if they noticed her.

"But, sir! I just went to bring him back!" Jo retorts.

He cuts her off with a wave. "I'm not angry about the sneaking out to fight demons, though you are too young. You certainly aren't the first students to sneak out to try their skills a little early." His eyes seek out the old lady's and they share some memory. Then his face hardens and he leans back to glare down his nose at the two delinquents. "Wanting to fight demons is good, even if it is a little premature. But, when you knew she was a Beacon and brought her back to the school, why did you lie about who she is?"

Chi turns white while Jo looks at the floor. The headmaster waits for them to answer.

Is this really the time to dole out moral lessons? Whip the puppies later – if we live that long.

But he waits until Chi finally answers. "So we wouldn't get into trouble."

"Precisely. And who does that help?"

"No one. Just us."

"Exactly. You hid the truth so you wouldn't get into trouble. It was cowardly. Had you come forward and told us we had a potential Beacon on campus, we would have known we needed to step up our protections."

Chi looks as if he's going to be sick. Jo hasn't lifted her face from the floor so I can't see her expression.

There is one more beat of silence as he skewers them with his steely gaze. "I just hope you live long enough to appreciate this lesson."

"Now," The Sarge cuts in briskly. "What do we do now?"

About time.

She turns in my direction and a sky-blue laser beam hits me. Thank God she doesn't have two. "You're Mary Porter's daughter?"

"Yes."

"So she didn't die."

"Not then, no," I answer carefully.

Her eye hits the old man and he picks up where she left off, turning to me. "When and how did she die?"

I swallow. "Two years ago. She was... attacked." I try to block the visual. "Now I know something demonic did it, but I didn't at the time." All this is true. True like the tip of an iceberg.

"I'm sorry, child," The Sarge says, and her sky-blue eye is soft now. "She was a wonderful girl."

I nod. She was wonderful. "How did you think she died?" I ask.

"She was taken captive while on patrol with her mentor. He didn't make it." She exhales. "There was nothing we could do. We built her shrine, as we do in these situations, and, one day, her candle was lit."

I don't know what that means and let her see my confusion.

"The candle's kept lit by the Inheritance," she explains. "When a Templar dies, the Inheritance leaves their body and lights the candle."

But my mom didn't die, so how could her candle light if she was still alive? But The Sarge has already turned back to the headmaster and half-sentences ricochet between the two as they finish each other's thoughts. I wonder why they bother speaking out loud when they can apparently read each other's minds. I'm glad, though. Unlike them, I'm not a mind-reader.

"It can't just be…" she starts.

"…because she's a Templar," he finishes.

"They wouldn't trade one hundred weapons…" Her.

"For just one." Him.

"Unless that one was a nuke." Her.

How long do people have to be together to manage this particular feat?

"There's something special about her." Him.

"For them to want her so badly."

"So we can't let them have her."

YES! YES! YES! I almost dance.

Jo cuts in, alarmed, "But the children…"

Shut up, Jo! There's more where those came from.

The Sarge's mouth tightens then she lets out a breath. "Jo, I know it seems bad, but we can't make deals with the devil. I promise in the long run, we will lose."

Jo sputters trying to collect herself enough to shout, but the lady puts up her hand. "We have a plan. Several, really. We're not going down without a fight."

The headmaster takes over the explanation. "Right now the students are back under the school. They'll go out another tunnel – scouts are determining which ones have been compromised. For now, we stall and give the exodus another opportunity. Eventually the demons are going to realize we aren't going to turn her over and they'll attack again. Hopefully reinforcements will get here in time to help."

"How can we help?" Chi, of course.

The headmaster turns proud eyes on him. "We need you to get Meda out of here. In case we... in case reinforcements don't arrive in time."

"Me, sir?"

"You're younger and faster than anyone left. You're skilled at sneaking off school grounds." Really, a joke now? "And we need everyone else to hold the school for as long as possible."

"Why can't we just send her with the children?" Jo, cutting in.

The headmaster shakes his head. "I don't want to put all our eggs in one basket." He looks to Chi. "She's what they're really after... I'm afraid what I am asking is going to be very dangerous."

"Then I want to go, too." This, unexpectedly, from Jo. I had no idea we were such good friends.

"It's too dangerous," says Chi at the same time the headmaster says, "But your leg."

Jo has marshaled her arguments. "My leg slows me down barely at all – I can keep up with the human."

She can't keep up with me, of course, but no one else knows that.

Jo turns to Chi. "And two protectors are better than one. I already saved your life once today." Chi turns red. "If I hadn't been there earlier, you'd be dead."

"I'm sorry, Jo," starts the headmaster, "but you shouldn't be fighting in your condition." She tries to cut in, but he holds up a hand. "I know you want to help, but you can help keep the children calm as they sneak out."

I watch the headmaster tie Jo's ego to the tracks, then The Sarge comes through, driving the train. "In fact, you should have already evacuated with the other non-combatants."

I wince at "non-combatants". Jo's head is going to explode, I can tell.

And why shouldn't she come along? I've seen her fight and she's pretty good even with her leg. Part-girl, part-machine – all ninja. Two defenders are better than one. She might slow us down a little, but if it comes to outrunning the demons, I could always just leave her behind. What is that old adage about outrunning a bear? You don't have to run faster than the bear, just faster than the other people you're running with. I cast a look at Jo – seems to me having a cripple along could be advantageous.

"I want her to come." They're all surprised, especially Jo.

"But Meda–" the headmaster starts.

"No. I want her along. I've seen her fight and she's good," I say. The headmaster and The Sarge exchange looks and hope dawns on Jo's face. "She can keep up with me, for sure. And I trust her."

The two old people's eyes are on each other and I can see a whole conversation being exchanged. But Jo's eyes are on me and the gratitude that's in them is almost embarrassing.

"She comes, or I stay." My threat is empty (so, so empty) but they don't know that.

"Fine," The Sarge finally says. She looks at Jo. "It's dangerous. Are you sure you want to do this?"

Jo nods her head resolutely.

"So be it," The Sarge says, then turns to the bank of computers. "Christophe?"

A man seated at a screen answers without requiring any elaboration. "Beth says east tunnel is clear and Hez is almost to the Sylva sewer, no blocks yet. The exodus is just arriving into the main."

On the monitors, the demons all open their mouths in sync and we hear the voice through the walls. It's not clear enough to make out the words, so a computer operator hits a button and it comes over speakers.

"Well?" they say. They draw out the word so the "lllll" sound seems to roll on forever. The headmaster gives a little nod to The Sarge and she gives him a grim nod in return – more wordless messages being exchanged. Then she dives in faster than someone her age should be able to move and steals a kiss from him. He smiles as she shuffles us out of the door, then follows us out.

Over the PA system we hear the headmaster speak. "We're looking for the girl. She's either dead or hiding."

"You had better find her soon or we will search for you," the demons threaten.

"We'll fight you and she would die. You don't want her dead, do you?" There is no answer, but I guess that's better than the wrong one.

"You have fifteen minutes," they respond.

"It's a big school. We need at least an hour. She could be hiding anywhere."

The negotiations continue on as we race through the school. Jo takes the lead this time, probably trying to prove to The Sarge that she can keep up. Meanwhile The Sarge's lips move a mile a minute with instructions. We're to go through the tunnel to the Sylva sewers. There are a dozen different exits we could take, but the one marked with crosses has been checked and seems clear of demons. Some bikes are stashed at the Iron Snake bar, keys hidden in the tank of the men's toilet (ew). We pause as some kids are forced to trade their cleanish shirts and jackets for Chi's, Jo's and my bloody ones. The girl I steal from not only has abominable taste, but is also smaller than me, so my new pink Care Bear tee is snugger than I would like. The leather jacket's cool though. The Sarge doesn't come with us all the way down into the basement, but turns around once our orders are complete and starts heading back up to command.

We swipe our way into the museum from earlier, but this time it's a hive of activity, packed with all the evacuees. The emergency lights are still on, casting the room in a ghoulish red. The children whimper and clutch their backpacks like they're life-preservers, more panicked-looking than when I saw them on the stairs. I guess even six-year-olds can figure out it's bad when your evacuation route is shut off. A dozen or so pregnant women direct the children towards a narrow tunnel. It's only a few feet wide so they have to travel in single file, slowing their escape to the pace of a four-year-old.

Chi pushes us through the crowd in the opposite direction, leading us towards our own escape tunnel. As we pass, a few children clutch at Chi and Jo. My companions smile too brightly and lie that everything is going to be OK. One big-eyed, tear-stained toddler compels me to do the same. I add a pat on the head.

We make our way to the edge of the room, towards the long wall lined with bookcases, where it's a little easier to move. The bookshelves are empty now and I notice the glass display cases are as well – the artifacts and grimoires no doubt evacuating with the people. Abruptly Chi stops and we have a second serving of Meda sandwich.

"Jo, take her out. I'll catch up," he says and starts weaving in the opposite direction, a salmon joining in the school traveling upstream.

"What are you…?"

"Jo, just *go*," he says, over his shoulder. "I'll catch up." She recognizes – brilliant girl – that now is not the time to argue, and confines herself to the flightiest "Fine!" ever gritted out. Chi peels off and we continue through the crowd. Eventually we push through a door into a hallway and leave the masses behind. The bunker-like cement-block walls slash the crowd's noise to nearly zero. We walk briskly, Jo throwing a look over her shoulder every once in a while, probably looking for Chi. The only conversation between us is the tap of our feet.

Pit-pat, mine say.

Pit-thunk, hers reply

Pit-pat, mine insist.

Pit-thunk, hers maintain.

Pit-shuffle-shuffle.

My little skip and slide earns a funny look from Jo. What? It's tiresome the way they argue.

"So…" Jo starts awkwardly in the quiet. "Thanks for what you did up there." There's none of her usual anger or sarcasm – without them I almost don't recognize her voice.

She must not realize I volunteered her for a possible suicide mission solely for my benefit. "No problem."

I must not have kept the irony out of my voice because she rolls her eyes and stops, forcing me to, too. "I'm not stupid, I know it's dangerous."

Ah, there's the Jo I remember! But then the irritation fades back out. "I know that fighting demons is dangerous." She jerks her head towards the evacuees. "I know that better than any of *them*." Her eyes flick away, aiming at the ground but I know that's not what she sees. Then they come back, locking on my face. Her hands curl into fists. "And I want to do it anyway. I *have* to do it." Her hands relax. "Anyway, you're the first person to ever think I can do anything." She snorts. "Other than keep babies calm. So… thanks for that."

It's true. I was sincere when I said she was a good fighter and I thought she could help keep me safe. I don't know what to say and, really, if we keep on this way we might become friends and then where would my plan to toss her to the bear be? So I just nod. She offers me a tentative smile in return. A real one.

I return it.

We reach a stainless-steel round door, the kind with the steering wheel in the middle. The door is framed on either side by shelves scattered with backpacks. Jo turns the wheel and the door releases with a slight hiss. She swings it inward with a small grunt – the door is nearly a foot thick. Blackness gapes on the other side. I blink a few times waiting for my eyes to adjust, but there is nothing to see but darkness.

Jo passes me a backpack from the shelf with a quick "Supplies," in explanation and gestures for me to go first. Where she wants me to go, I have no idea. Into the abyss?

"Climb down the ladder," she explains. I stick my head out of the door and see a metal ladder bolted into the wall. I throw a leg over and start climbing down. She follows, but pauses to pull the door closed after her. I have to slow down and wait for her, but I don't mind. I'd rather Chi catch up with us sooner than later.

The ladder seems to go on forever and the air temperature drops as we descend. The voices in the earbud start to break up, then disappear altogether. My foot reaches for another rung and finds the ground instead. I ease off the ladder and feel grit and pebbles crunch under my feet. The inky blackness is impenetrable. I wave a hand inches from my face. Nothing.

There's a scuffling as Jo awkwardly climbs off the ladder, then I hear zippers. When a Maglite clicks on the light is blinding.

"There's one in your pack too," she whispers and I know we're out of the secured school zone. She holds the light so I can see and I pull mine out.

"Where are we?"

"An old mine. One reason why the founders picked this place – there's a warren of them."

I flash my light around and see that we are in a large cavern with a lot of smaller tunnels branching in every direction. I follow Jo to one on our right and she points her Maglite to a plain, unevenly carved cross. It is almost unnoticeable; it could be a natural crack in the wall.

"If we get separated, follow these, they'll take you to the sewer."

I nod, then realize that she can't see me and answer instead. We duck into the narrow tunnel and I know why they didn't take the children this way – other than the long, dangerous ladder suspended over a hundred-foot drop on to solid rock. The ground is uneven and rocks roll under our feet, but we can't keep the light trained on the ground without hitting our heads on the equally uneven ceiling. It makes the children's tunnel look like a spacious hallway. While Jo does well enough on flat ground, half-bent makes it hard for her to compensate for the lack of bend in her leg. It's slow going, but still Chi doesn't catch up.

We've probably been on the move for close to twenty minutes when we hear a noise in the tunnel, the rhythmic scuffling of feet, moving fast. My hopes lift for a half-second, thinking Chi has caught up, then come crashing down. The footsteps are coming from the wrong direction. Someone is in the tunnel ahead of us – and they're coming closer.

The demons have found the tunnel. I flash my light behind us, frantically trying to remember where the last side-shoot was. Not recently and not in sight. Jo is doing the same, only in front of us. She grips my arm and points her flashlight to a hole in the wall about thirty yards ahead of us. She starts hobbling forward, but I hesitate. I can't slide around Jo in the narrow tunnel so I'm stuck at her pace. Without her I might be able to run back to the last side-shoot before the newcomer reaches us.

I see a break in the darkness. The glare from the newcomer's flashlight is lightening the darkness but is not yet in sight, like false dawn. He's close; Jo's not going to make it. Still, she wastes several precious seconds to turn back and make sure I'm coming.

Suddenly, I am.

I race forward and catch up with her. We click off our flashlights, not wanting to give ourselves away. We can see our destination by the intruder's light. We are running, as best we can, bent over. I'm gripping her arm, shoving her weak side with more power than her leg can manage. We are moving faster, but not fast enough. The light is getting brighter; the entrance to the tunnel is ten feet away, eight, six, four. We are just diving in when the intruder comes around the corner.

We are caught, dead-center, in the blinding glare of the flashlight.

"Jo?" A boy's voice. Not a demon. Jo turns and tries to block the blinding light from her eyes. The newcomer realizes what he's doing and drops the beam.

"Who's there?" she demands. The pumping panic makes her voice harsh.

"Hez," the voice answers.

"Hezekiah?" Jo asks and squints into the dark.

I can see him now, a boy of about fourteen or fifteen, with a mop of too-long hair and a machete-sized knife in his free hand.

"Thank God," she says. It's more gusting air than words.

"The Sarge sent me on to scout the tunnels. For you guys, I guess."

"Yeah. They sent you?" Jo says, holding her hand over her heart. My heartbeat's a little wild too.

"Faster than a fogey or a double."

Double? Oh, pregnant woman.

He grins, as if that's something to be proud of. "Well, I gotta get back, I'm supposed to help guard the kids," he says importantly. We step into the recess so he can slide by, but Jo puts a hand on his arm and he stops.

"Be careful, Hez."

"Of course," he says easily and she releases him. "Good luck," he says with a cheerful wave.

Jo is not cheerful when she responds. She is suddenly ancient, sorrows written on her face like wrinkles. "You too."

We don't leave, instead we stay perfectly still as she watches his small form disappear, his silhouette outlined by the bouncing beam of his flashlight.

After all that terror, it's a pretty anticlimactic encounter, but I can't say I mind. Jo collapses against the wall and takes a couple of deep breaths. I do the same. We start off again, but we haven't gone far when we hear voices echo in the tunnel behind us. Hez and Chi. We keep moving and it's not long before Chi catches up with us.

"Where have you been?" Jo hisses.

"Supplies."

"There were supplies at the door."

"Other supplies," he says mysteriously.

"That's just great–"

Oh, for pity's sake. "Shhh! You can fight as much as you want once I'm somewhere safe." They both quiet down and we move on.

Our path becomes even more complicated as we go and we have to watch for turns – there are a lot of them. I swear, I think we looped around the mountain twice. The ground starts to slant upwards towards the surface, which means it's warmer, and my legs start to burn with exertion. The earbud begins to crackle back to life, but there are no voices.

At least, not at first.

"Meda…" a voice entices, sing-song and smooth. I stumble and Chi grabs my arm to steady me. I look up and his expression is grim. I turn to where Jo has stopped. Her back is rigid and her hands are fisted. She turns to face us. Her eyes shine.

"Meda, come baaaack," the voice rolls. "We have the school. We will peel your friends apart and only you can save them…" There's screaming in the background.

Chi's hand on my arm shakes; Jo covers her mouth, stricken.

"Or maybe you don't care, but are you alone? Maybe your friends care–" More screaming. Tears roll down Jo's cheeks and she shakes uncontrollably. Chi brushes past me and puts his arm around Jo. She collapses against him for a half-second, but then jerks away as if burned. With a frustrated scream, she rips out her earbud and stomps on it furiously.

Chi is stone. His jaw is granite, his eyes are coals, his spine rigid marble. His movements are shattered-shale sharp as he pulls the bud from his ear and slips it in his pocket. I do the same. We follow Jo.

Twice we stop when we think we hear noise behind us, but when nothing attacks, we continue. Finally we reach another vault-type door marked with a sloppy, barely recognizable cross. Chi turns the door's wheel while Jo holds her flashlight so he can see. I sweep mine from side to side in the tunnel behind us, watching for any followers. I hear the door open with a rusty squeal and turn around to follow them into sewers.

The sewer is perfectly round, like a giant brick-walled pipe. More pipes jut into ours, raining down slime to collect in the two-foot-deep pool of cloudy brown sludge that sits in the bottom. Chunks float in the sludge and cling to the wall at the water line. More chunks are crusted to the wall at the high-water mark – right where I want to put my hand to keep my balance. And it smells. Oh, God, does it smell. I gag and stick my nose in my shirt.

The Teenage Mutant Ninja Turtles lied to me. The sewer is emphatically not somewhere you want to live, let alone eat pizza in. I feel like I have a fairly high gross tolerance, but this is way out of my league. We troop along the pipe, doing our best to stay out of the ick.

We round the first bend when we hear a screech behind us. A familiar rusty-hinge screech.

Someone followed us into the tunnel.

A shared look flies among us and we break into a run, heedlessly splashing through the soupy mess. Our eyes are peeled for crosses and, when we see the first, we turn sharply, then the second. I'm glad for the turns now, they will make us harder to track.

Somehow the footsteps persist.

We turn at one more cross-marked corner but it's a dead end. The only tunnels leading out are too small for us to fit, even if we could kick our way through the disintegrating metal grates. Chi points up. There's a manhole cover above, marked with a cross. I look for the ladder.

The only problem is, there isn't one. We're trapped.

Twelve

Chi presses himself against the wall (gross) at the corner, both of his swords in his hands. I'm tucked behind Jo, as far away from the entrance as possible. We click off our flashlights and I miss my vision – without it, I swear my nose gets more sensitive and the heinous smell is even worse. We wait, crouching in the dark. The instant our pursuer comes around the corner, Jo and I are going to blind him with our flashlights while Chi attacks.

We don't have to wait long. The bouncing beam of a flashlight lights up our little tunnel accompanied by a fast-moving splash of feet in sludge. Only one set of feet that I can count and I smile. One we can handle. The light gets brighter and I can see Chi's outline. He's smiling too, that violent, vicious smile I love. He must count one set of feet, too.

Our pursuer breaks around the corner. We flash our lights and Chi leaps – then drops his weapons and windmills, trying to stop. He can't and slams into the form that is way too small to be a demon, and they both hit the side of the tunnel with a grunt, but fortunately, don't fall into the sludge. Chi pushes himself off to reveal Uri, the professional tag-along.

Less terrifying than annoying, but I still have to stop myself from killing him. Seems only fair: he scared ten years off my life, so I should take ten years off him. He's so annoying someone's bound to kill him before he hits twenty-two, so killing him now would make us even. In fact, he might even be thirteen, so that would put him a year up. What can I say? I am the soul of generosity.

But I can't, so I just snarl at him. Jo reads him the riot act and Chi welcomes him like a long-lost brother.

There's rope in our supply pack so Chi boosts Uri through the manhole. He ties a rope somewhere above and we climb out. After the sewer, the crisp evening air of the mountains smells especially sweet. No matter the season, it makes me think of apples.

It's twilight now and we're on a quiet side street in what I guess must be downtown Sylva. I can just make out a white building with a dome, complete with statuary on top. Definitely a downtown-like building. The chant of crickets and the distant drone of cars are the only sounds, and we try to keep it that way by not speaking and moving stealthily. There's an entire demon army a few miles away and there's no telling whether they left someone to stake out the town. They know the Templars have tunnels – they managed to block one off.

Chi and Jo must have previously taken the thirty seconds necessary to memorize the tiny town's layout because they don't hesitate in leading us to the Iron Snake.

The Iron Snake is a small dive in a brick-and-green strip mall, complete with neon signage and, of course, a cardboard "Bikers Welcome" sign leaning crookedly in the window. Fortunately, it claims to be both bar and grill, so we're allowed in, despite being minors. We still get looks as we stroll into the dark interior, but maybe it's not our age so much as the accompanying stench that draws all the attention. It's not exactly a family place, though the patrons are having burgers with their beers. The food actually looks pretty good and it occurs to me we missed dinner. I hope Chi and Jo have a plan for that – I get cranky when I haven't eaten. You wouldn't like to see me cranky. "Hangry," Mom called it – although when she called me that I was too hangry to appreciate her cleverness.

We make a casual beeline for the bathrooms, earning a suspicious glare from the bartender. Chi and Uri fetch the motorcycle keys while Jo and I hit the ladies' room to clean off the sewer slime. I stick my entire foot, shoe and all, in the sink and turn the tap on, then do the other. We regroup in the hall, Chi waving the keys triumphantly, and we take the emergency exit out of the back.

Behind the bar are six bikes covered in an army-green tarp. The genius who left the keys didn't label them so we try them in all the locks before we find two that fit. Only two because there isn't a tricycle for Jo and I don't know how to drive a motorcycle. As I've said, pavement is a worthy foe and I don't plan on taking her on. I climb on behind Chi, cringing at the smell emanating from the back of his jacket, then pause as I hear a roaring in the distance. I look up to see Jo and Chi grinning and I realize what the noise is.

Motorcycles, lots of them, in the distance. Reinforcements are reaching the school. Chi and Uri kick the cycles to life and we get the hell out of dodge.

Once again I find myself thoughtful on a motorcycle ride away from a human–demon bloodbath. I sense a habit forming and resolve to nip it in the bud before it gets any further.

The demons want me – badly. That demon licked my blood at the insane asylum and it shocked him. Something about my blood must have told him I am half-Templar, or otherwise different. The question is: Why does that make them want me? More importantly, how do I make them un-want me?

The Sarge told us to go to a Templar base located in rural Wisconsin, but I'm not sure that's the best plan. Eventually they'll figure out I'm not a Beacon and the questions will roll in – questions I don't want to answer. In Wisconsin they might even have their own way of determining my Beacon-ness, or rather lack thereof. Chi said the other American chapters don't have Beacon Maps, but that doesn't mean they don't have anything. Besides, wouldn't the demons assume that's what we would do? Go to another Templar stronghold?

I don't particularly want to become a sitting duck for either of my two enemy armies. Instead, I revert to my earlier plan – find out as much about my past as possible and go from there. Probably into permanent hiding. The first step is clear, however: find Luke Bergeron.

Two butt-vibrating hours later we pull off at a Wal-Mart. Uri's the cleanest so we send him in for clothes. I'm hoping everything I've seen him wear until now has been a secret joke on his part. I'm pleasantly surprised when he returns with a replica of what I've been wearing – jeans and a T-shirt, this time black with a cartoon dinosaur saying "Nom, nom". When I see the pink T-shirt Uri picked out for Jo, I wonder if Uri has a death wish. Jo's eyes promise violence if I say anything, so I manage to swallow my laughs and don't say a word. I don't need to say anything though, because really, a shirt like that speaks for itself. I make an imaginary camera with my fingers and snap a picture to treasure always. She sticks her tongue out at me. I snap a picture of that too and, to my surprise, I think I see her smother a smile as she rolls her eyes.

Our next stop is a roadside cafe to eat and plan. We slide into a vinyl booth as far away from the few other patrons as possible. Since the restaurant is roughly the size of a shoebox, that's just outside of touching distance. Fortunately the nearest couple are in a heated debate concerning each other's lineage and don't care about a pack of high-school students. The way they're going at it, we might get lucky and get dinner *and* a show.

We order off laminated menus to a waitress who chants our order in some kind of hash-house dialect. Once she leaves, we are quiet. The lack of sleep last night, the adrenaline dump, the two hours of numbing vibrations have taken their toll. But there's something else to it – in their cases, if not mine. Pinched mouths, pale faces. Glazed eyes watching private screenings of horrific replays. Jo looks away. Chi casually wipes his face. Uri puts his head down on the table and Chi puts his arm around him. Suddenly I'm glad they came with me, even Uri, because it means I know they're alive.

The food comes, they pray and I wait. Then I eat but they mostly just poke, as if their waffles are mysterious washed-up sea creatures.

We're somewhere in Tennessee, en route to Wisconsin, and I need to turn this ship around. The only problem is: How do I convince my escort? I could leave them behind, but there's safety in numbers and I have no idea how to find Luke. I decide to improvise.

"So… what's the plan?" I ask, invading their tortured silence.

"What do you mean?" Chi asks, poking his waffle. "We're heading to Wisconsin."

"Do you think that's wise?" I don't want to jump in with an alternative plan – I'd rather they do it. It's usually a good idea to let other people think my plan is their plan. I have enough brilliant ones that I don't mind missing out on the credit.

"I don't think so," Jo says, thoughtful. This surprises me. Up until now Jo has been the plan-follower.

"What do you think we should do?" An honest question.

Jo sets her jaw and meets everyone's eyes. "I think we need to find out more about Meda's mom."

Apparently my plan *is* someone else's plan. We're all looking at Jo with surprise. I mean, I like it, but I'm not sure what her motivations are – certainly not to keep my status as a half-demon secret.

"Think about it," she says, setting down her fork and leaning forward. "The demons want Meda, possibly because she is a Beacon." Even with all the evidence, she doubts my saintliness, clever girl. "They want her so bad they attacked our entire home base, which they've never done before. If we take her to another one, they'll just attack them too."

"But, this time we would be ready for them." Chi thumps the table with his fist.

"So what?" says Jo, killing Chi's moment. "We still have a big battle, lots of people die – then what? We move again and they fight us again?" Jo shakes her head. "The only thing that makes sense is to help her figure out what Beacon thing she's supposed to do and help her do it. It's the only way to keep everyone safe," her eyes hit mine, "including Meda."

There's a moment of silence as they all examine me for impending greatness. I wish I'd had a chance to comb my hair.

"So what does that have to do with her past?" Uri asks.

"Don't you think it's an awful big coincidence that Meda is a Templar and a Beacon? I've never heard of someone who was both. And why didn't her mom ever tell her she was a Templar? Why did Mary fake her own death? It doesn't make sense." She shrugs. "It gives us a place to start in any case." She turns towards me, asking wryly, "Unless you happen to have some great Nobel Peace Prize-worthy plans that you'd like to share with us?"

Ha, no, not exactly. I shake my head.

Chi mulls it over, but he likes it. It's the kind of dangerous and heroic plan that appeals to him. Finally he concedes, as does Uri, predictably.

"So, Meda. Tell us what you know," Jo says and they all turn to me.

I think about it. "I don't really know much. Mom and I moved a great deal, from city apartment to city apartment. She worked a lot of crap jobs and I was homeschooled."

"Did she have any friends?" Jo asks. "Anyone she spent a lot of time with? Who might know something?"

I shake my head. "She didn't have many friends." I tap my chin. "*Any* friends, actually, now that I think about it." That didn't strike me as weird at the time. After all, I didn't have any, either. I wasn't allowed to mingle with other people, although Mom planned on letting me start. At fifteen, I was starting to gain pretty good control over my… darker impulses. But it didn't occur to me to wonder why she didn't have any friends. Or why we moved so often.

It seems stupid now, all the questions I didn't ask her.

They look unimpressed by the amount of information I have to offer.

"And you said she was murdered?" Jo asks and I nod. "And you were the one who found her?"

The memory makes my mouth dry. I nod and take a sip of water before answering. "We were living in London` at the time. In a basement flat. She was... torn apart. Nothing was stolen." Images flash before my eyes. Red pools, staring brown eyes, her hand in mine. And the rage that nearly brought our apartment building crumbling down. Someone places a hand on my fist. Jo.

"It does sound like a demon. They break their... prey open to eat their souls," she says gently. As if I didn't know.

"What have you done since then?" Chi asks, changing the subject.

"Not much." Talked to ghosts, murdered bad guys. "Traveled around, took a few jobs to get by." Stole money off my victims. Got myself thrown into insane asylums. "Just drifted." I smile. "Nothing Nobel-inspiring, unfortunately." Now is the time to make my proposal. "I think I know where we should start our search." I pull out the picture of my mom and Luke and slide it on to the table so they can see. "Judging from my mom's shrine, this guy knew her better than anyone." Then I add, to sweeten the pot, "And I don't know who my father is." I know enough to know it isn't this guy, but I let them draw their own conclusions.

Jo doesn't recognize him and looks to Chi.

"Luke Bergeron. He doesn't come back to base much. Not married, no kids, so just stays in the field."

"Where in the field?" Jo asks, but no one answers. "So how do we find him?" She sits back and taps her plate with her fork in thought.

Uri's eyes are narrowed and his tongue peeps out of the corner of his mouth as he thinks. "The Sarge would know where he's assigned."

"I don't think we can call the school. They're either still fighting or evacuating with everyone else." Or dead, but Jo doesn't say it. "Besides, even if we could get hold of her, it would just get us an escort to Wisconsin."

"Anyone on the Council would know." Chi this time.

"But how would we get in touch with them?" Jo.

"Don't they have cell phones?" Me.

"Don't need them – they use magic," Chi explains. "Magic we won't have until we're Crusaders."

"Don't your parents ever call?"

"Yes, but they call my room."

"Like a landline?" It occurs to me that none of the Templar teens suffer from the strange growth on their hands that garden-variety teens do. "You guys don't have cell phones? Really?"

Chi says, "Vow of poverty, remember?"

"I hadn't noticed you toting one around," Jo remarks. No vow here, just poverty. And no one to call.

"How do you call your parents then?" I ask.

"I don't," Chi says. "It's too dangerous for them to keep a phone. Instead, I ask a Crusader to let my parents know to call me. They get back to me as soon as they can."

Uri nods along, but Jo looks away. As with me, parents, or lack thereof, is a sore subject.

"So we need to find a senior Templar who will help us contact Luke," I say.

Jo answers. "Back at the battle are the only ones I know of, but by now the school is probably evacuated, and they'll be gone." Or dead. But again she doesn't say it.

"So that leaves us stuck with Wisconsin. The only place we're sure to find Templars," Uri sums up, crestfallen.

"Let me guess, they don't have a phone," I say and Jo answers.

"Oh, they do." Thank God, a break. "But we don't know the number and it's not the kind of place that's listed."

I slam my head on the table.

Uri jerks his head up. "Wait!" We all look at him. "The Sarge keeps a spreadsheet of all the known Beacons and who's assigned to guard them. I worked in her office last summer. We don't need her; we just need that spreadsheet."

"Uri, that's brilliant!" A rare compliment from Jo. Uri hops up and down in his excitement, making the vinyl bench squeak. "If we know who Luke is guarding, we know how to find him."

"So where's the spreadsheet?" I ask, praying the obvious answer is wrong.

"On The Sarge's computer. It's password-protected, but I know the password." He grins triumphantly. I hate to spoil Uri's moment, so I don't point out the obvious problem.

The Sarge's computer is back at the school – which is currently a war zone.

Thirteen

A daring, death-defying quest to retrieve the Holy Spreadsheet from a battlefield of Good versus Evil, this sounds like a job for...

Someone else.

Fortunately, I picked up a pack of self-sacrificing lunatics who see no problem with that. Even better, they don't want me to go with them. I'm too valuable. The discussion goes something like this:

Asinine solo plan where I risk it all to save the planet! Chi.

Rude comment. Jo.

Fake attempt to be included in dangerous mission. Me.

Slightly less asinine plan involving the two of us. Uri.

Rude comment. Almost-sane plan using Chi and me. Jo.

Overprotective response. Chi.

Reeaaally rude comment! Jo.

Cringe-worthy comment about Jo's leg. Chi.

Head explodes. Near homicide. Jo.

Life-saving intervention ending the debate and getting everyone to agree to Jo's plan. Me.

And the crowd goes wild!

That last bit might be a slight exaggeration. But I do get them to agree that Jo's plan makes the most sense. Chi and Jo misspent most of their delinquent youth breaking out of the school then sneaking back in and, if there is an attack, two are better than one. Hopefully, by the time they drive the two hours back to the school, the battle will be over. Who has control of the school is the biggest question – since death is worse than detention, they'd rather it be the Templars.

Uri is disappointed not to be included, but his ego (and mine) gets a boost when Chi explains that someone has to protect the priceless cargo.

It's after eleven by the time we finish planning and leave the restaurant. I assume we're going to dine-and-dash, which is worrisome since the waitress looks mean and wiry, but fortunately there's cash stuffed in each supply pack. It was how we bought the clothes, if I'd been paying any attention. Uri and I are stashed in a cheap motel with the important task of sleeping. It's the kind of division of labor I can really get behind.

The motel is pretty awful, but we're limited to the kind of place that will rent to teenagers. It was new in the '50s and since then there has only been a half-hearted attempt at upkeep and a heartless attempt at decorating. The wallpaper is peeling; the bathroom is moldy. The two queens are covered in teal and pink floral bedspreads pilled more than any addict. No TV. And the smell... I'm not cruel enough to describe it.

Chi and Jo come in with us and our packs are reorganized. They contain flares, flashlights, thermal sheets (like a big sheet of aluminum foil for trapping body heat if you are caught in the cold), rope, knives, power bars, a map of the mountains, $500 in cash and a 9 mm handgun. No good for demons, but they aren't the only bad guys out there.

Chi fumbles with his packs and I feel his eyes on me periodically. He's stalling for some reason.

Jo grabs her pack to head out and turns to Chi. "Ready?"

"Uh yeah, just a minute." He looks around. "I gotta go to the bathroom." He's a terrible liar. He's up to something. "You go on out – Uri, will you start the bike for her?"

And the two of us are alone. I must be that something.

The instant the door closes my suspicions are confirmed. He turns to me, his blue eyes intense and the words come out quick. "Look, Meda, I know you're not as defenseless as you seem."

Crap, maybe he's not as stupid as *he* seems. It must be because of the bodies at the school. I tense to spring, to run, but hold still. In the pregnant pause lies are born in my head, woven by clever spiders to be spun from my mouth.

But he surprises me. "Will you look after Uri for me? He's tough, but he's just a kid. And don't tell him I asked." His mouth kicks up in a half-smile. "It'd hurt his feelings."

No, he really is that stupid.

An engine roars to life outside. Jo's waiting for him. I'm confused but I don't relax. He knows I'm hiding something but he asks me to babysit?

"Why?"

"Because I trust you."

Mystified, the word comes out unbidden, "Why?"

He shrugs. "I'd rather risk wrongly trusting you and dying, than to wrongly distrust you and turn my back on someone who needs my help." He didn't even have to think about it.

Chi might be an idiot, but it's a heroic kind of idiocy.

"Chi!" Jo shouts impatiently from outside. "If I'd known it was a number two, I wouldn't be wasting gas!"

She's a classy girl.

"Well?" Chi asks me.

"Sure."

"Thanks," he says, then grabs his pack and ducks out of the door. He climbs on in front of Jo and they're off.

It's a two-hour drive back to the school, probably an hour or so to sneak in and out, then two hours back. They leave us just before midnight with plans to be back by 5am.

If they aren't back by 6, we are to go to Wisconsin.

Uri and I take turns showering. Uri bought sweats for everyone, so I put on a pair and another black T-shirt. I think the only women's underwear Uri's familiar with is his mom's because he supplied Jo and me with panties in the parachute style. I don't tease him though – it probably took more courage for him to buy girls' undies than to sneak out of the school during the demon siege.

It's been a hectic couple of days with only a few hours of sleep in the last forty-eight. I lie on the grungy queen I'm to share with Jo, but sleep doesn't come. Instead I count bugs, like sheep, except these are real. Then I search for shapes in the water stains on the ceiling. I hear a huff from Uri. He's not sleeping either. The glowing red numbers of the clock are too bright: they tinge everything with blood. 12.15. Five hours and forty-five minutes left to go.

I lie there until they reach 12.45, then give up.

"Uri – you asleep?" I know he isn't.

"No."

"Wanna get some air?"

It's like I offered the kid a lifeline. "*Yes*."

We pull on hoodies, sneakers and, in Uri's case, his weapons, and slip outside, locking the door behind us. We're still in the mountains, so it's cold, and our breath comes out in small clouds. Uri has his hands fisted in his pockets, probably more so he can hold his weapons than to keep his hands warm. He takes his role as bodyguard adorably seriously, an earnest Labrador puppy guarding a wolf.

The Mountain View Motel is backed up against a steep drop to a river and shares a parking lot with a mom-and-pop gas station, which is closed this time of night. At some point someone must have tried to make the hotel more tourist-friendly and built a children's play area. It's right next to the river cliff so either the owner was stupid or hated children. It's mostly rotten, but the swings seem sturdy enough to sit on, though I won't risk more than a tentative sway.

I decide to point out the elephant in the room, but I give it a clown hat to make it funny. "Twenty bucks says Jo kills Chi before the demons get a chance."

It works and a slow smile stretches across Uri's face. "Naw, she wouldn't kill him." He settles on to a swing next to mine.

"Yeah, you're probably right," I say. "Then she wouldn't have a ride."

Uri laughs. "She wouldn't anyway."

"She would. I'm pretty sure she hates him." When she isn't lusting after him.

"They don't hate each other, they've just hurt each other." Not what I expect from a thirteen-year-old kid. I raise my eyebrows. "What?" he says defensively, "You can't hate someone you'd be willing to die for."

"Tell me, O Sensei, how did you get so wise?"

He blushes. "My mom explained that to me when I, ah," he looks down and his hair flops in his face, "was mad at her."

Ah, I get it. He shouldn't be embarrassed though. I don't think you can consider yourself a teenager unless you scream "I hate you" at your parents at least once. At least not a proper one. I change the subject. "So, tell me about Beacons."

"What do you mean?"

"Well, are they saints?"

He cocks his head and looks at me. "Are *you* a saint?"

"Do you think I'm a Beacon?"

He nods instantly. "Yes."

"Why?"

He thinks about it, his big puppy-dog brown eyes studying me carefully. "You're special."

"How do you know I'm not special-bad?" Shut up, Meda.

"I prayed about it. God says you're good."

"He does?"

"Yup."

Sounds like I'm not the only one with a pair of flaming britches. The Lord himself has a pair. "Well, then, I can safely say that Beacons are not saints," I say and Uri laughs. He kicks off but the play set sways ominously, so he stops.

"Saints probably are Beacons, though," Uri says. "But Beacons can be anyone. It could be a scientist who cures cancer, or a foster parent who raises a lot of damaged kids. Sometimes we'll watch a person for their whole lifetime and never figure out what it is they did."

"Maybe they never did what they were supposed to."

"Maybe," Uri agrees. "They're just people and all people are flawed. I think most Beacons are good people, but no one's perfect. Take Einstein. He was a Beacon, but he also thought up the atomic bomb."

"Are your parents guarding a Beacon?"

"Yeah."

"Don't you miss them?" I had my mom for only thirteen years, but I had her all the time for those thirteen. Maybe I'm luckier than I realized.

Uri watches, his feet scraping the dirt, his hair flopped forward so I can't see his face. "Yeah. But it wasn't so bad until the last year or so. I used to see them three months out of the year, one week in every six."

"Doesn't it bother you?"

He looks up. "Sometimes. But anything worthwhile is worth making sacrifices for. Besides, I'll get to spend all eternity with them, once our work here is done."

Mom won't be where I am going. Even if she is, she probably won't want to see me. Time to change the subject.

"Who are they guarding?"

"A scientist at a pharmaceutical company."

"What disease is he working on?"

"Breast cancer, but that doesn't mean there'll be a cure. Could just be that he'll discover something that will lead to something else. Or maybe it's not related to that at all and he's going to save a baby from a burning building."

"So you don't even know what you're protecting?"

He shrugs. "The good guys, isn't that enough? After all, we don't know what *you're* supposed to do," he points out. I feel a little sick to my stomach. Must be all that grease.

I catch a flicker out of the corner of my eye. I tense and Uri does the same, catching my movement. But it's not a demon, it's a ghost.

Great.

"What is it?" he asks, hands back in his pockets.

"Nothing. I just thought I saw a movement. It spooked me. Why don't we head back in?" I say it quietly, partly to scare him into doing what I want and partly because I don't want the ghost to notice us.

The silvery-smoke girl is around seven years old – or rather was. Her hair is a bunch of tiny braids and she wears a long nightgown that twines around her ankles like a cat. She moves in that relaxed, distracted manner of children when lost in their own world. She carries a bunny-shaped Easter basket with floppy ears. Uri and I hop off the swings, but the ancient wood creaks loudly. I wince as she turns, alerted and curious. I instantly turn away pretending I don't see her. But it's pointless. They always know. I curse silently.

"Come on, Uri, let's go." We start walking back around the motel. The girl catches up and prances around us on her toes. I refuse to look at her. She tries to touch my hands, but I snatch them out of reach, startling Uri. He knows something's not right. We go faster.

We slip into our room and I close the door and lock it. Not against her, that would be pointless. She breezes right through. They can't go through living things, but short of that, nothing can stop them. I sit on the bed and stuff my hands in my pockets. She sits down next to me and watches the bulges in my pockets like she's a cat and they're mice.

Ghosts can't talk, at least not to me, but if they touch your fingertips they can show you images from their life. It's like watching a TV that only shows home videos and someone else has the remote. Their favorite show is My Grisly Death.

Because the ghosts who bother me are always murder victims and they always want me to get revenge.

I always do it. It's how I find my meals and I'm not really given a choice. Ghosts are amazingly pesky creatures – you can't lock them out and you can't keep your hands balled in your pockets forever. But I don't have time now. She'll just have to find someone else.

She edges closer, a warm, sweet-scented mist at my side. I edge away. She comes closer, I edge away. Uri watches.

"Lumpy bed," I say, but his expression says he doesn't buy it.

The ghost girl gets impatient and sticks her face in mine, trying to force me to look at her. I close my eyes and pull back, twisting away.

"Are you OK?" Uri asks.

"I have to sneeze." Maybe my dumbest lie to date, but why else would I be twisting around with my eyes closed and my hands in my pockets? I jump up and beeline for the bathroom. I close the door and she follows right through it. That's fine, this time I want her to.

Like all ghosts she's painted in glowing silvers and greys, so saying she's black would be a misnomer. Her eyes are as big and hopeful as I feared. I'm her only chance for justice.

"Go away," I hiss.

Her eyebrows draw down and her lower lip starts to tremble. She looks like a kicked puppy. Then she shakes her head at me and smiles, delighted, and comes closer. I guess she doesn't think I could possibly mean it.

"I said, *go away*."

"Meda? Did you say something?" Uri, he's on the other side of the door. Great.

"No. Must be the thin walls." I wave my hands to shoo her but it is a mistake and she dives for them. I shove them back in my pockets and growl at her.

"Meda?"

Oh, for cripes' sake.

I open the bathroom door, boxing her out so she can't get to my hands. Uri's on the other side.

"I just… need a moment to myself," I say.

His face softens. "It's OK. I'm scared for them, too."

I open my mouth to correct him, but change my mind and push past him out of the bathroom. "I'm going to get a soda from the vending machine. You want one?"

He starts to follow me – a good bodyguard would – but I guess my plea for alone-time changes his mind and he stops. "Sure."

"What kind?"

"Orange."

"I'll be right back." I walk across the room with my hands firmly in my pockets as the wispy girl shadows me. As I slip out, I see Uri moving towards the window. I glance back as I walk towards the main building and see him peeking between the blinds. I turn the corner, out of sight, but instead of going to the lobby I cut around the side of the building. Then I wheel around on my annoying tag-along.

"Look," I say sternly to the ghost. "I have my own problems. I can't go chasing down your bad guys for you. Go find someone else." She ignores me in favor of my pocketed hands. Her eyes are big and full of stars.

I kick at her as I would a cat. She's a ghost so I can't do anything but stir her air. She doesn't notice. I walk away and predictably she follows.

Ghosts.

Uri will start to worry if I take too long. "Fine," I say, I pull my hands out and she dives for them, but I shove them back in my pockets before she can reach them. "First, some rules. I can't go after them right now."

Her eyes get the kicked-puppy look.

I continue. "But I promise I will go after him as soon as I can," provided I'm still alive. The lower lip protrudes again and the starry eyes fill with moonlight tears. "That's the best I can offer. Take it or leave it."

She waits for me to cave, but I am made of stone. "That means no following me. Not even a little."

She nods, not meeting my eyes. I keep my hands in my pockets and wait for her to meet my eyes, then glare to let her know I mean it. She looks sulky but nods again. I take a deep breath before sliding my hands free. I lift them as if touching an invisible glass between us, the barrier between the living and the dead. She touches her silver fingertips to mine and I fall down the rabbit hole.

The last thing I see before my eyes are traded for hers is Uri's face, whiter than the ghost's in the moonlight.

You might think, given my hobby, that I would enjoy watching the things ghosts show me, like hunters watching *Buck Commander* on the Outdoor Channel. But I don't, and hunters probably wouldn't either if the show was shot from inside the deer.

And, like the deer, this little girl was very, very innocent. At least the deer never believe the hunters love them. But this little girl and her murderer… It's sick.

And, anyway, he had bad form.

He'll get what's coming to him. I will see to it. What I do to him will make what he did to Annabel seem like an act of kindness.

I drop back into my body, which lies seizing. I open my eyes and Uri's panicked face is above mine, in front of a water-stained ceiling.

"Meda? Meda?" His voice breaks. I blink.

"Uri," I say stupidly. The whole thing is very disorienting.

"Should I call the hospital?" The phone is clenched in his hand. I tilt my head, taking in my surroundings. We're back in the hotel room. Uri must have carried me, impressive for such a little guy.

Hospital? "No." I clear my throat. It's sore from all of Annabel's screaming. I am me, the ghost is gone. My brain sluggishly cranks into action. Uri would have seen me talk to myself then watched me collapse. "No, Uri, I'm fine." I sit up. The room swims a little then settles back into focus. "I'm fine," I repeat.

Uri looks unconvinced. I grasp for an explanation.

"I have epilepsy. Seizures."

His eyes narrow. "No, you don't. I saw you talking to someone."

"I hallucinate?" I didn't mean it to be a question, but it comes out as one. Uri shakes his head. When all else fails, try the truth. "Can you keep a secret?"

"Yes."

"I see dead people." I don't get a laugh from him. "I'm not kidding. I see ghosts. They tell me things."

Uri tucks his chin in surprise. "Things? What kinds of things?" He's taking it better than I expected. I guess when you grow up fighting demons your worldview is a little more flexible than the average person's.

I gingerly push myself up until I am sitting upright on the bed, then slide back to rest against the headboard. "How they died. They want me to find their murderers." I shake my head to clear the remaining fog and Uri puts a concerned hand on my arm.

"And do what?"

Torture them to death. "Make sure they don't hurt anyone else." Uri senses the ambiguity in my answer, so I go for the straight lie. "Turn them in to the police, point out evidence, that kind of thing." Disembowel them; drown them in regret and blood.

Uri's face lights up. "That's it, Meda! That's what you're supposed to do! Catch bad guys!" He pauses, thinking. "But why do we need to keep it a secret? We need to tell Chi and Jo."

I don't know why I can see ghosts, but since I haven't met any Templars who can do it, I have to assume it's from the demon side. I can't risk Jo finding out and putting it together. She's too clever by half. "Because..." Come on brain! "Because, the ghosts told me not to tell anyone."

"But you just told me."

Stupid brain! I scramble. "Only after you caught me. I'm not supposed to go around telling people."

Uri digests this and I try not to hold my breath. "But we have to tell them. This means we know your Beacon mission and we don't need to find Luke."

Eek! Can't have that! "Not exactly. I mean, Jo said I'm the only Beacon to ever also have been a Templar. What are the chances, then, that my Templar-ness isn't related to whatever my Beacon mission is?"

He cocks his head. "What are the chances that you can see dead people and *that's* not related to your Beacon mission?"

Touché. Clever little bugger, isn't he?

"Maybe they're *both* related," I suggest.

Uri settles back on his heels and taps his chin. Point – Meda.

"Can other Templars see ghosts?" I ask.

"Not that I know of," he says, then pauses, thinking. "I think demons can, though."

Danger!

His face brightens. "Jo could probably tell us."

"We can't tell Jo." We absolutely can't tell Jo. "The ghosts made me promise." He looks like he's on the fence, uncertainty making him look even younger. "How about this – I think we still need to find out about my mom's past, because it could be related, so our current plans don't change, but I'll see if the ghosts will let me out of my promise."

Uri scrunches his face, thinking, and again I try not to let him see how important his decision is to me. Finally he nods.

"Promise?"

"Promise," he agrees. I relax back on the bed.

"Can you tell me about ghosts? Since I know already?"

I don't see the harm, so I tell him. He flops back on the bed, hands behind his head.

I don't really know that much. Ghosts mostly have a one-track mind: get the bad guy. They all seem to carry some sort of bag or, in Annabel's case, a basket. Once, I asked a ghost what it was for. Actually, I asked a lot of ghosts, but only one ever answered me. That's that whole annoying-ghost thing I was talking about. In any case, he showed me.

While the video I most often get is a horror, the basket contains what most people would choose to film to celebrate their life. Birthdays and Christmases, trips to the beach, new puppies, parents, children. But it's more than just a memory. Memories are flat and faded. This is like living it for the first time.

"Why do they collect them?" Uri asks, twisting his head to look at me.

"I don't know," I answer honestly. "Maybe they showed up to Heaven too early and St Peter wouldn't let them in." I hold up my hands as if to stop someone. "No Vacancy." I shrug and continue lightly. "They have to do something to pass the time."

Uri doesn't laugh. He's back to staring at the ceiling and his forehead is scrunched as if he's trying to read answers etched in the stained popcorn-paint. Then his face relaxes. "I think I know. Their ends are so horrible and early that they get to relive good memories to replace their last, bad one. You'd want your last memory to be something good, something you wouldn't ever want to forget."

"How could dying *ever* be something you wouldn't want to forget? The ones I've seen..." I shiver. "I don't want to experience it the first time, let alone over and over."

"Oh, I don't know. Old and surrounded by family, or doing something heroic – in a battle, or rescuing someone." His voice gets really soft, a little dreamy. "Or sacrificing yourself for someone else. That's something you'd never want to forget."

I don't agree, but I recognize that Uri is a rather deep little kid.

He twists again. "So, do they, like, watch people in the shower?"

Maybe not so deep.

I laugh. "I guess, if they wanted to. But I haven't noticed any ghostly Peeping Toms. Like I said, they have one-track minds. At least around me."

"How many are there?"

"Not that many. Eventually they go away. I never see them again after I k–" err, "catch their killers."

"How long have you been seeing them?"

"Forever. But they didn't start bossing me around until my teens."

"How many have you helped?"

I close my eyes. Images of the bodies I separated from their souls are stacked in my mind like cordwood, toe-tag forward so I can remember the specifics. They don't deserve a burial, not even in my mind. Except one.

Everyone makes mistakes.

"So, how many?"

Hundreds. "A few dozen, probably."

"Wow."

Our conversation drifts along, then we start inventing games to keep us occupied. By 4 in the morning, we're hungry again. The food vending machine is broken, so instead we cook and eat imaginary food. If one person can guess what the other person is having, then they get some. I'm terrible at it. I guess hamburger like ten times in a row. Finally, Uri throws me a bone and makes a hamburger but I guess steak tartare. He's good at it though. I think he cheats.

"Cherries jubilee!" he shouts triumphantly, rising off the bed and pointing.

"Get outta my head!"

The clock creeps towards 5 and our game lurches and slows. Gourmet meals become fast food as our hearts abandon it. Finally we trail off altogether. Chi and Jo should be back any minute – if all went well.

Uri traces the designs on the bedspread and I fight the urge to stop him. Some things should never be repeated. The sink-drip taunts; the minute hand teases. I crack the window and night sounds slip in. The elephant in the room is so studiously ignored he develops a complex.

5 becomes 5.30. Uri locks himself in the bathroom.

5.30 becomes 5.45 and Uri comes out. He tries to hide his face behind his hair, but I can tell his eyes are red. We're supposed to leave without them at 6 but neither of us packs. He widens the window and the room turns frigid, but I don't close it. Morning birds and highway sounds assault my straining ears.

Then we hear it, the growling rumble of a motorcycle. I beat Uri to the door, but not by much. I fight the locks and pull it open. Jo climbs off the motorcycle and Chi pulls off his helmet. I let out a breath I didn't know I was holding. They're fine, they're in one piece.

Until, that is, Jo decks Chi in the face.

Fourteen

I'm gonna go out on a limb and guess from context that things could have gone better. Since Chi made it back alive, I guess I owe Uri twenty bucks. Then again I really don't think the mission is over until they're back in the hotel room. Judging from the homicidal glint in Jo's eye, I still have a chance.

Unfortunately she doesn't hit him again, but the verbal swings come fast and furious.

"Of all the unbelievable, stupid risks to take–" Jo attacks.

"I saved your life!" defends Chi. He's off his bike now and holding his nose which is already shrinking back down to normal size. Templar healing, nice. Without the violence, the battle has been downgraded to a tennis match.

"You did not!" Jo hits the ball back into Chi's court.

"I did! They were going to cut your head off!" Chi. Fifteen-love.

"They were not! They were going to *try*, but I had it under control." Fifteen-all. "And, in coming to my 'rescue', you left your back wide open. If I hadn't been there, you'd be dead!"

Aw snap. Fifteen-thirty.

"That's the second time I've saved your life," she continues.

She's wrong. Actually it's the third – I would have killed him the night we met if she hadn't shown up. I don't think it's a good idea to point that out, though.

This is all very entertaining but no one has spilled the necessary information. "Time out!" I call, hands in a "T". They both stare at me blankly, "Did you guys get the information?"

"Yeah, of course," Chi says.

I step back. "Carry on." I was being facetious, but they do. A furious match like this needs popcorn. I imagine a batch and munch while the show continues.

"You were moving too slow. You weren't going to get out of the way in time," Chi with a backhand. Thirty-all.

"Well, don't bother next time. You can't even take care of yourself!" Jo with a vicious return. Thirty-forty.

Uri pulls the door closed, then joins me on the curb, wide-eyed and watching the battle. He catches my hand movements. He points and mouths "popcorn"? I'm telling you, the kid is a savant at this game. I nod and offer him the imaginary bag. He takes a handful.

"Look, you have to face reality about your injury, you can't just pretend it doesn't matter–" Chi. Forty-all.

"I can! I mean, it doesn't!" Jo trades some rage for intensity. "Look, Chi, can't you understand? If I can't stand on my own two feet then I don't want to stand at all."

"You just expect me to let you *die*?" Chi rocks back on his heels; he definitely doesn't understand, but I do. Those of us who live with twisted bits like to think we can overcome them. In Jo's case she probably can – even if he did save her life today, she has still saved him three times to his once.

"If it comes to that, yes, but it won't." She's fierce, she means it. "I can take care of myself."

Chi loses it; his hands are waving in the air like a madman's. "And you're supposed to be the smart one! That's the *stupidest*–"

Jo turns beet red, her pleas are over and it's all rage. The next bit is gritted out. "Your life is charmed – the Prince of Mountain Park, the Golden Boy, while I'm just the cripple." Game. "You don't have any idea what it's like to lose your family, your future, your *leg*." Set. "You've never lost anyone, or anything!" And match. Chi turns white.

Both pant, saying nothing, and the silence stretches as Chi grasps for words. When he finally finds them, they are soft and small. I haven't nearly enough life experience to understand his expression. "You're wrong. I *have* lost."

Somehow I don't think he means the tennis match.

Jo starts as if slapped, staggers back a few steps, then turns and runs. Maybe Chi won the match after all.

Chi drops his head in his hands and pulls at his hair in frustration. He turns to me. "Go after her, would you?" I hope he's kidding, but it doesn't look that way. I leave the rest of my imaginary popcorn with Uri – I need my hands free for self-defense. I follow the trail of angry muttering to the edge of the parking lot and into the trees. She's stomping around and scaring the squirrels.

"Men!"

"Err yeah – men!" I commiserate.

"I don't need him babysitting me. Who does he think he is?"

I hope that's a rhetorical question. She punches a tree. Probably empty agreement is safest. "Um, yeah."

"What an *asshole*. He almost died!"

"Yeah, asshole."

She turns on me, eyes narrow. Her bullshit-o-meter must have alerted her to my lack of sincerity and I'm in imminent danger of replacing the tree as her punching bag.

I scramble. "Don't look at *me* that way. I totally would have let you die."

In hindsight, I could have phrased that better.

She stands frozen for a minute then snorts. Then her snort erupts into a laugh. She laughs and laughs, collapsing against her wooden victim. She finally takes a breath. "Thanks, Meda – I think."

"Any time," I say deadpan. "Mean it." That sets her off again. She slides down the tree and sits at its base. Unsure what to do now, I sit with her.

"I guess I owe Chi an apology," she says out of nowhere. "It's not Chi's fault. I mean, almost getting himself killed is his fault, but not the last of it. My family, my leg." She starts to shred a leaf and it wants me to point out it's not *its* fault either, but I bite my tongue. To our relief she throws it down. "I just get so mad sometimes. I'm never going to be a Crusader, never get married, never do anything."

I don't get the connection. A weak leg isn't that big of a deal. But it seems rude, and dangerous, to interrupt her embittered monologue.

"But who do I get to be angry at? The demons? They're constantly trying to destroy mankind and, if at all possible, Heaven too. There's enough reasons to be angry at them – my leg's superfluous. The other students, the Crusaders for how they treat me? They're not trying to be cruel, I am damaged. They're so very kind, so full of pity. I'd rather they hate me than feel sorry for me." Ah, that explains why she's so horrible to everyone.

Another leaf becomes her victim as she continues. "How about God? I've dedicated my life to His service and everything is part of His plan. If He has decided that I best serve His needs as a cripple, who am I to say it should be otherwise?" She looks up, meeting my eyes. It's nice she remembers I'm here. "I'll tell you who's left. Me. I can hate myself for feeling the way I do, for being unable to accept it. But when you hate yourself for hating yourself – how the hell do you get out of that?"

She looks at me like I have the answer. And I kind of do, actually. After all, I'm practically an expert on self-hate and hers is pathetic. She hates herself for being upset that her dreams are ruined? It would be weirder if she did happily accept her fate.

So I offer her my sage advice. "Quit being such a whiner."

Not what Jo is expecting and she draws back. She's been coddled, everyone else tiptoes around her. I'm not the coddling kind. "This pity party is pathetic."

Jo's face turns an ominous shade of purple and she jumps to her feet. "*Pity* party? I'm sorry if my problems aren't—"

But I cut her off and climb to my own feet. She's giving self-hate a bad name. "Yes, you are sorry. You're angry at yourself for being angry that all your dreams were taken away? Give me a break!"

"What do you expect me to do? Rejoice that my life is ruined?"

"No, you're not listening. I don't care that you're angry that your life is ruined. You'd be an idiot if you weren't. Hell, I don't even like you and *I'm* angry about it. I'm just saying you're stupid for being angry for being angry – that's ridiculous."

"But—" she sputters.

"Do something productive with your anger instead of stomping around snapping at everyone." Actually, I hope she doesn't take that advice. It's pretty entertaining to watch, when I'm not the focus of it. "Take it out on the demons."

"No one will let me." She sulks, but it's half-hearted.

"Yeah, I've noticed. They've been not letting you for the past two days." That wins a limp smile. "You want to fight demons? Stop whining and do something about it."

She pauses, looking at me like she's seeing me for the first time. "Ouch," she finally says.

"Yeah, well, you needed to hear it. It's good for you."

"My best interests at heart?"

"Yeah. Good intentions."

We both recall the last time we talked about good intentions – and she pulled a knife on me – and smile. "Thanks, Doctor." She takes a deep breath and changes the subject. "But you're a liar." She pauses. I am a liar, but I wonder which one she's talking about. "You *do* like me."

I'm surprised to find she might be right.

Before I can think of a response, she changes the subject. "It'll be harder to fight demons once things are back to normal."

"Things get normal around here?"

"They'll never let me have full Crusader status. I'll be a desk Knight. My leg *is* a liability." Her voice gets really small. "I think Chi really did save my life."

"So what? You saved his, twice." Three times. "So you might die. If that's OK with you, what can they say about it?"

"The basic fighting unit is the pair." Her mouth twists. "The couple, actually."

Isn't that the same thing? I don't have time to ask before she continues.

"I'll never have a partner. I couldn't take one even if someone was stupid enough."

I point out the obvious. "Chi's stupid enough."

"I couldn't be responsible for the death of my partner. Besides, Chi's not stupid, he's... naive."

"There's a difference?"

"Naivety is cured with time. Stupidity is terminal."

I laugh. "Fatal in a Crusader."

"For sure."

I cast her a sideways look. "You don't have any naivety left."

"I guess the demon ate it along with my leg," she says lightly. Then there is a long, sobering pause. "And my parents."

For the first time, with sudden clarity, I understand why Mom let me kill only bad people. I recall an argument we had. I was soul Hungry and impatient. Hangry.

"Everyone dies," I'd said. "Why does it matter if it's a car wreck, a clogged artery or me?"

"Meda!" Mom was too horrified to manage more than that.

"God kills indiscriminately. Why can't I?" I'd been snotty in that way only tweens can manage.

Her mouth snapped shut at my blasphemy and, when she responded, it was with a tone I'd never heard from her before. The memory alone gives me goosebumps. "God has his reasons. Good ones." Her brown eyes leveled me. "So will you."

I did as she said – with one glaring exception – because it upset her if I did otherwise. And I understood, in an abstract way, that it was wrong. Good people don't do things like that, so I didn't. When it became apparent that I was not, in fact, a good person, I continued – partially out of respect for my mother, but also because of ease and habit. When you have dead victims pointing out their murderers, it's not like it's a challenge. Thanks to human nature, I will never starve.

But now I understand what I had taken before as rote memorization. Every adult knows $E=mc2$, but only a scientist understands it. I was becoming a scientist on human nature. It's a comfort, now, to know that I haven't left a trail of Jos.

I look back at her now. "You're still smarter than Chi."

She snorts. "I spent two years bedridden with nothing to do but study. But Chi is..." she searches for the word, "good."

"What does that mean? You're not?"

"Not like him. He trusts people."

I feel as though that makes him stupid, not good, but I keep my mouth shut.

"He'll sacrifice himself for what he believes in. He's brave."

"You're brave."

"No." She smiles wryly. "I'm angry and borderline suicidal. It functions like it's the same, but it's not."

"He abandoned you. I don't think that's particularly good."

She's startled. "No, he didn't."

"Uri told me. You used to be best friends."

"Uri told you Chi abandoned me?"

"Yeah–" but actually he never said that. "No, actually he didn't. Chi didn't ditch you?"

"No." A pause. "I ditched him."

OK, now I'm really confused, because it's obvious to a blind man that she has the hots for him.

She looks down and a brown curtain of hair obscures her face. "Meda, the basic fighting unit is the couple."

Couple, not pair. Oh. Her earlier distinction becomes clear.

"That's why both parents are out in the field at the same time," she continues. "Whoever I marry will either have a position at the school or a weak, one-legged partner. Neither option is fair."

Wow. That does suck. "But, now that you're going to fight demons–"

"Chi already almost died today because I was too slow."

"But–" I start but she shakes her head. She doesn't want to hear it. She has a point. It's going to be a struggle just to be allowed in the field. And her leg does make her weaker than, say, that bimbo Rachael.

"Besides," she slants me a sideways look, "I thought you and Chi were…" she trails off suggestively.

What? Oh, the kiss. "Nah, I just did that to piss you off."

Her mouth twists. "I figured." She studies me. "But… you're sure?"

Love really is blind. "Yeah." I smirk. "I can do better."

She hits me, but it's half-hearted. "I prefer you to Rachael," she says, but I can tell she's relieved.

"Well, obviously."

I think Jo's making a mistake. I think it should be up to Chi, since it'd be his life at risk. But I can understand her not wanting to be responsible for the death of someone she loves. I understand better than she could possibly imagine.

Fifteen

Jo and I trudge back to the motel room and slip inside. At our arrival, Chi stands up from his spot on the bed. "Jo..." he starts, but she flinches away, as if his outstretched hand were hot iron. He drops his arm and his eyes are full of hurt as he watches her stalk into the bathroom. I follow before she can close the door.

"I thought you were going to apologize," I whisper.

She squeezes toothpaste on to her brush, not meeting my eyes. "I said I owe him one, not that he's going to get it." Then her shoulders slump and she braces herself on the sink. The toothbrush comes perilously close to falling from her hand. If it touches the bathroom floor, we'll need to torch it. After a deep breath, she forces starch back into her spine. I watch the vertebrae stack themselves straight like children's blocks. Hazel eyes meet mine in the mirror, and I can't describe the things I see there. I'm not human enough to understand. "It's better this way, Meda."

I'm unconvinced, but I can't argue when her eyes look like that. I leave her staring in the mirror, closing the door softly behind me. I am even less convinced of her course of action when I see Chi. He's slamming around belongings, jaw locked. Fire to her ice. He kicks the bed leg then covers his eyes and takes a few deep breaths. Uri and I look at each other, caught between the two brewing storms.

Awkward. Team Meda needs to pull itself together.

Finally, Chi visibly wrestles himself under control and Jo comes out from the bathroom. She's calm and composed, like nothing has happened – an ice-capped volcano.

"We need to talk about our next move," she says coolly.

"Fine," Chi bites out. I hate that word.

Jo turns to me. "Luke is guarding a Beacon named Exo Greer." The look in Jo's eye suggests she has some bad news. I wait for the shoe to drop. "Unfortunately, the database doesn't keep exact addresses for the Beacons for security reasons, so we only have a city."

Still he should be easy to find. How many parents hate their kids enough to name them "Exo"? Jo's eyes flick uncomfortably to Chi's. Oh, there's another shoe.

I look to Chi and he drops it. "He's in Washington, DC."

Demon Central. Un-effing believable. My jaw flaps in the wind.

"On the plus side, it's the last place the demons would expect you to go," Chi offers and I look at him like the lunatic he is.

"Oh, it's not that bad, Meda," Jo says. "We'll get in, make contact, get out. It's a big city and it's true – they won't be looking for you there."

No, you're right. Traipsing into Demon Central is a *good* idea.

"Would you rather not go?" Jo has no patience tonight.

"I have an idea," Chi says. "Why don't you all stay behind and I'll go."

Hardly. I need to talk to Luke, especially since I don't know what he could reveal. I open my mouth to answer. Jo cuts me off, red-faced. The volcano bubbles through the ice.

"Why don't *you* all stay behind and I'll go?" She snaps and Chi's jaw hardens again. The two of them face off, eyes locked, fists clenched.

"Children!" I say. "Knock it off. We're all going. I'm the one who needs to talk to Luke."

Chi breaks first and turns to me. "Well, if we're all heading into Demon Central, I guess it's a good thing I got us a secret weapon." His voice is full of challenge. He knows whatever he's about to show us is going to piss Jo off – and he's looking forward to it.

"Really?" Uri pipes up.

"Yup." Chi kneels stiffly by the bed and pulls out something wrapped in a sweatshirt. "I told you I was getting extra supplies." He unwraps it to reveal... I cross my fingers and hope for a rocket launcher.

"An old book?" I ask.

"You stole a *grimoire*? Are you *insane*?" Jo, of course.

"Nope."

"The exodus is supposed to have that."

"*They* have all the rest of the grimoires, *they* have full Crusaders, *they* have the rest of the senior class. *We* have a Beacon to protect that is wanted by the whole host of Hell."

Chi's actually talking sense.

"Yes but *we* can't protect it. If the demons get their hands on it..." Her face summarizes the potential horrors. "Besides," she snaps, "I bet you can't even read it."

"Nope," Chi says easily and Jo opens her mouth. Possibly to scream. "But I bet you can."

And she swallows it and chokes.

"You're taking advanced ancient languages, right?"

Jo blushes. "Ah, yeah, but–"

"But what? Can you or can't you?" he challenges.

She sticks her chin in the air. "Can."

"Good." His smile is tight.

I clear my throat. "So what will it do? What's our secret weapon?"

Chi turns to me. "This grimoire contains the Inheritance ceremony."

I still don't get it. I can tell by Jo's expression that she does.

"Meda," she says slowly. "The secret weapon is you."

"What do you mean?"

"You're a Beacon and a Templar," she says earnestly. "The only one like you I have ever heard of. Ever. We've already decided they're related, right?"

I nod and Chi picks up the explanation.

"So doesn't it make sense that somehow your version of the Inheritance could be somehow special? Change-the-world-for-the-better special? What if it's like a version of what Zeke has – shooting demon-killing light?"

"Is Zeke a Beacon?" Not that it really matters, since I'm not either.

"No," Chi explains. "So it follows that yours would be even bigger than Zeke's."

Uri, behind me, gasps in awe like he just saw a firework.

"How do you know I just won't cure cancer and my Templar abilities are just normal?" I'm stalling, but thinking. Of course I'm not a Beacon, but why shouldn't I accept the Inheritance? How could having extra demon-fighting skills be bad? Especially if compounded by my already awesome demon abilities?

"We don't," Jo says. "But what have we to lose? It wouldn't hurt to have one more fighter on our hands. Someone the demons don't expect."

She has a point and, as Chi pointed out, the whole host of Hell is after me. Extra skills could come in handy. "OK, let's do it."

"Well, we can't do it *now*, now," Jo says. "I have to figure it out first – study the spell."

"When then?"

"Hopefully by the time we make it to DC."

"Hopefully?"

She pauses awkwardly, and I narrow my eyes at her, waiting for her to come out with it. "Other than basic protections, I've, err, never actually done magic before."

Great. Just great.

"We need to get some sleep before we do anything," Chi says.

At the mention of sleep my body remembers how tired it is. We all creep off to be hounded by nightmares.

When I wake up, the room is empty except for Uri passed out on the other bed, hugging a pillow with his mouth hanging open. It shouldn't have surprised me, but Jo even sleeps violently – I had to snatch sleep between kicks.

The clock says 1.52 and the sun slipping around the curtains says it's afternoon. I blearily stumble to the door in search of the others and the sun blinds me. When my vision clears I find Jo sitting on the cement. She leans against the brick of the motel and the grimoire's propped open in her lap. A notepad and a pen sit on the ground beside her. She doesn't even glance up as I come out.

"Chi went to get food. We'll leave as soon as he comes back. You should probably wake Uri."

Good morning to you, too.

I stumble back inside for bathroom rituals and Uri's awakening. A motorcycle's grumble announces Chi's return. I'm thrilled to see he brought back food from Sugar Burger. There aren't any stores in the UK or the northeast where Mom and I bounced around the most, or at least there aren't many. I suspect the South hogs them to punish the North for the Civil War. Just a theory I'm working on.

After breakfast we pack and get on the road. Jo reluctantly climbs on behind Chi. She'd probably be more comfortable sharing the motorcycle with a viper than Chi, but Chi's a better windbreak than Uri. Why does she need a windbreak? Because she reads on the back of the motorcycle. Fortunately, I think it distracts the rest of the motorists from noticing my suspiciously small driver. We give Uri the only helmet with a visor, but since he can't be more than four-feet-eleven inches and 105 pounds, I don't think his disguise could withstand a close inspection.

We stop again to eat at dinnertime, then again as we enter DC around 11pm. As we pull up to the restaurant, I can't believe it.

"Sugar Burger? Again?" I mean, I love it, but we had it for every meal. Chi climbs off his bike and holds his hand out to help balance Jo. To no one's surprise, she ignores it. Chi's mouth tightens and his movements are sharp as he unclips his helmet.

"The founder's a Beacon," Uri answers.

"Really?" I wouldn't have figured a fast food owner, but then again, he'd done a lot more to improve my life than, say, Gandhi.

Uri's entirely sincere as he answers. "How could their food *not* be divinely inspired?"

Another good point. My mouth waters.

Chi orders as we use the bathroom and idle around in the lobby. There's a little coin-operated toy machine, so Uri begs some cash and we all end up shelling out the 50 cents for cheap toys while we wait. Uri becomes the proud owner of a temporary tattoo of a fat-baby angel.

"Lame," he complains, but sticks it on his shoulder anyway.

I pop open my plastic egg, and inside is a tin heart. Mr Wizard heard my prayer! But what's this?

"It's broken." Damn you, Mr Wizard.

Jo peers over my shoulder and plucks it from my hands. "No, it's not. Haven't you ever seen these before?" She struggles with the thin, cheap chain, then frees the mass of slick shiny snakes into two necklaces. Suspended from each is half of a heart, cracked right down the middle. "See, *best friend*."

She hands them to me and, indeed, each heart has one of the words. Great, so I have two broken necklaces.

She laughs at my expression and explains. "You take one half and your BFF gets the other." She points to where they hang between us, one from each of my hands. "You want 'best' or 'friend'?"

"*You're* my best friend?" I'm horrified.

She raises an eyebrow. "Oh, I'm sorry – you have someone else in mind?"

No. "Wait, I'm *your* best friend?" An interesting accusation.

She snorts. "I think you might be my only friend. I don't know if you've noticed but…" her voice drops to a whisper, as if she is imparting some great secret. I like secrets. "People sometimes find me hard to get along with."

Well, that's no secret.

"Naw. I don't see it." My eyes are wide and innocent.

She laughs. It's hard to hate someone who so freely embraces their horridness.

"So which do you want?" I ask as I dangle them between us, tin tokens of friendship between a demon and its hunter.

"Obviously, this one." She snatches up the one that says "best", leaving the other one to me. "I think it best defines me as a person," she says loftily.

I rub my fingers over the small scratched letters before slipping it around my neck. *Friend*. I wanted this one anyway.

The restaurant is closing so we have to eat somewhere else. That's fine with us – we need to make some plans and the empty restaurant is not ideal for covert discussions. We move to a Wal-Mart parking lot and look disreputable while we munch sandwiches under a street lamp.

"So how's it coming with the spell?" I ask Jo.

She lets out a breath that says "not good" before she answers. "It's a pretty complicated spell, and…" she fidgets. Jo never fidgets. "It might be pretty dangerous if I get it wrong."

My sandwich pauses on its mission to my mouth. "How dangerous?"

"It's one of the most important spells we have. Crusader Puchard's been doing it for the last fifty years and he makes it look so easy, but… well, it's really not. I'm not sure we can go through with it."

Well, that explains why she pulled her nose out of the book – she's given up.

She continues, bossiness creeping in to replace the uncertainty. She looks to Chi and Uri. "I think we should find Luke while Meda's still human and wait to do the spell until we're back at school." Slight hitch – for all we know there is no school any more. "Or wherever we go after, and have a Crusader do it."

Chi shrugs, his mouth full of food, and I'm not sure Uri's listening. He's bouncing around – playing hopscotch by himself? Regardless, he doesn't look like he's going to object to Jo's plan.

It's up to me then. I won't be going back to the Templars with them, so if I want the powers to fight off the demon hordes, I need Jo to do it. "How dangerous though? Will I die? Or will it just hurt?"

She considers that, her head rocking slightly back and forth. "I've never heard of anyone dying from a mis-spell, but then, no one's ever done it wrong as far as I know. If someone has – well, it would be in the histories, which I don't exactly have right now."

"But how far are you from finishing the translation?" Chi asks for me.

She doesn't look at him and answers stiffly. They really need to get over each other. "Not too far off. I'd say I have about three-quarters of it done. But it's written in a cross-contaminated version of medieval French and Latin. I'd need a dictionary to finish it. An obscure dictionary."

Dead end. I shift it to the back-burner.

"So how are we going to find Luke, or rather, Exo Greer?" I ask.

"Google," answers Uri. "Beacons tend to do something newsworthy – CEOs, charitable organizations, scientists, valedictorians."

"We don't have a computer," Jo points out.

"We could buy one," offers Uri.

"I don't want to blow all our money. We don't know how long this is going to take. Then we'd have to find internet somewhere, set it up..."

"We could steal one," suggests Chi.

"Really? We're going to become muggers?"

A light dawns in my head. "Nope. We need a computer with internet access and a dictionary. I know where we can get both – at the same time." They all turn to me. "The library. And it's all free." I wait for applause.

"It's after midnight," Jo says flatly.

I'm undaunted. "Better yet, no crowds," I say. "And a little B&E is better than mugging someone, right?" Yes, folks, I am talking to the good guys.

"OK," Jo agrees slowly. "How do we find a library?"

"One that has medieval French dictionaries," adds Chi.

"Easy," I answer. "A university library. There's at least two I can think of in DC – American and Georgetown. And, as a plus, they're both already full of disreputable-looking teens."

We're all suitably impressed with my brilliance.

I actually spend a lot of time in libraries. When you're a homeless drifter, they're like a living room away from home. I also like to break in and sleep there – lots of reading material and comfortable couches.

Plan in mind, we all climb reluctantly back on to our motorcycles. Jo stopped studying once it got dark and now drives Uri on his motorcycle. They worked out a system where he is the legs, and she is the of-age licensed driver. It feels a little surreal to be worrying about something as common as the cops.

As we get close to American University, in a stroke of good luck, we see a sign for Wesley Seminary. A seminary is bound to have access to the dictionary Jo needs – she is translating a religious book after all – and a small seminary would probably have a much less impressive security system than a place like Georgetown. We follow the green signs.

The seminary is (or maybe was) part of American University and squats on a corner of its small campus. The building could have shared an architect with the Templar school – a cement-and-brick box with narrow windows. The building is silent; this corner of campus is dead at 2am on a cold Monday in March. Our motorcycles are painfully loud, so we drive past and park a few blocks from where we intend to commit our crime.

As a general rule, people tend to not alarm windows that no mere human can reach, which is great for those of us who are not mere humans. Or even for those of us who are pretending to be mere human who hang out with others who aren't mere human. Chi climbs an obliging tree, puts on Uri's helmet, wraps his arms in his leather jacket, and dives the ten feet right through a second-storey window, shattering it on his helmet. The rest of us crouch in the bushes, but when no police or security comes, we climb up the lowered rope. I pretend to struggle and feel ridiculous. And, strangely, guilty.

The second floor is a long rectangle filled with tables, shelves of books and study carrels. One wall is lined with glass-windowed study rooms, and a door marked "Technical Services" that probably leads to offices. We take the stairs down to the first floor, which has a circulation desk and, what we really need, a bank of computers.

Jo pulls up the catalogue and finds the dictionaries she needs, then heads upstairs. She says something about needing light and looking for an interior office with no windows. Chi, Uri and I stay to Google the crap out of Exo Greer.

Round one turns up nothing. Fortunately, I am rather adept at finding people. Ghosts can be very clear on some things but annoyingly vague on others – like the exact current location of their murderer. The library has access to some newspaper databases, so I start searching specifically through local DC news sources. Twenty minutes later, I hit gold. It's a local neighborhood newspaper called the *DC Townie* from two years ago. Turns out Exo is a girl's name. Really, it shouldn't be anyone's.

St Albina's Orphanage Seeks Runaway

Local St Albina's Orphanage reports that ward Exo Greer, twelve, disappeared late Wednesday night. Greer has a history of escape attempts, so her custodians do not suspect foul play. The girl suffers from schizophrenia as well as Tourette's Syndrome and requires medication and constant care. If you see this girl, call 911. Do not attempt to approach.

Next to the article is what must be a school photo but more closely resembles a mug shot. A greasy-haired pre-teen girl in a black sweatshirt glares from the page.

Great. We're searching for a mentally ill runaway. She could be anywhere. In fact, the only information we have is where she is not – St Albina's.

I share the information with Chi and Uri, but they're less worried than I am.

"She has to be in Washington, DC," Chi explains. "Remember, Luke is on assignment with her and he had access to the Beacon Map. If the headmaster wrote Washington, DC, then it must be Washington, DC."

Now that we have some more information, we start researching St Albina's. Maybe she was caught and taken back. Interestingly the orphanage was in the news quite a lot following the girl's escape. Former employees were discovered to have been embezzling money and another one was caught on film abusing children. Overall a pretty nasty place. Following the scandal, the place was shut down – another dead end, we can't go there to ask questions.

When we exhaust all our options, Chi and I decide to check on Jo's progress. Uri stays behind, still researching. Jo is locked in a back office with a bunch of dictionaries spread out around her.

"How's it coming?" Chi asks and Jo holds up a hand for us to wait. She finishes writing something down, then looks up at me – not Chi.

"I think I almost have it… but I still don't think we should go through with it."

"Why not?" I ask.

"It's not just some quick hocus-pocus, it's some serious magic. And…" she finally looks at Chi, "do you remember all the oaths that we took the night of the ceremony?"

Chi thinks. "Yeah, blood swears to dedicate our lives to the Order, and all. So?"

Wait a minute, what?

"Well, those aren't part of the ceremony. I mean they are, but not part of this spell. They're separate." She's looking at Chi, waiting for him to understand.

"So?"

"So I don't have those," she says, frustrated.

"So what?"

I know "what" and it makes me very happy. No blood-oaths for this little monster.

Jo gives up and rolls her eyes. "So we're going to be giving Crusader powers to someone who has no obligation to the Order. Do you get it now, genius?"

So much for being best friends. I am all righteous rage for about five seconds, but it's hard to maintain when I know she's right. I pretend injury anyway. But my reaction is nothing to Chi's.

He explodes. "You know what, Jo? I might not be a 'genius', but I'm not some idiot leper either." He steps closer to her, and she stands, staggering a little in her haste, wanting to be on equal footing, I guess. "But you know what? I'd rather risk trusting someone once in a while, than storm around telling people what dirt I think they are." He's inches from her face now. "I put up with it from you because you once were my best friend in the whole universe, because I keep hoping that one day, you'll stop being such a twisted bitch and become who you once were." He waves his hands and a bitter bark of laughter escapes him. "That given enough time you'll get over it. But I won't stand here and let you treat Meda like she is some kind of evil monster. That you would rather she dies than trust her."

The color drains from Jo's face, but Chi isn't done. "You don't deserve to be a Crusader – and it isn't because you don't have the legs, but because you don't have the heart."

Jo is stricken. She looks at me and I flinch away from her expression. She's right not to trust me. I'm not trustworthy, I am evil. I am dirt, but Chi crushed her for me. I'm the one who belongs under his feet.

Rage spent, Chi looks as guilty as I feel. If her hurt makes me feel this way, there's no way he's immune. His voice softens, "Jo–"

She cringes away from him, shaking her head, then shoves past him, running away.

Chi facepalms and makes a frustrated sound. He kicks the desk, then sweeps his arm across it, throwing everything to the floor. Man version of tears, I think.

I love good torture as much as the next demon, but this is getting ridiculous. Jo spends her days hurting the man she loves in an attempt not to hurt him and Chi wanders around baffled, setting himself up again and again for her crushing blows, not understanding why his best friend keeps kicking him down. For him, it must be like a body-snatcher stole her away. She walks and talks, but she's not Jo. Not his Jo. But he can't stay away. They are tied together and, the more one struggles to be free, the more it hurts the other.

I'm pretty sure I'm about to violate every BFF girl code out there, but from what I've seen on TV no one seems to take girl code very seriously, anyway. Besides, for once I have good intentions: these two need to get out of their own way.

"Chi," I say and wait until I have his attention. He stops his vicious desk attack and leans heavily on it instead. He turns to look at me. I take a deep breath. "Jo's in love with you."

I think I could have hit Chi with a baseball bat and gotten a lesser reaction. Under other circumstances, the expression on his face would be funny. Actually, it still is funny – bug eyes, gaping mouth and skin an odd shade of puce.

"Go kiss and make up."

His brain starts functioning again and he straightens. "What?"

"Kiss her."

"Why would – I mean… That doesn't…" he runs his hand through his hair, making it stand wildly.

"Sorry, was I being unclear?"

"Um, but–"

"Kiss. Her."

"Are you insane?" He looks hurt, like I jabbed him with a stick. "She hates me."

Wow. Really. I sigh – it seems I must spell it out. "She's in love with you. She doesn't want to be because of the whole Crusader-fighting-couple thing. She thinks you won't want her fighting by your side – too weak." I tap my leg.

He just stands there. The gears in his brain lurch unevenly as he tries to process. "Does not compute" flashes on his forehead.

Maybe if I try in Latin? "Iss-kay er-hay." OK, so it's only pig Latin. Sue me.

"But–"

Maybe in song? "*You know you wanna kiss the girl –* whoa-whoa!" *The Little Mermaid*-style.

"Ugggggggggh!" He throws up his hands and stomps away. Which would be great except Jo had stomped off in the opposite direction. Ah well, there's only so much I can do.

Jo comes back minutes later, red-eyed and set-jawed. I feel sick.

"Jo–" I don't know what I was planning to say, but it doesn't matter because I don't get any further.

"No, Meda, he's right." She fingers her half of the necklace. "I do trust you." Her eyes meet mine and I have to fight not to look away. She sets her jaw. "Let's do it."

And we will. Because I need to protect myself from the demons.

It's not because I can't bear to admit the truth to her.

I have done far worse things, I tell myself. This is nothing. But at this moment, it doesn't feel that way.

Chi comes back with Uri in tow as I am cleaning a space on the floor. I explain the decision because Jo refuses to even look at Chi, let alone talk to him. Chi, on the other hand, doesn't take his eyes off Jo. He's a scientist searching for evidence to support a crazy, world-changing hypothesis. His world, at least. Uri notices something big happened and looks from Chi to Jo and back again. Then he turns to me, his eyebrows near his hairline.

Great, I was hoping everyone would be distracted while casting potentially fatal spells on me.

We finish clearing a space on the floor and Jo motions me to lie down. She spends the next fifteen minutes defacing the carpet with symbols in a black Sharpie.

"These are protections. If something goes wrong... well, these might keep you from dying."

Great.

Once that's done, she kneels next to me. She licks her lips and swallows. "The spell consists of six parts, the first four are the hardest and it's going to burn. You have to hold as still as possible – if we lose contact, I'll have to redo that section. The good news is each section is half as long and half as painful as the previous. The last part is only about fifteen seconds long and hurts hardly at all, but the first..." She trails off with a wince.

I can do the math. Six sections, the shortest at fifteen seconds – so the longest is eight minutes and agonizing. My face must convey what I think of that, because she pats me awkwardly on the shoulder. I find Jo's attempt at being understanding the scariest thing of all.

"In any case, no matter how much it hurts, you have to hold still – or we have to do that part again." She flexes her fingers and shakes them loose. I've never seen her so nervous.

I nod to show I understand. She needs to calm down or I'm toast. "It's a good move in the long run," I say encouragingly.

"Right," she says, but she doesn't sound convinced.

I force a smile. "Hey, Doctor – surgery doesn't ever feel good, but it's good for you." I call back our discussion on intention, letting her know I trust her.

She smiles back weakly, but it fades as she kneels next to me. She shuffles her notes one last time. She pulls her knife from under her jacket and with a deep breath cuts across her palm. I smell the blood as she rubs it between her hands, washing them in it.

Her mouth tightens as she meets my eyes. "If this winds up killing you, it was an accident, I promise."

I must look terrified because the corner of her mouth kicks up and she ends by teasing, "And... well, I told you so."

With that promising remark, she presses her hands to my chest and I burst into flames.

Sixteen

I wear napalm-soaked skin; my bones are fire-heated iron. My blood boils. A scream sticks in my throat like vomit, strangling me. Still my mouth opens, trying to do its part.

I lock eyes with Jo. Her calm face hovers over mine, telling me without words that I am not actually on fire. I try desperately to hold still, going rigid in my attempt, but shudders rack my body. Only the fear of having to go through a second of this ever again makes it possible for me to stay under the brutal heat of those small hands.

It occurs to me that maybe my body can't live through this. Maybe the demon half makes this process impossible and I am lying here in agony, dying, doing my best to sit perfectly still as I am roasted alive. But no, they told me it would hurt and Jo's face is so calm. A cool pool in a world on fire.

Besides, it's too late now.

So I go away. I drift through paintings I love, I swim through the swirling blue of *Starry Night*; I twirl through O'Keefe's flower petals.

I stay away from red.

Time creeps and crawls. I spend a month in Dali's *Persistence of Memory*, playing with melted clocks, a year among Van Gogh's *Irises*. I dance through Picasso's *Guernica*. I avoid *The Scream*.

Then, just as quickly as it started, the fire is extinguished. I open my eyes and see Jo's worried expression. "The first part is over. How do you feel?"

"Great," I croak. I've never felt less great in my life. She knows it and smiles.

"Then time for part two." She reaches out with her hands and I have to bite back a scream. She stops when she sees my face. "Four minutes. That's all, half as long, half as bad."

My breath is still coming out in panicked gasps. My body does not want round two in any way, shape or form. I force my breathing to slow. The worst part is over, it's all downhill from here. No matter what happens, I don't have to repeat that segment. The worst is over.

I stare at the fluorescent lights recessed into the ceiling. One more breath, then we go for part two. She reaches for me and I cringe away.

OK, two more breaths.

No, three.

"Meda – today." Apparently Jo can only do sympathy for so long. I give a stiff nod, but as she reaches forward, the light I'm focused on flickers out and we are dropped into darkness.

"What's happening?" I ask and, trembling, pull myself up.

"I don't know," Jo whispers, alert and staring into the hallway. Chi's already in action, moving out to investigate. Uri follows him out and goes across the hall to an office with a window.

"All the power's out," Chi calls.

Uri turns towards us from the window he's peering out of. His face is white with moonlight and terror.

"They've found us. I think…" his voice breaks, "I think we're surrounded."

Jo and I jump up, panic pushing the pain from the forefront of my mind. Jo grabs the grimoire off the desk and we all run out into the library. Unspeaking, we each take a wall, moving between bookcases to peer out of windows. How is it possible? How could they have found us?

I don't know how, but they have. Black suits, two to three deep, ring the building as far as I can see. They stand stiff and silent, black shapes in the black night. I can feel it now, the swell of power, unnoticed while I lay in burning agony. Not as many as were at the school, but if the building is surrounded… then there have to be nearly a hundred. I run to another window, and there are still more. I seek out Jo and Chi, shaking my head – no escape this way. They repeat the motion. We're surrounded.

"Meda," croons a sing-song voice from multiple throats. It's low, soft. It slides through the broken window. "Come out, come out, wherever you are."

I back away from the window. Chi, Jo and Uri do the same, coming to meet me in the middle.

"What are we going to do?" I whisper.

"Come out, Meda, or we will come in."

Chi answers, "Uri and I will hold them off–"

"You expect me to just run–" Jo starts but Chi cuts her off.

"No. I don't want you to run. I want you to finish casting the spell on Meda." He switches to me. "Let's hope you've got some badass skills or we're all dead." Then Chi locks eyes with Jo, weighing her reaction. "Then you can come back and we'll fight side by side."

This startles Jo and her eyes get big with a happiness that really doesn't belong in our present situation. "Really?" she whispers, hoping but not quite believing.

He squeezes her arm. "Really."

"Meeeeeeeda," the demons chant, sing-song and almost sweet. Jo grabs my arm and hauls me back to the office.

"I'll try to leave some for you," Chi calls after us.

Jo slams and locks the door behind us. We hear shattering glass as she shoves me back down into the circle. She awkwardly climbs on to the desk and shoves the grimoire into a ceiling panel, then half-jumps, half-falls to my side.

I have no time to take a breath before I'm on fire again.

Half as bad as the worst pain I've ever felt is still awful. And this time, I cannot go away to hide among the paintings I love. I need to know what's happening. I keep my eyes open and fight to stay still, but it's like trying to keep your hand on a hot iron. Not impossible – that's as much as I can say. Not impossible.

I hear fighting in the main room, grunts, screams, more breaking glass, crashing furniture. I hear Uri's childish scream, and Jo's eyes pop open and her chant hitches. She half-rises like she wants to run, but I grab her hands before we lose contact. She looks back at me, her eyes burn as hot as my skin.

The fighting gets louder as the pain dials down. We're on to the next section – two minutes. By comparison, this feels only like the worse sunburn I can imagine. Dull and throbbing. Less to distract me from the movements in the next room. The demons are in the hallway, but not to our door yet. Chi, at least, must still be alive, still holding them back. It's not clear about Uri.

Chi yells for us to hurry, but two minutes is two minutes. I hear Chi shouting orders, not to us.

Uri's still alive.

The pain ratchets down again – this section's only a minute long. The rhythm of Jo's speech changes and I can almost feel the excitement in it. I grip her wrists. Bodies slam against the walls outside the door, and a picture crashes to the floor by my head.

There are two more hard slams, then a strangled scream, cut short. A human scream. We both recognize it instantly, though it's not a sound I ever thought I'd hear from him.

Chi.

I see things in Jo's eyes I will never forget.

Demonic cheers echo in the hallway and a body slams into the locked door. Tears run down Jo's face, sizzling as they hit my skin, but she doesn't stop. We're on to the next set, only thirty seconds here, then fifteen more and it's complete. The words flood from her mouth. The door explodes, and we break eye contact to watch, though Jo keeps chanting. The pain dials down. Fifteen seconds, that's all that's left. Fifteen seconds. A middle-aged man enters, dumpy and dark-haired. Jo needs to stand and defend herself, but she doesn't. She stays on the floor where I lie, finishing the spell. Her fingers dig into my skin. There can only be seconds left.

He smirks and rubs his hands together, then with a hiss, he jumps for us. Jo waits to the last possible second, but has to break contact before she can finish the spell. She dives behind the desk as I roll towards the door, and the demon dives over me. He goes for Jo and I jump him from behind. I drag him backwards by his hair as Jo guts him. I drop the body and Jo passes me a knife. I fight down a shudder of revulsion, but hold on to it.

More demons bubble through the door like yellow jackets from a hive. The small room is our best asset because they can't all attack at once. Jo and I fight at right angles to each other, our shoulders bumping, keeping the desk between us and the door.

We manage to take the next two around the desk, but behind them, more stack up. One launches himself over the desk and I turn to face him head on. He impales himself on my knife, but the force of his dive slams me into the bookcase behind me. I shake him off just as another one dives – this time on Jo, who's already trying to hold off two coming around the desk. I rush forward and haul him off, twisting until she and I are back to back.

Another one comes over the top of the desk and drills into my side, sending me sideways. The demon swings at me and I duck. I hear Jo scream and twist in time to see her go down. I jump at her attacker, stabbing into his back.

But that leaves my own back exposed.

A brutal weight slams into the base of my spine and my legs give out under the pressure. I land on Jo, the dead demon between us, and our eyes meet for a brief second before I am hauled off her and slammed into the bookcase. The world goes dim as blurry shapes bubble over the desk in a wicked waterfall, blocking the light, blocking everything. I struggle, but sharp hands pinch and grab, pinning my arms to my sides.

The demons cheer and chirrup and I am loaded overhead and carried out on a river of demons. I twist and thrash, looking for Jo.

Please let her be alive, please let her be alive.

The sweetest sound reaches my ears – swearing fit to make a rapper blush. Jo's alive. I twist and spot her, carried as I am.

The narrow hallway squeezes our captors together and Jo reaches out her hand and I jerk my arm free and grab for it. We just touch fingers and she starts to mutter, still trying to finish the spell, but we are wrenched apart almost instantly.

With a squealing cackle, the demons slam me to the floor and my breath leaves in a whoosh. The last thing I see is a polished dress shoe poised for a kick. Pain explodes in my head, flashing red.

Then black. Shiny black, like the tip of that shoe.

Seventeen

I lift cement eyelids. I'm not dead. Hands press unevenly beneath me, lifting me, like I'm floating on a wavy pool. Flickering candlelight illuminates a ceiling painted with grey, red and cream. Writhing naked bodies, monsters, fires, blood and storms. I'm not sure if it's supposed to be an image of an orgy or Hell. The walls are black and slick.

I rock my head to the side. The two dozen creatures dancing around and seething under me aren't the same suited suburbanites who captured me. These creatures are young and wickedly beautiful. Lithe, dancing creatures, in stylish suits and gowns. All black, grey and red. I don't understand.

"What's happening?" I try to say, but it's slurred. Fortunately, the nearest woman makes it out.

"Ohhh, don't recognize us?" croons the elegantly evil creature. Her voice hums along my bones. "Those are our disguises." Her red lips curl into a smile. "Middle-aged people in suits can get away with anything. An invading army of demons looks like a banking convention." She laughs, a husky sound that gives me goosebumps. "Now our true forms." She indicates her beautiful, skimpily clad body and spins. "Well, anyone can see these are meant for no good."

"Where are we?" My voice is a little clearer now.

"We're off to zi-Hilo." That wicked, sensual smile again. "He has plans for you," she sings and strokes my face, long nails rasping across my skin.

"Where are my friends?"

"Shhhhhh, now." She lifts her hand and opens her palm. She purses her lips and blows me a kiss. Whatever is in her hand dusts my face and I sink back into darkness. "Nighty-night."

The first thing I become conscious of is the cold. A cold so deep my bones ache. I lie on a slab of ice. I try to move, try to open my eyes but I can't. I'm encased in ice. My breath comes fast and my heartbeat races, adrenaline rushes.

My eyes snap open. Everything's black. I wiggle now, the ice was all in my head, but I'm still cold. I pull myself up and notice I feel nothing but cold and stiff, not superpowerful. Quite the opposite, I'm weaker than I've ever been. And so Hungry it gnaws on my insides like a rat. But how can that be possible? It should have been weeks before it feels like this. How long have I been out?

My eyes start to adjust but I almost wish they wouldn't, because what I see isn't promising. Black floors, black ceiling, black bars – a cell. I push myself to my feet, but stumble.

The floor is a mosaic of black glass, but the tiles aren't square, they're all slightly... off. Not quite square, not quite anything else, just askew and oddly angled. They're polished to such a high shine that they work as black mirrors. A shattered Meda stares back at me from beneath my feet. The wall behind me is the same, as is the ceiling. There are no other walls to my cell, only bars. Outside my little cell are more cells, oddly shaped and arranged randomly with walls jutting out at odd angles. The ceiling is all different heights, low where I am, but in other areas multiple storeys. One is only two feet high. Anyone in that cell would have to lie flat. The dungeon is lit only by cone-shaped sconces that shoot bluish light to the ceiling. The room is a cave of shadows and dim mirrors.

I catch a movement out of the corner of my eye and spin, but no one is there. While spinning I see another, but it is a reflection of my reflection. I hold perfectly still and nothing moves.

Uri, Chi, Jo. They might be in here somewhere. If they're alive. I rush to the bars.

"I wouldn't do that if I were you," a voice rumbles through the black shadows.

I spin, but I don't see anyone. "Who's there?" I demand.

"Do you have to be so loud?" he asks, a wince in his voice. I notice he has an accent, but I can't place it. I find him in the darkness. His cell wraps weirdly around a misshapen corner and I see him sitting in the darkest shadows, leaning against a wall with his legs bent and his arms resting on his knees. His head is tilted back but I can't make out any specifics of his face. A human-shaped shadow.

Another prisoner and bars between us. Not a threat. I turn back to searching for my friends, hands out to test the bars.

"I'm telling you, that's a mistake." His warning is a half-taunt.

"What's it to you?" I say, but my hands hesitate. It's not like it would be out of character for the demons to rig the cell with nasty surprises. I look back at him.

"Oh, usually I enjoy a stranger's pain as much as the next child of darkness, but right now I'm trying to enjoy my misery in peace." His teasing tone says he's doing no such thing.

Still, I pull my hands away from the bars. Better not to risk it. "How long have I been out?"

"About an hour."

"Where are my friends?" I demand.

"Do I look like your tour guide?" I hear a smile in his voice. His eyes pop open now, the faintest slash of white in the shadows of his face. "Because I am not."

I'd like to hit him, but he doesn't have to fear me any more than I him. I turn my back on him and squint into the uneven darkness, webbed with bars. I avoid the sconces which blind me, searching the shadows for my friends.

"Jo," I hiss into the darkness. "Chi, Uri." No answer. I whisper again, louder this time. Still no response. Screw it. I open my mouth to yell.

"Please don't."

"Why not?"

"My peaceful misery, remember?"

"Do I look like someone who cares?" I say, mimicking him from earlier. "Because I'm not."

"The guards will come. They won't be happy." It's a warning, but his tone seems to suggest he doesn't really care.

"Ah, well, you should know, I don't live to make other people happy."

I see a flash of teeth. He's smiling. "I'm beginning to get that impression."

"If you just tell me where my friends are, I won't scream," I suggest.

"There are the negotiation skills our kind are famous for." He rises to his feet, abandoning peaceful misery for my charming company. He moves with compressed-spring energy, as if he's ready to pounce. My unwilling tour guide is about my age, maybe a year or so older, as he has managed a manly stubble. He's good-looking in a bad-boy kind of way – downright hot, really, not that I'm in a position to care. Impending death has a way of focusing your priorities.

Smooth skin, longish tangled dark hair, full lips, girly-long lashes, black eyes, black T-shirt, black jeans tucked into black combat boots. No wonder I couldn't find him in the dark. He looks like he's taken a beating recently, as a bloody cut splits the side of his lip and his left eye is swollen and discolored in the corner. A smirk teases the corner of his mouth and his eyes have a twinkle even in this dark hellhole that suggests he never takes anything seriously.

It dawns on me, what he just said. *Our kind.*

I crouch and snarl. "You're a demon!"

He kicks up the uninjured side of his mouth into a slight smile, unconcerned by my violence. Why should he be? I'm caged. "A halfling," he says, blasé. "So, yes, as much a demon as you are."

A halfling. The first like me I've ever met. A dozen questions come to mind, but I bite them back. Now really isn't the time.

The boy's smile stretches a little further. "Maybe more than you, actually, as I've already sided with the demons." He takes his smile too far and winces. I smell blood. "And I definitely don't hang out with Templars."

My eyes narrow. "How do you know my friends are Templars?"

"Because I'm undercover in an elaborate scheme to trick you." I glare at him, and he holds up his hands. "Relax. Because they're in the Crusader cells." He lifts his hand to point, and I twist to follow his finger. "They were awake when they were brought in, but then they made the guards unhappy. They're not up yet."

"How many?" I demand as I peer into the shadows. "How many did they bring in?" My heart races, afraid of what I will, or maybe *won't,* see.

"Three," he says. I can breathe.

Finally, I spot uneven lumps in a cell about twenty feet away, shadows slightly different from those around them. I can't be sure it's them, but there's no point shouting if they're knocked out.

"You sure that's them?"

"You have trust issues."

I ignore that. "Are you sure?"

"Two boys and a girl." He winces, "A really loud girl."

That's them. My breath is so big I have to tilt my head back to let it all out.

Now that my greatest fear has been allayed, I can pay more attention to the boy. I don't have a lot of weapons down here – might as well cultivate what resources there are. At the very least, he could be another body to toss to the bears. I take in his athletic build – unlike Jo, I'd probably have to trip this one. "So what are you doing here? You don't happen to be a good guy in disguise, do you?" I pause. "A really good disguise?"

He chuckles. "Hardly. Bad as they come, I'm afraid."

"Why, then?"

"Why should I answer?" He comes as close to the bars as he can without actually touching them.

"Because if you don't, I'll have to talk to myself." I pause, then add ominously, "Or sing."

"Sounds dangerous."

"You have no idea. You'll wish I was screaming."

That full mouth twists into a decidedly sensual smile. Trust a boy to turn it dirty. We're standing far too close, only a foot away from each other with only bars in the middle. Pain-inducing bars, but still. I take a step back and clear my throat. His smile stretches even further at my discomfort.

I decide to resume my spot on the offensive. "So why are you here?"

"I'm not such a good rule-follower."

"Like what kind of rules?"

He pauses, studying my face. "'Never, ever kill your own'."

"Own what?"

"It means other demons."

"Why not?"

"We're evil and violent with ferocious tempers. If we were allowed to kill each other, we'd be extinct in a week."

I can see that. So far, I've certainly wanted to kill every demon I've met.

"So you killed another demon?"

He smiles, white teeth dance in the dark. "A few."

"Why?"

"I didn't like their attitude," he says shortly. Apparently, he is done sharing. I'm not done being curious.

"If you hate them so much, why do you play for their team?"

He cocks his head sideways. "Because it's what I am." That wicked smile is back. "Evil."

"No, if you're a halfling, then you're only half evil."

"Half evil, half human." He raises an eyebrow. "But humans aren't exactly good, are they?"

No, they aren't. Even my friends are borderline delinquents.

"I decided a long time ago not to fight it." His eyes drift off to something I can't see. "There's no point. In the end…" He snaps back to the present and the smile is back. "It's more fun to be bad, anyway." He leans closer to the bars and I catch his dark spicy scent, chocolate and cinnamon.

"Even if you periodically end up in a demon dungeon?"

He laughs. "I hardly think you can judge, Good Girl – how's that working out for you?"

Touché. I stick out my tongue. He chuckles and the sound dances down my spine.

"So what's your name?"

"Not Good Girl."

He raises an eyebrow. "Bad Girl, then."

I roll my eyes.

"Pretty Girl," he suggests and I open my mouth to speak, but he beats me to it. "No, not pretty." Ouch. "Flowers are pretty, sunsets are pretty. No, you're not pretty. You're…"

I don't think I want to hear what I am. "Meda. Meda Melange."

He laughs.

"What's so funny?"

"Melange. It's French for mixed – so appropriate."

Mom, you're hilarious. "What's your name?"

"Armand Delacroix." Before I can move, he snatches my hand from between the bars. I try to tug away, but it's too dangerous. He bends over my hand like he's going to kiss it, but then pauses and looks up at me through his eyelashes. "At your service," he murmurs and presses his too big, too soft lips to the little joint. I flush and jerk my hand back the instant he loosens his grip.

"French?" I ask and he tips his head in acquiescence. I wipe my hand on my jeans. "So, Armand, what happens now? Do I get a trial or something?"

His eyes laugh at me. "You're a captive of Hell. They're not big on justice here."

"So, what happens?" I'm not sure I want to know.

"If you're lucky, they'll let you sell your soul and become one of us."

"I'm not that easy to boss around."

He shrugs. "That's only if you're lucky anyway. If you aren't... well, it's safer for them to just eliminate the problem."

Maybe I'm easier to boss around than I thought.

"Anyway, if they do decide to convince you, I recommend you don't fight it." The bitterness is back. "There's no point, especially not for someone with your... nature."

That doesn't sound good. "Will they torture me?" *Was that puny thing my voice?*

"In a fashion."

"What does that mean?"

"It's torturous, but... they only remind you of your own nature. They'll starve you – these cages suck the life out of you. In a few hours, it will be like you haven't eaten in weeks. In a few days, you will be starving. By next week, you will be insane. Then, they tempt you with what you will always want most. Freedom from the Hunger, freedom from the constraints of humanity." His voice gets husky, seductive. "We're really not so bad, you know. We're you, if you let yourself be who you were born to be. We're creatures of temptation, not torture."

"I'm not like them. Like you."

"Aren't you?" His voice is a taunting caress. "You look like temptation to me."

I open my mouth, but he continues. "Don't you dream of violence? Of power?" His voice casts a spell. I can see it, a life draining in my hands, the soul billowing free. "You don't dream of that perfect moment when a brilliant soul filters through you like cascading rainbows, that moment of absolute freedom when you need nothing?" His accent thickens as he talks.

I shake myself free. "Pshaw – who would want that?" I say shakily and he laughs, the spell broken. "But anyway, they can't be so great, you just told me you kill them regularly."

"Not regularly and not because they were demons. Because they pissed me off." That annoying eyebrow quirks again, "Or have you never met any humans the world would be better off without?"

I don't want to talk about that. "My friends will never turn."

His eyes meet mine, his tone is flat. "Then, they will die."

"But–"

"You can't save them; you can just not die with them."

"But–"

"They can't just let demon-hunters walk out of here. Do you think your friends would react any differently if they had a demon hostage?"

I remember the Crusaders butchering the frozen demons.

He laughs again, a bitter sound. "At least the Templars have a choice – they can stop being Crusaders at any time. But there's no choice for demons, not after you sell your soul, and there is never any real choice for halflings. We're born evil. We are what we are and yet they slaughter us." He cocks his head and it appears he can be serious. "How do you do it? Be friends with them? Don't you ever get tired of pretending to be someone else? Of all the restraints?"

Yes. "No."

"It's like trying to put a leash on a wolf."

It was. "It's not so bad."

"So a wolf can be housebroken. Who knew?"

I hiss at him.

"Meda? Is that you?" A weak voice whispers. My dark companion ceases to exist for me, I'm at the bars and just barely catch myself from touching them.

"Uri?"

"Meda? Where are we?" I squint into the darkness. A shadowed lump is upright.

"A demon dungeon – don't touch the bars." Uri doesn't answer, but I hear panicked panting, so I add calmly, "Pretty cool, hey?"

"Cool?" he squeaks.

"Just wait till you tell the other kids. They'll be so jealous."

"Jealous," he repeats but his voice is steadier. "Why are you all the way over there?"

I dodge the question. Armand notices and smirks. "Are Jo and Chi in there with you?"

"Yeah."

"Well, wake them up." I hear Uri move around shaking them and saying their names.

"Meda?" It's Jo this time.

"Hey Jo, Chi, I'm over here."

"Meda." Jo's voice is panicked. "I didn't finish the spell. I need a few more seconds–" I shoot a look at Armand and cut her off.

"I noticed." No new superpowers here. They are about twenty feet away, and there's another cell between us and a jutting wall blocking part of their cell from my view – and Armand from them.

"Don't touch the bars," I add, in case Uri forgot. I hear Jo talking to Chi.

"We'll get out of here," I hear Chi say. I notice he doesn't say how.

"Meda, how long have you been awake?" Jo asks.

"Just a few minutes. There's another prisoner down here."

"There is?"

"Yes," Armand says.

"A halfling," I warn. Jo makes a disgusted noise, filled with enough hate to make me wince. "He's the one who told me not to touch the bars. I haven't actually tried it." I add.

There's a miniature explosion and Chi curses. So Armand wasn't lying. Good to know, especially since I didn't have to risk my skin to find out.

"Definitely don't touch the bars," says Jo. "What are we going to do?"

"What can we do?" I return. Nothing, but the word hangs unsaid.

"Are we going to die?" Uri whispers so faintly I can barely hear.

Chi is the only one who answers. "Not if I can help it."

No one is reassured.

Jo chokes down her hatred of Armand enough to pepper him with questions. Her tone is a quarter-step above a sneer but he seems more amused by it than insulted. His tone in response is polite, but his eyes dance. It's a joke to him, their trying to escape.

Chi tries wrapping his hands in his shirt to touch the bars and learns the painful way that doesn't work. He tries wrapping the whole shirt around the bar and only holding the very ends. He learns the (slightly less) painful way that doesn't work. He gets pissed and kicks the bars as hard as he can. That definitely doesn't work and he flies across the cell.

Hours pass.

I pace the cell like the caged tiger I am. Armand tries to talk to me, but he's only a distraction. I ignore him. Harder to ignore is the growing Hunger. It claws at my insides like a living thing. It was a rat, then a cat, now it is a crocodile, snapping at my innards and twisting. I smell chili-sprinkled mango, pot roast and, by far the most irresistible, popcorn – the sweet scents of my friends' souls.

These thoughts are not helping. I squat and pull my hair, then look at Armand. He eyes my friends, wearing the alert look of a stalking lion. He catches me watching and relaxes with a chagrined smile.

I pace, Jo swears, Chi electrocutes himself again, this time with his shoes on his hands. The only one who is silent is Popcorn. I mean, Uri. He is sitting cross-legged on the floor tracing his face in the glassy floor tile.

"Dollar for your thoughts," I say and he looks up.

"Not a penny?"

"You get what you pay for."

Uri smiles, then idly taps the floor. "I was just thinking that there's nothing to worry about."

"Whoa – you were robbed, that's worth at least a twenty. Can you tell me why?"

"Because there's a plan."

"You have a plan?" He's sounding way too philosophical for the ol' nail-file-in-a-cake type plan, but one can hope.

"No." He half-smiles. "God has a plan."

Blast. He's got no reason to help me out.

Uri continues. "And I was thinking…"

"Yay, BOGOF," I tease. Buy One, Get One Free.

He doesn't laugh. "No matter how this ends, it was worth it."

"What was worth it?"

"The adventure. Fighting demons. Meeting you. Being a part of it all."

Jo starts paying attention. "Don't talk like that, Uri," she snaps. "We're not dead yet."

For once Uri isn't afraid of Jo. "No, and I hope it stays that way, but if it doesn't… well, it was enough." His eyes meet mine. "I don't regret anything. Better to die for something I believe in, than live for nothing at all."

If that's The Plan, frankly I'm underwhelmed. Uri would be too, if he knew the truth. That it's all a lie. He thinks he's going to die trying to save a Beacon, but in reality, it would just be for me.

I feel Armand's eyes on me, because he knows. I don't look at him, because I swear if he smirks I will rip his head from his shoulders, bars or no. Instead I force a weak smile for Uri.

"I don't regret anything, either."

That's the biggest lie of all.

"Can we stop planning our own funerals and figure some way out of here?" Jo demands but her voice breaks.

And that's when a door across the room slams open.

Cut into the side of the tallest wall, probably three storeys high, is a crookedly carved staircase with no banister. As it reaches the bottom, it twists away from the wall into a free-form spiral that disappears into the floor. We all watch with bated breath as in dances a collection of giddy demons. Six or seven of them, mixed men and women, darkly beautiful in shades of grey, red and black.

They giggle and squeal, and one of them laughingly shushes the others, as if they're drunk high-schoolers sneaking home late. We all stand at alert, watching their erratic yet graceful descent. I uselessly hope they'll continue down the stairs, to the floors below, but they don't. When they step from the staircase, I shoot a look at Armand and he's rigid. I wonder if they're coming for him. No, I *hope* they're coming for him. They look like they're out for fun and I don't want any of us to be their toy.

They sidle, twist and dance between the maze of bars and walls, running their hands along them as they pass. The bars in the empty cages must not be switched on.

That might be good to know, later. They come to a decision point. Left takes them to the Templars, straight brings them to Armand and me.

The demons pause, giggling, whispering and pointing. Three women in twisted ball gowns and four men in macabre suits, all appearing to be in their twenties. Jo and I meet each other's eyes. She's pale and fear adds more chili to her mango scent. Chi subtly steps between the others and the door. I hold my breath; the thud of my heart keeps time. One beat passes, two.

I don't know what I want the demons to decide.

Their smiles shine whitely in the dark, mixing with the spots in my vision. I need to breathe, but I can't, their decision is too important. Finally, finally, they come straight. Me or Armand. My knees tremble; fear and relief – a contradictory cocktail threatens their stability. My eyes meet Jo's again and she's at the bars of her cage. Chi's hands are on her shoulders, holding her back. Uri's eyes are wide in his very young face and, even from here, I can see him shake. The stiffer he tries to hold himself, the more the tremors rock his frame. Jo reaches out and pulls him to her side in a fiercely protective hug. Uri, the oldest child I have ever met, who tries so hard to be the brave hero, curls into her side like a toddler, burying his face in her shoulder.

The weirdly beautiful procession enters the corner of my vision. Me or Armand.

It stops in front of my cage.

Me.

I lock my knees and turn my attention to my guests. They return my regard, cocking their heads curiously, like crows. The one in front, a woman with sharp features and silky curls, eyes me. Black rhinestones, stuck to her skin, climb across her cheekbones in swirling designs. Her gown clings and plunges, stark black against ivory.

"So you're what all the fuss is about." Her voice is beautiful and cultured. It rains down softly. Acid rain. My response is a drought; I say nothing.

"What are you doing here, Serena?" Armand asks blandly.

She cocks her head sharply towards him. "Ah! Armand." She sidles over. "How are you liking your cage?" She smirks and dances her fingers close to the bars, but doesn't touch them.

Armand bares his teeth.

"That's unfortunate," she fake-sympathizes, her eyes dancing in delight at his predicament. "Maybe if you were a good boy they'd let you out to play more often." The others giggle and cackle, hiding sharp-toothed smiles behind hands.

"You're not supposed to be down here," Armand says coldly.

Her eyebrow arches. "Yes, Armand, *you* should give *me* pointers on what I should and should not do." The others don't bother to try to hide their glee any more, the laughter bubbles free.

"If zi-Hilo finds out–"

She lets out a trilling laugh. "Why don't you tell him then? Oh wait, you can't get out, can you?" She smiles meanly. "Pity." She sashays back over to me. Armand takes a step forward, but stops. There's nothing he can do.

She stares, contemplating my face. "You're a pretty little thing, aren't you? Not surprising really, your father..." She sighs in ecstasy and holds her hand to her chest. "But I see your mother in there too." She slides a slender white hand between the bars and tries to caress my face. I move like lightning and almost bite her finger off. She pulls back and eyes me sourly. I smile and bat my eyes.

"How do you like your accommodations? These dungeons are a sort of a hand-me-down of hers, from mother to daughter. How sweet." She pauses as though to think, exaggeratedly cocking her head and tapping a shiny black fingernail on her chin. "Though she was over there, with your friends." She waves in their direction. I hold still but she doesn't elaborate why.

I don't want the others to know what I am, even if we never escape. Even if we die. I don't want to watch their expressions change, horror and hate replacing the friendship. Fear *for* me replaced by fear *of* me.

If I die, I want someone to mourn.

"Speaking of your friends..." She trails off and her smile is full of things I'm afraid of. My blood turns to ice, my heartbeat races, my knees rebel. A flood of fear douses my desert; I can't stay silent.

"If you touch them..." I growl, but no threat has ever been emptier. Her smile says she knows it. Wild fantasies of ripping the bars free, then ripping her smile free of her face, dance through my brain. Kicking, biting, pulling, twisting, ripping, ripping and ripping. *Fighting*. But I can do nothing. I am trapped, helpless.

Her smile spreads wider and she wiggles her fingers at me. "Too-da-loo."

I pant in my hate. In my fear.

They stroll, painfully slowly, towards my friends' cage, taunting us all, giving us time to think about what's going to happen. Serena tosses smiling glances over her shoulder, at me, drinking in my hate, my fear, my helplessness. Armand says my name, but I ignore him. His tone hasn't the urgency of a plan, just soft notes of attempted comfort. Those are useless to me.

The demons sniff the air, murmuring appreciatively, and their movements become more energetic. A pack of bloodhounds, excited by the scent. They begin to dance and circle the cage, and, to my surprise, touch it. I look to Armand.

"Templar cages are for Templars, not demons." His voice is tight.

The bars won't keep my friends safe. My breath comes in horrified pants. Shallow and fast.

The giggling demons lean into the bars, reaching out to pinch, grab and claw. It's a game to them. The cage must also weaken my friends because they can't keep up, can't dodge all the hands. Nails slash across Jo's arm and I scream with her. Something inside me snaps and I scream and rant and rage – but I can do nothing but add to the cacophony. I shut my eyes and drop to my knees, only to open them again and crawl forward. I can't watch, but I can't do anything else.

Blood splashes on the black glass floor and the demons become frenzied. They yip and jump and dance.

One grabs hold of Chi and jerks him into the bars. Jo tries to rescue him and she's caught as well. The demons pin them to the electrified bars where Chi and Jo can do nothing but seize and bleed.

A demon with a too-bright grin twists on the prison door handle and it opens under his hands. Three demons slide into the small space. Uri fights and scrambles, but there's nowhere to go.

They drag Uri out. I stop breathing.

They lock the door behind them. They have no plans to put him back.

The demons release Jo and Chi and they collapse on the ground, but not for long. They jump to their feet and lunge and scream, slamming into the fence, taking shock after shock. All my shocks are internal. An unseen hand creeps into my chest and mangles my heart. Squeezes it like a chew toy, ringing out warped sounds of protest. Rubs it raw, beats it soft – into a squishy pulp. It was so tender and young, it didn't stand a chance.

Uri stops struggling long enough to look to me. His ancient eyes lock me into place and I stand frozen as he mouths. "No regrets."

My heart starts beating again, in painful lurches. It's crippled, twisted and weak, but it will beat for him, for his last minutes alive.

"Give 'em hell," I mouth back. Uri grins and then goes berserk, clawing and kicking and fighting. A demon screams in pain and drops from the herd not to move again. Still, they pull him down the stairs, scuttling with their small prize like a herd of ants carrying their catch below.

It is horrific to listen to Uri scream.

But it is worse when he stops.

Eighteen

The world is dim and my ears are filled with the limitless sound of the ocean. I am painted in black; a hole gapes where my heart should be. I try to put my hand in it, but it feels solid.

"Meda!" hisses a voice, snapping the world into focus. "Meda!" I blink and the room sharpens. A shattered version of myself stares back, my reflection on the shiny ceiling. "I told you not to touch the bars!" I turn. Armand.

I vaguely remember now, throwing myself at the bars, to get to Uri.

Violent sobs fill my ears, but they aren't mine. I'm numb. I push myself up until I'm sitting, shaking my head to drain out the sea. The sobs are Jo's. She's bent double on the floor of her cell, rocking in rhythm to the sad soundtrack of her own making. Chi has checked out. Even from here I can see the dead look in his eyes, the shiny tracks of tears.

Jo screams as loud as she can into the ground and that snaps Chi out of his trance. He crouches to curl his arm around Jo. She shoves him off violently, knocking him to the floor and jumps to her feet.

"Have you had enough *adventure* yet?" she screams at him.

"Jo." He stands and reaches for her but she shoves him away, then she hits him. A wild swing he easily could have dodged.

She takes two staggering steps away from him, her palms pressed into her eyes. Then she whirls to face him again. "Is this what you wanted?" Violent tears course down her face. "He was just a kid. He never should have been here – *we* never should have been here!" She flies at him but her leg gives out and she collapses against his chest. Still, she tries to hit him again, but he wraps his arms around her – not to hold her back, but just to hold her. Her rage dissolves into tears. They run down her face, little rivulets of sadness that escape from the raging torrent flooding through her heart.

I can't see Chi's face; it's buried in her hair. His broad shoulders shake. He holds her while they cry.

I stand in my cell, alone.

"He could still be alive," Chi whispers brokenly, his arms wrapped so far around her he nearly hugs himself as well.

"He's not," Jo says, her voice as dead as Uri's. Even now, she's willing to face the hard truth.

And she's right. Uri is dead, because I'm looking at him. His soul, stripped of life, creeps up the stairs, shining with a brilliance that hurts my demon-dark eyes. His face crumbles as he watches Jo and Chi. He takes a step towards them, then pauses and cocks his head as if someone whispers in his ear. He grins. Then he turns and shoots me a jaunty little wave before exploding into the sky like a firework, soaring straight towards Heaven.

With Uri's light extinguished, the next hours are very dark.

When the doors open again, they come for me. There are six of them, but unlike the last party of naughty teenagers, these scuttle silently. Jo and Chi are yelling in defiance, but they might as well be tree frogs for all the attention they're paid.

When the demons reach my cell, I'm ready for them, a seething pool of bubbling rage. I snarl and hiss and prepare to attack. The hate in the hole where Uri used to be roars. But the one in the lead waves his hands and I am frozen stiff. I can do nothing as they chain my arms behind my back and haul me out of the cage. Once I'm free of the bars a rush of demon strength pours through my veins, I am unfrozen but I cannot break the bindings, though I try. I thrash and kick and scream. As I go, my eyes meet Armand's.

Give in, he mouths, as they drag me away. I bare my teeth in response.

The demons force-march me up the twisting stairs, their hands wrapped so tightly around my upper arms that their nails dig in. I jerk and twist, trying to toss at least one off the stairs. I crave the crack of skull on stone, but they stay steadily by my side. At the top of the stairs stretches a hallway, but I can't see where it leads because it twists and undulates like a snake. The ceiling arcs over us like that of a cathedral, supported by stone pillars and painted in a richly-hued fresco – a macabre version of the Sistine Chapel. Sconces illuminate it from below, dramatically highlighting some spots while leaving some parts sneakily in shadow. I don't study the mural, but my brief glance captures beautiful monsters, fire and writhing humans. Teeth seem to be a prominent theme.

More hallways branch off ours and high-ceilinged rooms are visible through arched doors. My dishonor guard scuttles and crawls around me; the echo of our feet on the marble floor sounds like a drumbeat, like the bum-da-da-drum beat-out before an execution.

We turn off into another smaller tunnel, then a few more. Hall after hall looks the same and they twist and turn, climbing up and down, making it impossible to keep my bearings. Still, I optimistically try to memorize the way, in case I escape. Finally we come to a hall that is nothing like the others. It's rectangular and small, and looks like it was hewn straight from stone. The walls are rough, more cave than hallway. It slants downwards steadily, and the air gets a little cooler.

At its bottom is a rusty, round metal door with a barred window in its center. It's padlocked, but one of the demons, an androgynous creature in a crooked suit and heavy eyeliner, unlocks it with an iron skeleton key. It swings outwards, revealing a long stone tunnel. I can't see the other end from where I stand.

I start fighting again in earnest. It's pointless, six on one and with me bound, but I'm not one to make things easy. I arch hard and catch a woman on the nose with my head. Her nose crunches and she squeals. I smile at the sound. They may have the last laugh, but I'll have this one. Two more demons replace her and they throw me into the tunnel backwards. I land hard on my bound hands, as they slam and lock the door. Again I'm caged.

I rock off my hands and realize the cuffs are gone. They just dissolved from my wrists. Demon magic at work. I jump to my feet and I push on the door. I shove with all my might but it doesn't give. I scream at my escorts on the other side, but they stand impassive. I twist and take in my surroundings, looking for another exit. At the tunnel's mouth, the endless black is alleviated by curtains outlined in light.

I don't want to go towards the light. Seems like a bad idea, but I have no choice.

I can hear them now. Hissing and burbling. Giddy squeals. The crowd – not human, I realize, but a demon mob – awaits my arrival. Whatever they have planned for me will be a public spectacle.

I clench my fists and think of Uri. I will give them a show they will never forget.

I stride towards the curtains. With each step my outfit morphs and dissolves. My bloody shirt and ripped jeans are exchanged for a black ball gown that billows and swishes behind me. Like everything down here, its beauty is dark, sensual and wrong. The silk slithers and strokes, the beads are metal studs, the netted edges are uneven – torn, not cut. I am looking through a little veil on a cap like one would wear to a funeral. Not inappropriate, but usually the corpse doesn't wear it. My footsteps on the obsidian floor turn from thuds to clicks as my sneakers become heels. I don't stumble, I am too powerful, too graceful with the flood of demon energy. I am a sacrificial lamb dressed appropriately for the ceremony. But I am not a lamb – there's a reason it has never been "sacrificial wolf". My heart pumps. That dark side of me ignores the whole sacrifice part and focuses excitedly on being the wolf.

I reach the tunnel's end and pause. The Hunger's ready for the bloodbath, but the rest of me is not. There must have been a signal on the other side because the crowd hushes. All is silent, but for the thud of a heart beating its last in my ears and harsh breathing I realize is my own. I think of Uri. I think of revenge and my breath comes under control. I will die, but I will make them pay.

The black curtains swish open for my final act.

The lights are blinding and the crowd is deafening. They stomp, cheer and whistle. I blink and my eyes adjust. I'm center stage in an enormous arena. Seats tower around me, several storeys high, wrapping all around the circular floor where I stand. They teem with hundreds of demons, a roiling sea of black and white with brilliant spots of red. The floor is an intricate pattern of black, grey and white marble. On the far side of the arena, seated on a raised ebony throne, is the handsomest man I've ever seen. He looks near forty, but has the strong jaw and full hair of a younger man. He rests on the throne with the easy, confident posture of someone who gets what he wants. Elegant white stripes streak from his temples and, on his head, a steel and obsidian crown twists and stabs the sky. He stands at my arrival, rising fluidly to his feet, and strides forward, his black silk robe billowing behind him. He's magnetic, dazzling.

I crouch and snarl. I will rip his crowned head from his shoulders.

He stops mere feet away and extends his hands.

"Welcome home, daughter."

The crowd goes insane.

Not exactly what I'm expecting. It confuses me out of my crouch. "Daughter?" the word whispers out unbidden. I search the man's face, but other than the white skin and dark demon eyes, I find nothing in his face of me. He smiles. Do I smile like that? I don't know. My father. I have a father. A father who murdered my friend.

Uri.

Not my father – a sperm donor.

"We've had quite the time finding you." Laughingly disapproving. *I am such a naughty girl, aren't I, Daddy?*

"How did you find me?" I stall so I can think. I don't really care how they found me. It's done and I'm here.

"Your blood. Hal-Karim tasted it the night you met."

The demon that licked me. Was it only a few days ago?

"The sense of it was fading, as it does, so we lost you until you showed up in DC." He smiles. "It's destiny that you came here while he could still sense you."

Destiny or stupidity. "You kidnapped me."

"No. You aren't our hostage. You're our guest." He waves his arms expansively and the crowd burbles.

"Ah, well, I was confused by the whole room-with-bars. Do you usually keep guests in the dungeon?"

He chuckles. I'm so cute. He raises his perfect eyebrows. "Would you have stayed otherwise?" *No.* "I needed a chance to explain."

"You killed my friend." Uri – my heart is his gravestone. His name is carved there.

To my surprise, the demon frowns and shakes his head. "I'm sorry about that. I didn't know what they were planning." His eyes are as soft as their darkness will allow. "But you have to understand – he killed friends of those who killed him. You know how hard it can be to resist revenge."

Oh, I know. My nails dig into my palms.

"They wanted to go after the rest of your friends, but once I found out, I put a stop to it." He shows his teeth. "They were punished."

He stopped them from killing Chi and Jo? "Why?"

"Why? I feel like that should be obvious by now, Meda. I don't want to hurt you. You belong with us, your family. Your kind."

I think of Uri. I understand the demons' motivation – I pulsate with it. But I've never been empathetic. I'm hurting, my friend is dead. I understand, but I don't care. I'm still angry. "No, I don't."

"Don't you, Meda?" He cocks his head. "Then where do you belong?"

"With my mother's people." But that isn't true either. I don't belong anywhere. "It's great to meet you after all these years, Pops, but you're a little late."

"Meda." He shakes his head. "I never abandoned you, I never knew about you." His Beautiful eyes plead for me to understand. "She didn't tell me – she just took off when she…" his mouth twists, "got what she wanted. We only just found out about you two years ago. A place was destroyed by a great deal of demon power, we went to investigate. It was your home, Meda. I recognized Mary… and you. We've been searching for you desperately since."

They've been searching for me desperately for two years? A light explodes to life in my head – the big thing the demons are looking for is me. For a half-second I wonder if it's because he wanted to find his daughter, and not because I'm a half-Templar.

But then I remember that it doesn't matter. It wouldn't matter if he cut off a limb for me. Mom was the guiding star in my life. She wouldn't want me to go with him. She hid me from him for years.

"No."

"Meda, you belong with us." His voice is stern now, as if explaining the obvious to a child. "Surely you know that. Your own nature screams for it. Don't make me remind you."

Remind me?

Suddenly the low burn that is my Hunger bursts to life with an intensity I have only felt once before. It beats, pulses and pounds through my veins. The crocodile becomes a dragon thrashing under my skin. The ravenous ache is all I can think about. My skin can't contain it, my mind can't stop it. It pulls my body into a stiff arch, my elbows lock, my knees turn to stone. It scorches along the web of nerve endings until every inch of my skin is on fire. I would peel it from my bones if it would end the pain.

But zi-Hilo is asking for something so much less.

"Beloved daughter, don't make me ask this way."

Then the fire has gone, as suddenly as a blown-out candle. I'm left weak and panting, but I no longer want to rip the skin from my body. That's something at least.

His voice is soothing, cool after the fire. "You can't tell me you aren't one of us. The Hunger won't let you lie."

"Some," I pant, "way to show you care, Pops." Pain always pisses me off.

"You need to remember who you are, Meda. You're not one of them." He puts his hands behind his back and paces in an arch around me – but stays out of reach. Clever man. I turn away to show my disrespect, but follow him from the corner of my eye.

His voice changes from stern father to enticing salesman. "And, Meda, we can make it go away. Forever. No longer would you be a slave to your Hunger."

I can't help it, I look up at that.

He half-smiles. "Everyone here, Meda, is plugged into the source. We've a direct line to the afterlife. We're constantly fed; we never feel the need, the pain. We're never forced to murder." His eyes crinkle charmingly at the corners. "Although sometimes we can't resist." The crowd chuckles.

Hungry, Hungry, Hungry. The word dances through my head. The intense, screaming agony is gone, but the Hunger is not. It's banked but hot.

"And Meda, if you don't join us, we can't let you go. You're too dangerous." He pauses. "But I could never kill my daughter."

I shiver. His words are sweet, the intent is not. I will be locked here forever, not plugged in. Daddy's a shrewd negotiator. He showed me a preview of what I will eventually suffer. Locked up, no source of "food". Eventually I wouldn't be able to help myself. I would join to make the agony end. I would have no choice.

"No." The stupid word comes out.

"Why are you being so stubborn?"

I don't answer him. I owe him for nothing but a set of chromosomes. Somehow he knows why, anyway.

"It's your mother, isn't it? She turned you against me."

I almost laugh. It sounds like such a normal, divorced-parent complaint.

"Meda, I didn't want to have to share this with you, but…" He shakes his head in regret. He suddenly waves his arm. I duck instinctively.

"Meda, I'm not going to hurt you." He acts surprised at my reflexive cowering, like I should know he wouldn't hurt me. I try to pull myself together enough to give him the snotty face he deserves, but his next words steal all interest in that. "At least, not physically."

I don't like the sound of that.

A movement from above his now-empty throne calls my attention. A projection screen suspended on thin cables is descending from the ceiling. Some of the demons clap, excited for whatever show is to begin. There's some squealing as those seated behind the screen climb over others to try to get to a place where they can see. Light shines off their shiny silks and satins as they move. My father raises his hand and they go quiet and still.

"I think there's a lot you don't know about your mother," he says to me. "She was a guest of ours eighteen years ago. Captured and held captive. She succumbed to the charms of an incubus." He waves at himself, then his face twists. "Or so we thought." I don't know what he's saying. My mom didn't sleep with him? I'm not half-demon?

"But she didn't succumb, Meda. She *seduced*." He pauses, giving the information a chance to sink in. He's wasting his time, because I won't believe it. Mom? Seduce a demon? It doesn't make any sense.

He continues. "She wanted to see what would happen if there was a child. She always had an interest in science, you see." As if I don't know my own mother. "The old scientific debate of nature over nurture put to the test. Her hypothesis: A child of both Templar and demon could be raised to be good, but with the powers of a demon – the ultimate weapon in the battle of good versus evil."

He looks at me and I realize I'm shaking my head. I'm not a science experiment. Mom loved me.

"Don't believe me?" Again he looks sad, like he's actually sorry to break my heart. "When that building collapsed we sent people to investigate. They found a library of these." He waves his hand and a woman's face pops up on the screen.

"April fourth, 1999," she begins in a crisp professional tone. "Subject is four years and eleven months old.

Height 112 cm, the seventy-fifth percentile, weight eighteen kilograms, fiftieth percentile. Advanced coordination, but no physical manifestation of demon or Templar heritage." She continues with a rundown of diet and sleep habits, a breakdown of daily activities. Then she takes a deep breath and continues:

"There has been a setback in socialization. Risk to innocents has caused me to end it early. After four days in preschool, subject has shown an unusual amount of aggression towards another student…"

The face is my mother's. The subject is me. I shake my head. I don't want to believe it. This isn't a home video of a beloved child. This is a record of an experiment.

My father speeds ahead to another clip.

"Subject responds favorably to affectionate touching, but does not return hugs nor initiate any on her own. Will increase efforts and see if she can be trained to demonstrate human affection." I watch her mouth move, making familiar shapes. This is the mom I remember, not the laughing girl from the Templars' shrine. But at the same time, she's not what I remember at all.

Fast forward again.

"August seventeenth, 2003. Subject is eight years and three months old." Again there is the rundown of tedium. Then tension enters her eyes. "Subject demonstrates superhuman strength, beyond that even of a Templar. She lifted twelve repetitions of thirty-six kilograms. Subject also ran one kilometer in two minutes and twenty-seven seconds." Slight hesitation. "Faster than the women's international record.

"Subject's skin has taken on a metallic density; however, nails and hair are still human. She has a voracious hunger and I have increased her diet again, to a total of 2,200 calories a day. I am beginning to fear she may have a demon's appetite." She bites her lip. "The neighbor's dog disappeared a week ago accompanied by a sudden drop in the subject's appetite."

I ate him. He wasn't the first, but the first time I'd gotten caught.

He speeds forward again and I close my eyes. I don't want to see any more, but I can still hear.

"June fourteenth, 2004. Subject is nine years and one month old..."

"Stop it," I say.

"Height 141 cm, ninetieth percentile. Weight twenty-eight kilograms, fiftieth percentile. Caloric intake 2,600. Subject was introduced to a neighborhood cat..."

"Stop it!"

The recording stops, but my thoughts don't.

For a half-second I think it is some demon's trick, that they made it up. I cling desperately but it dissolves under the weight of reality. All the facts she listed were true. They couldn't manufacture such specifics.

Here I thought she was some rape victim who loved me so much she overcame the disgust. But that wasn't it at all. Not even close. I was a project, a weapon for the Templars. Hadn't I seen what they were willing to do, willing to sacrifice to win? Nothing matters as much as defeating the demons. Not even their own children; they are raised to be cannon fodder.

Pain lashes and stabs. My humanity is shredded. I was not her baby. I was her lab rat. None of it was real.

Subject does not respond to affectionate touching... will increase attempts to see if she can be trained...

My eyes snap open. It's not the lab rat's fault if the scientist's careless and gets bitten. The guilt-ridden ties that kept me chained to my mother unravel like rotten, rat-chewed rope. I am cast adrift on the violent sea of my rage, storm-tossed.

For the first time I am free.

Half evil, half human. *But humans aren't exactly good, are they?* Armand asked.

No, they aren't. I inherited monstrousness from both sides of my family tree. It is time to embrace it.

I arch my back, open my arms wide and screech at the ceiling. Screech, because something has to give, I don't have the control to stand there stoic and bear it.

The seething crowd screeches its delight back, bubbling with excitement. They want this, maybe more than I do. For me it is an escape from the pain. For them it is a future opened. They have been waiting to see which team the star player will choose.

I spin and swirl as they stomp and scream. I am flooded with hate, with rage. They are the soundtrack to my own vileness. I am not my mother's naughty child, I am Daddy's little girl. A princess of Hell.

"Now you see, Meda," Father says, his eyes alight. He's as excited as everyone else. "It was all a lie. Be as you are meant to be." He waves at someone and four demons drag some blindfolded humans from the tunnel behind me. I smell them before I see them. Smell their essence, their souls. Because I am denying myself nothing any more. I am a demon and I am Hungry.

The humans struggle and scream, and their fear scents the air. Their hate gives it a delicious, cinnamony edge. I will bathe in their screams and paint the walls with their blood. I hope my mother is watching. I hope she knows how horrifically her experiment failed.

The crowd chants. "Meda, Meda!" The pain, the excitement, the soon-to-happen action is what they crave. The bloodlust is taking over and already sensual creatures are slithering and sliding in near-sexual anticipation, a pool of writhing eels. I crouch and slither and scuttle. My dear daddy chortles in delight and raises his hands to incite the crowd to a fever pitch.

Two obsidian tiles rise slowly to become posts in the center of the room. The humans are chained to them, center stage, a mere dozen paces from where I stand. Their escorts step back a couple of paces, leaving a clear path between me and the humans.

My father lifts his hands and the room falls silent, but the frenetic energy is still palpable. Our audience is tense, each demon perches on the edge of their chair. I look at their faces, fanged and excited. A mirror, a thousand times, of my own.

"Meda – a gift, and a sign of your fealty!" Father says. The humans.

Oh, Daddy, I would be delighted. I prance over. The humans fight their chains, jerking as hard as they can. They shake their blindfolds free. Good. Now we can all see.

Something beats against the crazy rage of my mind, gentle butterfly wings pound as hard as they can to get in. But I have no interest in butterflies.

I run my claw – and it is a claw, though it might look like a weak, human hand – along the jaw of the human female, drinking her fear and meeting her eyes.

Then the butterfly's wings bang, and I know what the pretty creature is trying to make me realize.

I know those eyes. They're Jo's.

A wave rolls in, dousing the fire. I'm left trembling and cold.

"Meda, what's happening?" Jo, panicked, twists and the scent of her fear washes over me, almost firing me back up. I have to force myself to step away. "Meda?"

"Meda? What's the matter, dear?" It's my father. The crowd hisses and boos, but he silences them with a wave. I take another careful, controlled step away from Jo. The animalistic part of me, the part that thought it was finally free, fights caging. "Meda?"

"Meda?" Chi.

"Meda?" Jo.

They all want answers. Father thought I was won. Jo and Chi don't understand what's happening. They want answers, but I don't have any. I'm a reeling wreck. I meet Jo's tear-red eyes, then Chi's disillusioned ones. I don't have the words.

"Meda." My father now, commanding in tone. Going to tell me to eat my vegetables? "This is how you prove yourself," he says.

I never took well to being told what to do.

"My friends." My tongue is heavy, my voice is thick.

"No, Meda, they aren't." Back to the calming, loving father. The one that just wants the best for his little girl.

"Yes, we are, you evil, stinking–" A demon silences Jo. Painfully.

"No, Meda, they aren't. They don't even know you, don't know what you are, how can they be your friends?"

"Yes, we do." Chi, bold and heroic, if a little shaky. "Meda, I don't know what's going on here, but–"

"Shall we tell them what's going on, Meda?" Daddy asks. The crowd roars its approval. He waves again and the screen flickers back to life. It's my mother and I recognize the room behind her.

No.

I lock my knees because I have no doubt I will collapse if I don't.

No! But my mouth opens and closes silently.

"May fifteenth, 2009. Subject is fourteen years and eleven months old."

I scream and dive forward trying to stop what is about to happen. I can't watch it, I can't bear it. I'm hauled back by demons I didn't even know were behind me. A pair of Chi and Jo's escorts are now restraining me.

"Meda, what's happening?" Jo's voice trembles.

I don't answer. I can't answer. The face on the screen continues to talk, giving the details of the half-Templar, half-demon's abilities.

"You need to see this. You need to remember what you are," my father says.

"I'm half human," I say numbly. I try to make that matter.

"Half... Meda." Chi still doesn't get it. "Templars are human."

Jo is starting to. Her voice is edged in panic. "Meda, who is that?"

She already knows, but I answer anyway. "My mom." I don't watch her face as the ramifications hit. I don't want to.

My father's voice cuts in, calm and soothing. "You're not one of them, but I think you know that." I look away from the screen. We're not to the good part yet, anyway. My father's eyes are full of understanding. "It might be fun to play that way. We've all had our human moments. But they aren't real. They aren't permanent."

"I'm half human." I say it again.

"I'm not talking about your lineage. I am talking about a person's soul, some are just... dark, Meda. Most of the demons here were full humans." He waves to the crowd and there's a murmur of agreement. "But their souls have always belonged below. Because they are capable of truly horrific things. They're not wrong, Meda, the things you've done, the things you want. They are quite normal. Here."

Jo's screaming and Chi's shouting. Their two guards silence them so we can all watch the home movie.

My mom continues, her tone crisp and professional. "The subject has been interested in interacting with other humans. She is... lonely, I think." She pauses for a half-beat, her eyes downcast, but then the scientist is back. She clears her throat. "A commendably human emotion. I have hope that we can conquer her darker side, that she can be permitted to interact with others her age. She was too young before. Children don't have that kind of control, but at this age the subject should be old enough to…" My father fast-forwards.

"The subject hasn't had access to her secondary food source in over five weeks, but I can't delay her much longer without restraints…" Again my father fast-forwards. Apparently that's not what he's looking for. In speed-motion, my mother brings a younger me on to the screen. Jo starts thrashing, all her questions conclusively answered. I was younger then, plumper, with long shiny hair, but it's me.

My mother's talking to me, but he doesn't play that for us. He doesn't need to in my case, I remember. "We're going to beat this thing. Meda, you can do it. Just get past it." And other encouraging nonsense. Like my evilness is a cigarette addiction and I'm the Little Engine That Could. I try to fight her and go for the door. She holds me and pleads with me and I struggle. Then I give in. I always gave in to anything she asked. She was my world.

My father explains. "We're going to watch this in fast forward, as it takes quite some time."

Three days. It took three days. After two, I begged her to chain me to the wall so I didn't rip her to shreds. She gave in and did so. We watch it.

But in the end, the chains couldn't stop me.

Someone is screaming and begging for it to stop. The pain in my throat says it's me. I beg him not to make me watch.

In the video, I thrash against my restraints, and it could be a mirror because I'm thrashing against the restraining arms now, too.

"Please!" I scream.

I ripped the chains from the wall. I dove at my cowering mother.

My father pauses. If only I could have paused it in real life and just been suspended there, in mid-air, with her forever.

"Fine, Meda. But tell us what happens. Tell your friends what you did." Anything. Anything to make it stop. There's no reason not to.

"I killed her," I whisper. Dead.

"How?" he asks.

"I ripped her to pieces."

I hear Jo keening below the muzzling hand. I hear her chains rattle as she fights her restraints.

"Meda," my father whispers. He's a breath away from me. I stare into those demon-dark eyes. "You belong here. Don't you see?"

"I see."

"Your mother didn't love you. Let go of the guilt, embrace what you are."

"I am a demon."

"And your friends…" He trails off and we both turn to Chi and Jo. The demons release them and Chi starts talking instantly, unfazed by what he just saw.

"Meda, don't listen to them. You're not one of them. You're good–" Chi, foolish Chi. My father jerks his head and Chi is muzzled again, gagged with a cloth. Daddy doesn't want me to hear Chi's encouragement, as if it might sway me. He needn't worry. Chi's faith means nothing, because it has nothing to do with me. Chi's faith is blind. He doesn't see me. But Jo does.

Jo always has.

I meet her eyes. They burn with hazel-colored hate. Her voice is controlled and I see why – she has one tiny drop of hope left. Still she doesn't meet my eyes as she asks, they turn to the floor. "You knew all along?"

I squash it heartlessly. What's the point in lying? "Yes."

"At the school, all those kids died for you... you killed them." She can't digest it, doesn't want to believe.

Both sides of my family tree are monstrous, so why do I fight it? We just watched the proof that I will fail. No matter what, or who, is at stake.

I smile and it's all teeth. "Indirectly, but yes, I suppose you could say so."

It's dawning, a dark sun in Jo's soul. She says the last, the most damning accusation of all, in all our estimations. She meets my eyes for this one, and they beg for the lie.

"Uri died for you."

My heart is not Uri's gravestone. I am heartless, entirely made of stone. "Yes."

She jerks at her chains and screams. Profanity and insanity pour out of her mouth and I ride it like a wave.

"These are your friends, Meda?" My father, enticing again. "Why do you hold back?" The crowd is chanting and screaming again. The sound is sharp, yet rhythmic, almost musical. "End it, Meda. End it and join us. Everything you've done is a thing to be celebrated here, not hated."

Not hated. Freedom from my own self-hatred.

"Just end it, Meda." He waves at Jo.

End it. The roar of the crowd surges me forward. Jo's chained, but still she lunges. She's at the end of her leash, hate streaming off her in waves. I pause, inches away from her snarling face. Her eyes are red from crying. Crying for Uri. Even as I watch, more tears erupt as she shouts horrible things at me.

A surge of Hunger rolls over me, it burns and sears. Dear old Dad is concerned I'm on the fence. He is reminding me that eventually I won't be able to control it, and I will slaughter them anyway, only this time it would be after hours, maybe days, of agony.

And in exchange for killing them, I will live forever, never face my final reckoning. My past is filled with things I would rather not be held accountable for. Sell my soul, never be Hungry again, never die: the pain will be over. No more self-hate. Even if I wanted to, I can't help them. I need to look after myself.

Dear Daddy doesn't need to worry. When have I ever done anything else?

I lean in and drink in the scent of Jo's soul as she screams and fights and promises to rip my heart out. Her own heart thumps, swollen with sweet soul just begging to be set free and swallowed. I lean in…

But there, on her neck, is another heart. Cracked and made of tin. *Best*, its mate around my own neck.

Friend.

"I hate you! I HATE YOU!" she screams, spit rains down on my face, a shower of condemnation. I meet her swollen eyes for the last time, her eyelashes little daggers spiky with tears. The truth settles into my chest.

She's lying. I doubt she knows it, but she is. She isn't filled with hate. She's hurt. Hurt at Uri's loss, hurt at my betrayal. Salty sadness seeps from her eyes. Hate doesn't make tears, not like these.

And I notice then, that my own eyes are wet. I don't hate my mom, either. That's hurt, too. Because I love her, still. And even though Mom hurt me, she loved me, too. I know better than anyone how you can love someone and still hurt them.

"Fine," Jo screams, my favorite word. "Rip my heart out, you no-good *demon-ass-munching bitch*."

I laugh, she's always had a way with words. How could I kill a best friend who makes me laugh at a time like this?

"Demon ass-munching bitch? Really?" I hiss, inches away.

"And what do you think I should call you?" She casts a sneering glare at my necklace. "Friend?"

I grin, all teeth.

"Call me Doctor."

Nineteen

Time hangs.

We do nothing but blink at each other as the dust from my bomb settles. The world stands suspended as Jo and I think about life, death and friendship.

No regrets, Uri's last words. If I kill Jo and Chi, I may live forever and I may never be punished for what I've done, but I have no doubt that I will regret it. I'm angry that my mother treated me like a science experiment, but that's not all I was to her. And Jo and Uri and Chi mean more to me than just the means to an end.

They're my friends.

Doctor, I said, but I know Jo knows what I really mean. *Trust me*.

Jo told me the day we met that a knife in the chest is something completely different when a doctor's the one holding it. Because its wielder has good intentions. I now have her life in my hands, and I want her to know I have good intentions. Now. Finally.

But I already stuck a dagger in her heart with my lies. I, of all people, know she doesn't trust easily. I can see her choices battle it out in her eyes. Trust me or not? Am I her friend with the tin necklace, or am I an irredeemable demon? I don't blame her for having trouble believing the choice I just made. I'm having trouble believing it myself.

Our faces are frozen in snarls for our audience, but our eyes are pools of confusion.

And hope.

Another wave of Hunger washes like fire through my veins and I know what Dear Daddy is looking for. It's now or never.

I snarl and rip her chains free of the post. No longer chained, she leaps at me, tackling me to the ground, screaming profanities.

I hope she's pretending.

I laugh nastily and roll, so I'm on top, and slam her to the ground. She grunts as the wind is knocked out of her. The crowd is on its feet, screaming like South American fans whose team just won the World Cup.

I have my own reason to celebrate. Because, just barely audible over the demons' cheers, Jo whispers, "Hey, not so hard, asshole."

I try not to grin as Jo puts her hands on my shoulders and whispers the final words of the spell. The crowd's cheers start to falter, as they wonder why Jo isn't fighting back, why there's no blood. But the spell only takes fifteen seconds, not long enough for them to figure it out.

Then I feel warm, like I'm bathed in sunshine. Magnificent power swells under my skin, a sparkling warm-water wave. More power than when I am surrounded by demons, more beautiful than when I'm filled with a fresh soul. And I know it wants out, that I can't contain it all. I rise to my feet, pulling Jo with me.

I smile at my father. It's not a nice smile.

I explode in a blast of light. I see the truth register on his face just as the light swallows him.

I can't see anything, the light is too bright. Around me, I hear screams of both pain and rage. But the power doesn't hurt me and, as it fades, I see it doesn't hurt Jo either. The demons, though – it definitely hurt them. The ones in the front row took the brunt and the seats are filled with charred bodies.

Gee, I sure hope they hadn't paid extra.

The rest are still alive – hundreds of demons. They scream, no longer in joy and, after a minute of shocked hesitation, they come boiling over their fallen comrades, like a waterfall. Jo shoves me out of the way and makes for Chi, who is struggling against his chains and screaming for us around his gag.

Jo jerks at his chains, but they are made to contain a Templar and she gets nowhere. Nothing can contain me; I pull them apart as if they are made of tinfoil. Chi looks at me like he's never seen me before, his eyes wide with awe.

"Hey, Chi, sorry about the almost-eating-you thing," I say, hauling him to his feet.

He pulls off his gag and smiles. "No problem, I never thought you'd do it. You're a good person, Meda."

I smile back. He just might be right.

We run towards the tunnel we came through but the demons get there first, teeming over the low wall separating the spectators from the sport. We halt and spin but we're surrounded, trapped in the middle of the arena. This is the part that sucks about honorable sacrifice – the whole sacrifice part. The demons pace and circle, but none of them wants to be the first to attack. Jo slips her hand into mine and Chi does the same on the other side. They too, hold hands, a Bermuda Triangle in a sea of demons. We need a miracle to escape.

I feel the tension in their hands and I look at them. They're alight with the fierce energy they shared when we were surrounded at the school. I didn't get it then, now I do. I share it. We are going to die, but I'm going to get a piece of my own first. For Uri. For all my friends. I'm not saying I want to die. I'm not even saying that I'm ready to – after all, I think I'm just now getting the hang of this whole life thing. I'm just saying… well, Uri said it best. Better to die for something you believe in than to live for nothing at all.

"No regrets," I say and squeeze their hands.

"No regrets," Jo replies, returning the squeeze.

"No regrets," Chi repeats, then there's a tiny pause. "I always knew I'd die by your side, Jo – I just hoped it'd be in seventy years or so."

Jo's hand jerks in mine but she doesn't say anything. I look at her. Jo is actually rendered speechless.

A miracle, but not exactly the one I'm looking for, God.

"Now, Chi? You tell her this *now*?" I say.

His hand bounces in mine as he shrugs. "We said no regrets."

We did indeed.

The demons swarm. I'm stronger, faster, than they are, than I have ever felt. The small size of my hands shocks me, because I feel enormous. To my new eyes the demons seem so slow and clumsy, like toddlers. I am Godzilla – I mow them down like daisies in a field, Jo and Chi at my back.

Chi's not done. He grunts and ducks a demon's swing. "So Jo, you know I love you, right?"

Jo kicks out with her bad leg, catching a demon on the knee. He loses his balance and his head. "Chi, I..." Jo says and I recognize her "back-off" tone. The only thing more ridiculous than Chi choosing to tell her now, is her bothering to keep up the charade.

"Jo, we've got like a minute to live," I say, exasperated. I duck under a swinging arm and relieve its owner of his intestines. "I think you should tell him." Yes, I did just give love advice with a fistful of demon guts.

"Fine," Jo says, even though we are anything but fine. She dodges a demon's grab and hip-throws him in my direction. I give him a stay-down stomp. She pauses briefly to look at Chi, and I cover her back. She starts to respond when a demon dodges in on her left side. She ducks and rolls him across her back, and ends up shouting, "I love you too, Chi!"

Romantic, very romantic. Just like the movies. But it works for him – Chi grins, then ducks an attack, spins and kicks some guy's head off. You know, had I imagined a Chi–Jo love declaration, I would have pictured it amid demon decapitations. No sunset picnics for these two.

I'd like to say that we make our way free and despite all odds we manage to escape. But we don't. More come, unending. Jo starts to flag and I cover for her as they pile in, sensing our weakness. Chi takes a cut on his arm and he screams. My attention wavers and I lose a chunk of thigh. It starts to heal instantly, but it slows me. And still they come, swarming over the low wall from the seating area, flooding in from the hallways. Their screams and sneers turn to delighted laughs and cackles and I know the end is coming. Jo goes under with a scream. I haul her up and a demon jumps on me from behind. I pull his head off over my shoulder but his claws rake my face before he dies. Blood flows into my eyes, blinding me.

A demon tackles me from the side, my half-healed leg can't hold my weight and I go under. Black-clad bodies pile and writhe over me. I feel pieces of my skin being peeled away. Jo screams profanities and Chi cries out in pain.

I hope I'll see Uri, and I hope, I hope I'll see my mom.

As pain overtakes my body and numbs my mind, I strain to hear her voice over the laughs of my murderers. But I don't.

Instead, I hear the rumble of a hundred motorcycles.

Then I don't hear anything at all.

Twenty

I wake up. This in itself is news. On the other hand, I hurt so badly there's a good chance I'm in Hell. I don't recognize the ceiling I stare at, but then it's plain white, so who would? I make the effort to rock my head to the side but only manage a few inches before the pain is so bad I have to stop. I can see a window. It's sunny outside. That doesn't seem Hellish. The curtains, on the other hand… the artist in me winces. A mix of good and bad – I must be alive, among the humans. I smile. I black out.

When I wake up again, I know I am going to make it. I feel almost… well not *human* per se, but you see where I'm going. The room is mostly dark, but someone left the bathroom light on as a makeshift night light. I'm in a cheap hotel room – which explains the god-awful curtains – in a queen bed. Pill bottles, syringes, gauze and bandages clutter the nightstand. My arm is in a sling. I pull back the covers with my good arm and find I am naked except for my underwear and a ton of gauze. I'm more mummy than girl.

Water suddenly turns on in the bathroom and I scramble into a sitting position. I'm dizzy, but it doesn't slow me. I rip the sling from around my neck so my arm is free. My arm doesn't like it, but I prefer it stays attached and that's more likely if I can defend myself. I hope I'm with the Crusaders, but with demons you never know.

"Who's there?" I demand.

"You're awake?" I hear a female's voice before I see her. A slender woman comes out of the bathroom. I can see a blonde bob, but not much else, backlit as she is from the light of the bathroom. "Turn on the light," I say. She's taken aback by my tone, but flips the light on. She's in her mid-thirties, pretty, with light blue eyes. "Who are you?" I growl.

She smiles. Apparently in my current state I'm not much to fear. "I'm Caroline Dupaynes – Chi's sister." I see the resemblance instantly. I relax, then tense again.

"How is Chi? And Jo?"

"Good, they're fine. Awake already. The demons focused on you once you went down. Still, it was a near thing."

She doesn't need to tell me that. I was there.

"So, what did happen? How did you find us?"

She holds up her hand. "All your questions will be answered, I promise, but Jo threatened to gut me if I don't get her the instant you are awake."

My best friend is great.

Caroline disappears out of the door and I hear talking outside. I wonder if the person stationed there is to protect me or protect everyone else from me. They must know I'm a demon by now.

I hear Jo arguing with Chi before they even make it into the room. Caroline pushes Jo's wheelchair while Chi limps on crutches.

"Meda!" Jo says, as Caroline parks her next to my bed. Caroline then drags one of the chairs out to the hallway to give us some privacy.

"Hey, Jo. Glad to see you made it."

"Takes more than an army of demons to kill me."

"Naturally. Hey, Chi."

He grins. "Hey, Meda, looking..." he winces, then says, "alive." I stick my tongue out at him. "Alive" is about as much as I can say for either of them. They're also decked out in the latest in mummy-wear. In addition, Chi has a nasty row of stitches across his face, and Jo's good leg is in a cast. She follows my eyes and raises her eyebrows.

"Guess they thought it'd be funny if neither leg worked," she says, and I wince. "Nah, don't worry, doc said they got to it fast enough. It'll be fine. Until then, I'm stuck in this stupid chair while other people show off their crutches." She gives Chi the stink-eye, but she doesn't mean it.

Chi holds up his hands. "Hey, it's not my fault." Then he loses his grip on the crutches and they go crashing. Jo and I laugh. Things seem to have loosened up between the two of them. I look for evidence of happily-ever-after.

"You guys OK?" Caroline calls from the hallway. We all laugh harder. We're beaten, bruised and not a single one of us can stand up unassisted, but we are "OK".

"Fine!" Chi yells, and I laugh again. "Fine" about says it perfectly. Chi puts his hand on Jo's shoulder to balance himself and she jerks away. Chi doesn't seem bothered by her reaction, but it doesn't bode well for happily-ever-after.

"So, what happened?" I ask, then lower my voice. "Do they know what I am?"

Jo answers, still leaning away from Chi's hand. "Yeah. The Templars showed up – drove their motorcycles right into demon headquarters en masse. They started raining down holy water. I was still conscious enough to scream at them to stop." She meets my eyes, uncomfortably. "I had to tell them. As it was, if you hadn't been buried in demons, you'd probably be dead."

"Oh." I can tell she's worried about my reaction. "Well, maybe I should send the demons a thank-you card?"

She relaxes with a chuckle, tension broken. "Anyway, without the holy water, the battle got a lot closer. Then more demons came flooding in through the tunnels. The Crusaders just managed to haul us out of there and retreat." Her face gets tense. I don't ask how many died in our rescue.

"My dad?" I ask instead.

"Dead, we think," she says and watches me carefully. "It's hard to be sure, though. The Crusaders didn't have time to purify all the dead before more demons forced them out."

I shrug. Either way, he's just another demon to me. "How'd the Crusaders find us?"

Jo's and Chi's eyes meet. That rarely bodes well. "With the Beacon Map."

"The Beacon Map?"

"Yeah. They started looking for us when we didn't show up in Wisconsin. But, for some reason, we didn't show up on the map." Her eyes narrow briefly and my face gets warm. "Anyway, they thought we were dead, except the demons kept acting crazy. Something was going on, so they kept watching." I'm still not getting it. "Then they're watching the map, when all of a sudden a Beacon pops up out of nowhere, right inside the demon headquarters."

Beacon pops up right in demon headquarters... No.

"Who?"

Their eyes meet again. No, no, no.

"Who?"

Jo clears her throat. Oh no.

"You."

Sonofa– I collapse on to the pillows. I was just thinking I need more problems.

"This is good news, Meda," Jo insists.

"Yeah. Yet another reason for demons to hunt me down."

"On the bright side, it means the Templars won't kill you."

The look I give her must say it all, because she forces down a laugh.

"Well, without it, we would have died yesterday, so you can be grateful for that at least."

"When did you become so glass-half-full? Where's Angry Jo? We had so much more in common."

She laughs again. "She died five days ago."

"Hold a séance," I say crankily and she laughs harder.
I sigh. "So, what now?"

"Well, they haven't really told us. Sure, we saved the
day, but now we're back to being kids again." Chi this
time.

"And Luke?"

"He was here. They called him in for the attack on
the demon headquarters. But he had to get back to the
mysterious Exo. Apparently she lost her babysitter. He
agreed to come back and talk to you – but only you."

"So he knows?"

"We had to tell The Sarge what we were trying to
do when we got caught," Chi says, "but... Meda, Luke
already knew who you were. The instant we said your
name, he knew."

So my mom must have told him about me, which
meant they were still in contact, which means he might
know... But actually, it no longer really matters what
he knows. I mean sure, there are some things I would
like answers to, and there is more I would like to know
about my mom, but it's no longer life-and-death. I am a
Templar, I am a Beacon. I will be protected.

And as for my mom, whatever happened, whatever
her reasons were, they don't really matter anymore
other than as a way to know her better. She loved me,
no matter what, in her own way. And everyone has their
own way.

"When will I meet him?"

"As soon as you're feeling better, they're going to
recall him," Jo says.

"I'm better."

"I'm not going to argue," says Jo.

"You? Argue? Never."

I'm too battered to go anywhere, so we hang out in my room for the rest of the day, happy to be alive. Thanks to my new Crusader abilities, I'm already healing much faster than I would normally. I'm too beat up to tell if I gained any extra athleticism and, despite straining hard enough to nearly pop a blood vessel, I can't shoot any demon-killing light out of my hands, which is disappointing. Apparently the golden light that exploded from me at the demon headquarters always happens at the end of an Inheritance ceremony – it's just never been performed in a room full of demons so Jo had no idea it'd fry them like that.

Caroline continues to stand guard in the hallway, though she stops in to tell us Luke was informed I'm awake and will be here as soon as he can. Unfortunately, he's still trying to hunt down Exo and doesn't want to leave until she's found. Chi does his best to stay as close to Jo as possible, while she reacts like he has a repellent force field.

I kick the hornet's nest.

"So, what's the deal?" I look pointedly at the two of them. She's still in her wheelchair and he's sitting on the other bed, as close to her as possible.

Jo pretends innocence. "What do you mean?"

Chi ruins it by grabbing her hand, but she jerks it free. "Madly in love – can't you tell?"

Jo glares at him. "We are not."

Chi's unfazed. "Yes we are. You told me so yourself – can't backtrack now, darling."

She rolls her eyes. "I only said that because we were about to die."

"You meant it."

"No, I didn't. You begged me to say it."

Suddenly he swings from the bed and drops to his knee on the carpet – bandaged leg stuck out to the side, so they are face to face. "So you lied? You really didn't mean it?"

Jo's mouth opens and closes a few times. "I…"

"That's what I thought." He smiles and straightens back up and falls back on to the bed.

Once he's a little further away, Jo can apparently think again. "I meant it *at the time*. I thought we were going to die."

"Ah, so you only love me in deadly situations. Fine – I guess we'll just have to live dangerously. The way things are going, that shouldn't be hard."

Jo gusts in frustration, "Chi–"

"Yes, darling?"

"Stop calling me that!"

"Is there one you like better?"

"Yes! I mean, no. I mean, I'm not your 'darling'."

"All right – love of my life, but that's kind of a mouthful. One day, let's just shorten it to 'wife'."

Even I find that frightening, and it wasn't directed at me.

"Chi, stop it. I'm serious."

"So am I."

"Just stop it!" Jo shouts and tries to wheel backwards.

Chi's face gets serious. "Jo—"

"Stop it!" She awkwardly pushes at her chair wheels, and I think she might be on the verge of tears. She looks at me. "Help me – will you?" she snarls.

"Jo—" Chi starts again and Jo covers her ears. I push her out of the room. Once she's in the hallway, she shoves away from me. Caroline looks up from where she sits guard, baffled. I just shrug.

Chi's sprawled on the bed when I come back in, looking completely relaxed.

"That was kind of a dick thing to do," I say.

"She'll get over it. She's just trying to chase me off – for my own good. This time I won't be chased."

"Well, can't you at least wait until she is feeling better? She's in a wheelchair, for Christ's sake!"

"Are you kidding me? This is Jo we're talking about, the only person who could ever beat me. I need every advantage I can get."

"I thought you were trying to romance her. I didn't realize this is a war."

He laughs. "With Jo, it's gotta be both. A romantic assault." He puts his hands behind his head. "She wants what's best for me. I just need to make her realize that it's her."

And the drama continues.

Fortunately, Jo never figures out I outed her, so I'm cool with both my friends. The two of them continue their war – Chi marches on, an unstoppable juggernaut despite Jo's unrelenting cannon fire.

••••

Once we're healthy enough to travel, the three of us are packed into a van and shipped to West Virginia. With the school in Mountain Park compromised, the whole community is being relocated, but secretly. Now that the demons are willing to attack Crusader communities directly, they can't risk sending me to an existing school.

The Crusaders purchased a small valley in the mountains, on the top of another played-out coal mine. Apparently the escape tunnels worked so well they've decided to use that plan again. There's no school and, because of the secrecy, it's taking a while to move all the trailers and everyone in. The valley has a massive timber mill on one edge, hanging over a river and built into the side of the mountain in a series of ascending connected buildings like stair steps. It was built at least a hundred years ago and is half rotten – no, make that three-quarters rotten – and they're quickly renovating it to use as the school until a new, secure building can be built. It's hard to believe that there's a downgrade from Project Enlightenment.

When we arrive, the place is a hive of activity. Trailers are arriving and being put up, aluminum sheds constructed. Motorcycles roar day and night, but in small groups of three or four, so as to not draw attention. The older students have already arrived to help, but the younger ones have been sent to other communities until protections are in place. The students greet Chi and Jo, but I'm avoided or viewed with downright hostility. No one asks about Uri. They must know.

The adults have no idea what to do with me. As demon, Templar and Beacon, I am three times the average freak.

Apparently, the other chapters are being called to weigh in on the decision and, judging from the tone of the adults we come in contact with, this is not a good thing. Until then, I'm followed by guards. I point out I'm a Beacon, they point out that so was Einstein. Apparently, my destructive powers rival that of the atomic bomb.

But there's nothing we can do about it and, compared to demon prison, it seems like not much to worry about. We heal, and I am grateful for my new Templar abilities. Before the Inheritance it would have taken me months, not days, to recover from the injuries I'd received.

A week after I woke up, five days after we relocated to the new school, Luke finally arrives. But I don't speak to him. I have more important things to do. It's the day we hold a memorial for Uri.

There is no space large enough to fit everyone, so the ceremony is held outside in a field, at sunset. It's still early spring in the mountains, so it's chilly. The daffodils and crocuses have started to bloom and someone's gathered a near-mountain of them to place below Uri's memorial. Propped on an easel is a large wooden board, and at its center are a photo and a plaque, both illuminated by a silver-flamed candle resting on a small shelf.

Uriel James Green, 1998–2011. In the photograph they chose, Uri's got some crazy kung-fu pose going and he's grinning at the camera through his floppy hair. It feels out of place at the solemn event. It's perfect.

A eulogy is read, a prayer given. People step forward and mount their mementos, sometimes with an explanation, sometimes not. I have nothing to give him. The first friend I ever had, who died because of me, and I haven't a single token to give him. Nothing to mark our time together.

I cry. Tears flood and pour. I'm an ocean of sadness; my skin cannot contain it all. It drowns me, I can't breathe and my sobs have turned to gasps. There's no air. Suddenly Jo's at my side, holding my hand, and Chi's on the other. The ocean spreads between the three of us and I can breathe again. They don't say anything. We just stand together and mourn our friend.

Twenty-One

I'm sitting in the trailer I've been assigned, reading, when I hear arguing outside my door. Chi and Jo – who else? I pull myself up and head out into the living room, where my guard, Rebecca, sits reading a magazine. I give the middle-aged woman a polite nod and open the front door before they reach it.

"Hey, guys," I say, but am ignored.

"When will you get it through your thick head? I don't love you." Jo shoves him away.

"Nice to see you this fine morning," I add.

"As soon as it's true," Chi says to Jo, placidly.

"Hope you've had a good day so far." It's awfully uncomfortable not to exist.

Jo stops. "It *is* true." She turns to face him. "Listen. To. Me. I want us to be friends, but I have had it. I'm tired of your stupid games."

"Why, thank you, Meda," I answer myself since no one else is going to. "It's been lovely. And yourself?"

"That's fine with me, Jo," Chi says. "The last thing I plan on being is your friend." He grabs for her hand but she snatches it out of range, then gives him a shove. He grabs her wrists.

"I don't want to talk to you anymore," she says in desperation. "I don't want to see you ever again. Just leave me alone!" Her voice is high-pitched and frantic.

"Not gonna happen," he says easily. "Ever."

She jerks her wrists and he lets go. She opens her mouth, but closes it again. Her eyes are shiny. She looks to me (finally), but apparently doesn't know what to say there either. So she runs, or rather hobbles, as fast as her still-healing injuries will let her. Chi turns to me. "Hey, Meda."

"Looks like you're losing the war."

"Nah."

"Chi – I hate to break it to you, but she's been getting meaner and more upset – not less."

"That's because I'm getting to her. I'd be way more worried if she was calm. She's in retreat."

I am skeptical. "You sure?"

He smiles. "Yup." He's a madman, but, really, he's in love with Jo – it comes with the territory. "In any case, they want you in the admin trailer. We were gonna walk you there, but…"

Jo ran off in a fit.

"I'd still go, but, well…" He waves to where Jo went.

"She's in retreat," I supply.

"Exactly. I need to press my advantage."

"Got it," I say. Chi smiles in gratitude. "Good luck," I add. Rebecca apparently heard the conversation and is already standing, ready to escort me. We troop across the trailer park and listen for an announcement of Chi's death. None comes by the time I reach the admin trailer. The guard leaves me at the door.

Inside is a room with a bunch of tables and chairs. The trailer was used for meetings and as overflow space for people trying to organize the building of the new settlement. Right now it's empty but for a middle-aged man with sandy stick-up hair and a shell-shocked expression, leaning against a table.

Luke Bergeron. He's older, but I recognize him easily from the photos.

"Andromeda Porter," he murmurs. He straightens and wipes his hands on his dirty jeans.

"Melange," I correct him. "Meda Melange." My mother's name might have been Porter, but she gave me Melange. I'm not going to turn down any of her gifts.

"Right," he says, obviously unsure what to do with me.

I examine the man my mother considered marrying. Like most Templars I've met, he looks decidedly disreputable. Tall and lean with long hair, a full beard and a leather jacket with the Mountain Park insignia. If anything, he's even more disreputable than the average – the other Crusaders at least look as if they've thought about trimming their facial hair; he looks as if he's never even heard of the concept.

Noticing my regard, or maybe just because he wants to break the awkward silence, he explains, tugging his beard. "I'm undercover as a homeless person. To watch Exo."

"Oh." Scintillating. He has all the secrets of my past, and yet we talk about his hair. But he's a stranger. A strange stranger, and I don't know how to ask him about my mom. He gives me the same study.

"You look like her, you know?"

"No, I don't." My mom was girl-next-door sunshine. I am all darkness.

"Yes, you do. Not the hair color." His blue eyes crinkle in the corner. "And not in style, for sure. But your expressions – especially the one right now that tells me I'm full of it. That was your mom's favorite."

And just like that the dam is broken.

I don't know where to start. "Tell me everything."

"Your mom and I were best friends. Inseparable. She was..." Words fail him. I understand. "In any case, we were supposed to get married. Did you know that?"

I nod.

"Well, she was out on an assignment, during her apprenticeship, and they got her. Took her captive. I tried to rescue her – I swear I did." There's a hint of desperation in his eyes, like he needs me to believe him. I don't point out that if he'd succeeded, I wouldn't exist. "I would have marched into Hell itself for her, but the Crusaders wouldn't let me. They drugged me to keep me from doing anything stupid." He shook his head. "While I was in the hospital, her candle lit up. I was told she was dead. But I didn't believe it. I always thought that if she was, I'd know." He leans back against the table. I lean next to him.

"How did her candle light up?"

"You can renounce the Inheritance, after you've accepted it, and choose not to be a Crusader any more. You lose your special abilities and go back to being normal." He steeples his fingers and looks down at them. "Usually the candles of those people don't get a shrine. It doesn't really ever happen, and never by someone like your mom. She loved being a Crusader, it was her calling."

"If she loved it so much, why did she give it up?"

His soft blue eyes are on me. "She loved something more."

Me. He doesn't need to say it.

"She was afraid of what would happen to you. Afraid the Templars wouldn't listen, afraid they would make her give you up, or…" He shrugs. "We're not perfect, and you're possibly the biggest threat we've ever faced. Who knows what you're capable of?" He looks at me curiously. I don't really know what I'm capable of so it's not like I can answer.

He continues. "I found her, eventually. I tracked her down."

"How?"

"I knew her," is all he says. "She ran away from me." There is more in those words than I can describe. "But afterward, she made contact. We've talked over the last fifteen years. Mostly about you, Meda."

"Me?" My mom had a friend – a boyfriend? Someone she talked to, about me?

"You were her favorite subject. And she did it to protect you. She streamed me all her videos just in case anything ever happened to her. Or in case the Templars ever found the two of you. She wanted to have evidence of your character, of all the efforts she made to raise you to be good. Both her successes and her failures."

The science experiments were to protect me. Protect the world too, in case I turned out to be a monster, sure, but can you really fault a person for that? My eyes sting. They seem to be doing that a lot recently.

"Meda, I was watching the day…" his voice breaks.

I can't speak but I don't know what I would say, anyway.

He swipes his hand over his eyes. "In any case, I have something for you." He pulls a laptop out of a battered messenger bag. He turns and sets it on the table and opens it. He slides a chair for me to sit down in, then he starts a video. He doesn't sit, but stands next to me, his arms crossed.

On the screen appears my mother, in the basement room. I tense.

"Luke," she says and smiles. It's my smile. There's nothing businesslike about her in this video. "I want you to know I love you. I've always loved you." Luke turns his back to me, whether to give me privacy or him, I don't know. "What I've done to you hasn't been fair, and I'm sorry."

Her eyes are leveled at the camera. "This is even less fair."

She takes a deep breath before she continues. "I might be doing something dangerous today." Then she hurries forward. "I don't think it will be, I wouldn't do it if I thought it was. But just in case…" She takes another deep breath and stares straight into the camera. She has the look of a doctor about to deliver a terminal diagnosis – full of regret, but unable to change anything. "I want you to watch."

I hear a movement from Luke, but I don't take my eyes off the screen.

"I'm going to break Meda out of eating souls." She takes a deep breath and her eyes move back and forth as she thinks. "It's some sort of built-in addiction, and an addiction can be broken. She was too young to try before, but now she's fifteen. She's learning responsibility and willpower."

I remember Chi saying demons kill to get high. Mom didn't know it's the life that demons eat, not the soul. She didn't realize that the demons were constantly receiving life from Hell– "plugged in", as Daddy had said. She must have thought a demon's resurrection was a one-time thing, not a constant stream of "life". And how would she know? As Chi pointed out, they don't know much about halflings, other than the ones that play for Hell's team, and those'd be plugged in, too.

My mom spreads her hands on the table in front of her. "This will break her of her addiction once and for all. If there's any way for her not to hurt me, she won't. She's so human, so loving, you've seen it, Luke." She sets her jaw. "The demon side of her – she can overcome it. I don't want her to live her life carrying around this burden. Not if we can break the hold it has on her."

But we couldn't, or rather, *I* couldn't. I touch my fingers to her face.

She continues, her eyes are bright with hope. "And Luke, if I can break her of it, if I can *prove* it, she'll be safe from the Templars. Forever. And..." Her voice trembles. "And, maybe we can come home."

Home. Home to the Templars, to Luke. She waited the whole length of my existence to be able to go home, to escape her self-imposed isolation. The one she adopted for me.

"I'm not telling you this in person and I haven't called you in weeks, because I knew you'd figure out what I'm up to." She smiles slightly. "You probably have anyway and have been going crazy the last few weeks. I haven't checked my voicemail because I don't want you to try to talk me out of it.

"I know what I am doing. She loves me, Luke. She does. She'd never hurt me. But... if she does–" she looks dead at the camera and I see the tears shine in her eyes. "–find her, find my baby and tell her I love her and I'm sorry."

My baby, not my experiment.

She lets out a breath, and her face takes on a softness I've never seen. "I love you, Luke, and I'm sorry. I wish things could have been different for us, but I don't regret anything. I can't. You've always been my best friend, my confidant, and we will meet again. Luke, I–"

He reaches out and closes the laptop with a click, shutting it off, but he doesn't say anything for a few minutes. Then, thickly, "If you don't mind, I'd like to keep the rest just for me."

I nod.

I know I shouldn't ask, but I can't help it. This man is the biggest secret my mom kept – and that's saying something. "Why did you two never…?" I let it trail off, but he knows what I'm asking.

"She wouldn't let me. It would have meant leaving the Crusaders. She said she couldn't stay without giving you up, but she wouldn't make me leave." He snorts. "Make." He repeats and shakes his head, then looks at me. "She was real stubborn." He looks at the ceiling. "Anyway, the mission was more important to her than anything. Except you."

Even him. I don't say it. He knows it far better than I do.

"Anyway, I'll see her again." He looks at his hands. "One day."

After that we just talk. We leave the little room and stroll outside, both needing to escape the heavy air of the trailer. He tells me what she was like growing up, and I tell him what it was like to have her as a mom. We compare our versions of the same stories and they make us laugh.

He paints the picture of a side of my mom that I didn't always see but suspected was there. In his stories, she was happy and carefree, and quite mischievous. Apparently she was an ace prankster, and the tricks she played were legend – though only Luke ever knew she was responsible.

It's hard to think of my mom like that. Young, carefree and happy, and knowing the difference was me. She was only nineteen when I was born.

"It wasn't you, Meda–" Luke cuts into my thoughts. "–that changed her. If anyone's to blame, it's your father and the rest of the demons who took her from–" He stops and changes what he was going to say to simply, "–who took her. But even if they hadn't, Meda, she still wouldn't be that girl. Life has a way of happening to all of us, and we all grow up." A small smile appears. "I don't know any forty-year-olds sneaking out to prank their friends, no matter how easy their life is."

I let out a breath and change the topic. "Sometimes..." I don't want to say it, but he's the only one who might understand. "Sometimes, I forget what she looks like. I can't picture her. I'm losing my memories, and I just want to hold on to all of them, like a book, to read over and over again. I loved her, and yet sometimes I can't even picture her smile."

He looks thoughtful, not horrified, by my confession. "It's natural to forget, for the memories to fade. Your mom wouldn't want you to spend your life living in the past." A smile twists his mouth. "I've tried to remember everything. I remember all the important things, our first 'I love you', our first kiss." He grins, eyes twinkling. "*Definitely* our first kiss."

Then he takes a deep breath, his eyes on the ground in front of us as we walk. "But I also remember other things, things that weren't important at the time.

"I couldn't tell you what day it was, but we had been swimming like we'd done a thousand times, and we were lying on the grass to dry. Just a normal day, but I can lose my eyes and see the exact pattern the shadows of he leaves made on her skin."

He looks at me now. "Anyway, I want you to be careful, Meda. Careful you don't wake up one day, an old fool with nothing but the sun-dappled memory of a dead girl to keep you company. Your mom wouldn't want you to live like that. Remember people you have lost, but let them go. Let the memories fade."

It's obvious he hasn't let her go. "Wouldn't she want you to do the same?"

He smiles the caught smile of someone doing something they shouldn't. "Yes, but part of the fun of loving your mom was arguing with her."

"But I'm supposed to do as she says?"

"You're her daughter."

I pause, digesting that. "So... are you ever going to let her go?"

He looks up at the sky, and I don't think he's talking to me when he says, "No."

"But you just said she would have wanted you to move on."

He smiles. "Finally, a disagreement with her where I'll actually get my way." Then the smile fades, and he says softly, "But for you, Meda... I don't want that for you and neither would she. Remember the good times, honor her memory, but let her go."

I've been living with the guilt so long that it seems impossible. But I will try.

Eventually Luke has to leave, but we make plans to meet again.

After he goes, I continue walking. He didn't ge
someone to guard me when he left – on accident o
on purpose, I don't know, but I take advantage of m'
freedom. I walk the perimeter of the camp and think
about my mom. About Luke. About miscommunication:
and sacrifice. About mistakes. About good and evil.

I'm deep in thought and don't notice the arguing
couple until I am almost on them. Which is appalling
because Jo is, as always, *loud*. I try to retreat, but I'm so
close I really don't want to get caught – or interrupt.

"I don't know what you're talking about," Jo
says stiffly, backing away. He grabs her by the arms,
completely undaunted. I told you he's brave.

"You do. You love me, Jo."

"I don't." She won't look at him.

"Liar," he says softly.

She finally breaks down. Her collapsing face falls into
her hands. She cries. "It won't work, Chi. I'll be stuck at
the school–"

"Then call me Professor Dupaynes."

Ack, the horror.

"Be serious!" she says and he wraps his arms around
her.

"I don't care, Jo. We might actually make it to a ripe
old age that way." She cries harder. "But I don't think
it will come to that. Your brains and my legs? We're a
match for any pair out there."

"Chi, I'll get you killed!"

"It's because of *you* that Meda didn't kill us." Chi
kicks up his mouth in a half-smile and murmurs into

er ear, "How many times do you have to save my life
efore I'm allowed to like you?"

"I–" she starts to say before he tilts her chin up.

"Personally, I think three times is enough."

Four times. But maybe keeping some secrets between
riends is a good idea.

And then he finally takes my advice and kisses her.

I'm not going anywhere for a while, so I take a seat
while the soap opera that is the relationship between my
two best friends unfolds in front of me. In memory of
Uri, I pop some imaginary corn for the show and munch.
I just hope they keep it PG.

And suddenly Uri's beside me. Silver and smiling, he
sits on the bench next to me and takes a handful. He's
carrying the military supply pack, and pops some corn in
his mouth and some in his bag.

A good memory to save for later.

ACKNOWLEDGMENTS

A huge thank you to my parents, Bob and Mary, for all their love and support; to Wes and Matt for being the best and worst brothers ever; and to Diane for always being on the same page no matter how odd the book might be at times.

I'd like to thank all my critique partners, but especially Megan, Marlene, Reg and Ann for their early and constant support; the bearded ladies, Mónica, Stacey, Evelyn and Holly, for their tough critiques and persistent friendship; and Shiv for making my dream come true.

I would also like to thank my agent, Victoria Marini, and my editors, Ameya Nagarajan and Amanda Rutter, for loving my messed-up characters as much as I do; and the rest of the Penguin India and Strange Chemistry teams for their hard work in making *Cracked* ready for the world.

And lastly, I'd like to thank Raffi, Baird and 'the girls', whose companionship exercises my imagination every day, and Adam, for being the kind of man to which imaginary menageries make perfect sense.

ABOUT THE AUTHOR

Eliza Crewe always thought she'd be a lawyer, and even went so far as to complete law school. But as they say, you are what you eat, and considering the number of books Eliza has devoured since childhood, it was inevitable she'd end up in the literary world. She abandoned the lawyer-plan to instead become a librarian and now a writer.

While she's been filling notebooks with random scenes for years, Eliza didn't seriously commit to writing an entire novel until the spring of 2011, when she and her husband bought a house. With that house came a half-hour commute, during which Eliza decided she needed something to think about other than her road-rage. Is it any surprise she wrote a book about a blood-thirsty, people-eating monster?

Eliza has lived in Illinois, Edinburgh, and Las Vegas, and now lives in North Carolina with her husband, her hens, her angry, talking, stuffed dwarf giraffe, and a sweet, mute, pantomiming bear. She likes to cook, partially-complete craft projects, free-range her hens, and take long walks.

elizacrewe.com
twitter.com/elizacrewe

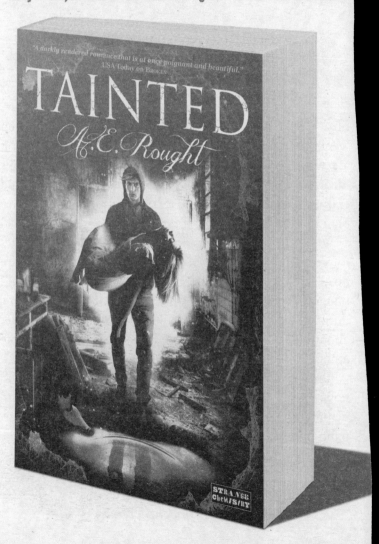

EXPERIMENTING WITH YOUR IMAGINATION

**Five years ago... the gods of ancient mythology
awoke around the world.
This morning... Kyra Locke is late for school.**

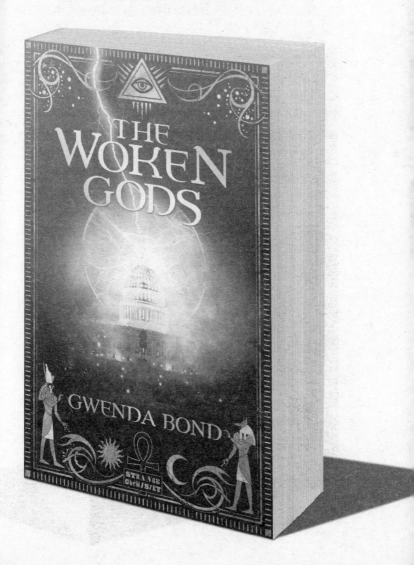

EXPERIMENTING WITH YOUR IMAGINATION

"A great mix of technical detail and breathless action."

Charlie Higson, author of the Young Bond series

JONATHAN L. HOWARD

"A highly effective, thought-provoking novel."
PHILLIP REEVE

KATYA'S WAR

STRANGE
CheMISTRY